THE KIOWA VERDICT

THE KIOWA VERDICT

Cynthia Haseloff

GUNSMOKE

First published in the US by Five Star

This hardback edition 2011
by AudioGO Ltd
by arrangement with
Golden West Literary Agency

ISBN 978 1 445 85643 8

British Library Cataloguing in Publication Data available.

Printed and bound in Great Britain by
CPI Antony Rowe, Chippenham and Eastbourne

FOREWORD

Like MAN WITHOUT MEDICINE, THE KIOWA VER-
DICT is fiction based upon an actual incident in American
history. I have taken many liberties in creating the characters.
Where we do know facts about the characters, I have incorporated them, and I have made use of the text of historical documents when they exist. The principal event is, of course, the
trial. Satanta and Adoltay were actually given separate trials at
the request of their counsel: Adoltay on July 5, 1871, and
Satanta on July 6. The same jury heard both trials. The verdicts
were the same. The trials are combined here for the sake of
space and dramatic effect. The transcripts of the trials, except
for the motions and S. W. T. Lanham's address to the jury,
are lost. Therefore, the trial is largely a matter of conjecture
based on the reason for the arrest of the Kiowas, on the known
witnesses, and on the ultimate outcomes of this journey toward
judgment and justice. I wish to thank John Lisle for his assistance in this recreation. In reality, the arrest and trials of the
Kiowa chiefs were a turning point in American history. It was
the beginning of the end for the Quaker Peace Policy and for
the Army's defensive posture. From this point, the old life of
the American Indian was truly doomed. The Army would push
them onto reservations throughout the West and keep them
there.

Cynthia Haseloff
Springdale, Arkansas
November 30, 1996

Prologue

May 17 - May 19, 1871
Fort Richardson, Texas

After an uneventful inspection tour of the western line of Texas forts — Fort Concho, Fort Griffin, and the abandoned Fort Belknap — William Tecumseh Sherman arrived at Fort Richardson, his next to last stop, late on the afternoon of May 17, 1871. Sherman did not like the fuss that went along with his four star rank and reputation. He declined quarters in the fort and pitched his tents near a small spring away from the buildings.

Down the road and across the way, he watched a group of wagons pull in from Weatherford, forty miles to the east. He learned that they were taking supplies to Fort Griffin, two days to the west. As Colonel Ranald Mackenzie showed him around, they talked informally about the persistent problem that had brought the general west — Indian depredations.

To this point, Sherman saw nothing that would cause him to think that the problem was more than exaggeration by the emotionally involved people on the frontier. He off-handedly suggested to Mackenzie that the protests could be thought of as little more than an attempt to draw troops away from their duties of occupation in the defeated State of Texas. His words drew the colonel out, just as Sherman had intended. Mackenzie had seen enough to know the horrors of Indian depredation were not exaggerations.

"It's a different kind of war here, sir. A few raiders can slip past our soldiers and hit a home or small party, kill and mutilate and carry off women and children, and be gone before we can get in the saddle. It's not like the War Between The States, sir . . . no regiments or battalions lined up with artillery and cavalry, no flags flying. It's easy to think nothing's going on. I mean five or six killed doesn't seem like much after Fredericksburg or Chancellorsville, but out here that can be thought of as a whole forward unit, and it's usually civilians, a family. You'll hear from some of these families tomorrow, after your inspection. I think you'll see these people are honest and straightforward. I've found they seldom exaggerate, more often understate, or just don't say anything, especially when they don't think they are getting an honest hearing. They are hard pressed, sir, fighting the Indians and the government."

Sherman watched the teamsters splashing in Lost Creek as the long sunset rested on the land. "Those men don't seem afraid to travel," he said.

"There's twelve of them," Mackenzie said. "And they are well armed. They know what can happen. But chances are a raiding party won't bother with them unless they have more men and guns. You see, sir, out here the enemy won't close with you unless he has the advantage. He'll just go somewhere else, and you'll never know he was there. Most of the time you don't know where he is. Men go out a hundred times without any trouble, then one day it's different.

"Britt Johnson, a teamster killed last February, had made dozens of successful trips. He had even gone into the Kiowa camps on three occasions to recover his family and captives from the Elm Creek raid in Eighteen Sixty-Four. I don't think anyone knew more about Indians than he did. But three months ago they got him and three other teamsters out on Salt Creek Prairie. The party that found him said there were more than a hundred shell casings around his body. He had fistsful of Indian hair in both his hands. The Indians cut him open

8

and stuffed his body cavity with his little dog. That's the kind of war we have here."

"You think the raiders are coming from the reservations around Fort Sill?" Sherman asked directly.

"A lot of Texas horses show up there," Mackenzie answered. "There'll be men at the meeting tomorrow who have seen their own well-marked horses at Sill, but couldn't get them back. It's an affront, really. These people are paying taxes to fund the Indian policy, and the Indians are stealing their property and killing their families."

After his talk with Mackenzie, Sherman wrote to General J. J. Reynolds, commander of the Department of Texas in San Antonio:

I do not doubt that some of the Kiowas and Comanches from the reservation do come down to Texas to steal horses, and they never object to killing and scalping when tempted, but these Indians are in the custody of the Indian Bureau, and the Army has no more control over it than the Post Office Department has.

He reread that, noting the exact truth of the situation.

If the Indians in the Fort Sill Reservation have many Texas horses with brands on, I will find it out at Fort Sill, and will labor to have the thing stopped through the Commissioner of Indian Affairs. Of course, it is a great outrage if the Indians who receive annuities from the United States make their reservation a refuge for stolen stock, and when the truth is ascertained some means can be devised to stop it, and of this I will write you from Fort Sill.

Still careful, still wanting to ascertain the truth for himself,

9

Sherman had used the word *if* twice in his letter to Reynolds. He was also still focused on the property issue of stolen horses. He had not yet met the Jacksboro citizens' committee on May 18th.

Heavy clouds with distant lightning hovered on the horizon beyond the headquarters building where Sherman accepted the sworn affidavits concerning stolen stock. Colonel Benjamin Grierson, commander at Sill, they said, had done nothing to alleviate the situation. *What could he do?* thought Sherman.

Among the papers, Sherman also found a "Statement of Murders and Outrages Committed upon the Citizens of Jack County by Hostile Indians." Each item on the long list included the date, the location, the number killed, wounded, or taken captive, remarks about the current situation of the captives. There were one hundred twenty-nine names on the list. Facts showed that hundreds of people had been scared out during the War Between The States. Young County had been de-populated to the point that its public records were removed to Jacksboro. The citizens' committee neatly upped the stakes for the general from horses to children and women and men, citizens due the protection of the United States — and to the very westward expansion of the nation itself.

With the poles driven deeper and the ropes lashed tighter at his tent, with the great prairie storm breaking over his head, Sherman wrote to his brother, John, of the Indian attacks.

This has been going on ever since we have had Texas, and now as much if not more than ever. People here, and the officers of the Army here, assert that these Indians come from the Indian Reservation, that they carry this stock to the reservation, and are then safe against pursuit. One of the worst practices here is the custom

10

of the Kioways and Comanches to steal women and children, and I have already had two mothers begging of me their children, as though I could help them. . . .

As though I could help them. . . . The words teased Sherman's mind as he lay on his bed, listening to the storm outside. *As though I could help them.* . . . Sherman sat up. What other business did a peace time soldier have but to protect the people as the country moved West? He ran his hands through his cropped red hair, scrambling it even more than usual. "Hell's bells," he muttered and stood up. He did not light the lantern, but took a cigar and matches from the box on the table.

Sherman did not like politics. He did not like waiting while the Peace Policy played out, and the Interior Department let the Indians bully the United States. It had been reported to him at his St. Louis headquarters that one of the chiefs, a Kiowa named Satanta, had defied the peace commissioners. He had said the only part of the white man's road he wanted was the breech-loading rifle and ammunition. That very astute Indian had noted that the government ignored the peaceful Indians and constantly sought to placate and win over the war-like. Sherman's mouth twisted.

Noises outside caught his attention. Smoking the cigar, he raised the tent flap. The seventeen black soldiers in his escort were lined up, roughly clothed, rifles in hand. "Brush the sleep from your precious eyes," said the sergeant, strolling through the rain like it was a sunny day. "Wake it up now, Kelso. Tuck in your shirt. There's Indians about, and up to no good at that. It's look sharp now or lose your scalps, but by God, better your own than the general's. They are getting the officers up, so you know it's bad. If that don't scare you sufficient, then you deserve to be killt by Indians." Sherman dropped the tent flap.

Sherman slipped in quietly to the meeting. His soaked aides-de-camp stood with Mackenzie and his officers around a map spread over a desktop. "You passed through that spot, day before yesterday, with the general. The teamsters weren't that lucky," Mackenzie noted. "Brazeal . . . that's the man who struggled in about an hour ago . . . says there were a hundred and fifty Indians. Some of the men escaped, made it to a wood. Gentlemen, at first light, I want scouts on every high piece of ground around this fort."

"Sir, can we even begin to defend this place? I mean, there are no walls, no protection," asked a Sherman aide.

"Gentlemen," Sherman's coarse voice came from the back of the room, "cavalry do not defend forts. They ride." He walked quickly to the front of the room. The officers cleared a place for him at the desk. "Proceed with your briefing, Colonel Mackenzie."

Again Mackenzie's fingers moved over the map, tapping Salt Creek Prairie. "This is Cox's Mountain, General. That's where they got Britt Johnson last February. In here somewhere they hit the Warren wagon train on its way to Fort Griffin."

"Those men down at the creek, night before last?" asked the general.

"That's right. You passed over the same route yourself day before yesterday. At first light, we'll send out scouts to check for hostiles." Mackenzie glanced at his officers. "I want this post secured immediately. Be prepared for any possible attack. Next, Brazeal's report must be checked out fully. Prepare your companies. General, I believe Fort Griffin should be notified."

Sherman rubbed his scruffy beard. "Call your clerk, Colonel. I'll dictate a letter with orders for soldiers from Griffin to join you. I want you to lead this party. Once you have ascertained the truth of the attack, you are to pursue these Indians.

You are to stay in the field with them. Take supplies for a month if necessary. I want to know positively whether or not these hostiles are taking sanctuary at Fort Sill."

Sherman was excited, not in any way that the men could really see, but they felt his involvement, his enthusiasm for pursuit, and for solution to a problem. Here on the Texas frontier, he was a commander of troops again. "Where do you want the troops from Fort Griffin to meet you, Colonel?"

Mackenzie told him.

Sherman rubbed a hand through his tousled hair, then looked up at the men still around the desk. "Well? Do you have work to do, gentlemen, or are you waiting for breakfast?"

The men quickly scattered as Sherman bent again over the map. "Our maps differ I believe," said a Sherman aide. "Perhaps we should verify. . . ."

"Forget that," Sherman said. "We'll use Colonel Mackenzie's information."

Colonel Ranald Slidell Mackenzie left Fort Richardson at noon on May 19, 1871 at the head of Companies A, B, E, and F of the 4th Cavalry — one hundred and fifty men with pack mules, carrying enough flour, sugar, coffee, salt, and bacon for a month in the field. The colonel carried signed orders from General in Chief of the United States Army William Tecumseh Sherman. They were very clear. Sherman had written:

I hereby authorize you to enter said reservation and, if the trail be fresh and you should overtake the party anywhere within thirty or forty miles of Red River, you will not hesitate to attack the party, recover the property stolen and any other property or stock in their possession, and bring them to me at Fort Sill. Should the trail

scatter and yet, in your opinion, lead into said reservation, you may in like manner come to Fort Sill that we may through the Indian agent there recover the stolen stock and get possession of the party of Indians who attacked this train and killed seven men as reported.

Sherman smoked under the porch roof as the troops rode west toward the site of the attack. The rain had not let up. "As if I could do anything, indeed," the salty general said to himself. "Indeed!"

Chapter One

Saturday, May 27, 1871
Kiowa-Comanche Agency

Issue day at the agency was trying, at best, for Agent Lawrie
Tatum. He knew that the Indians came chiefly for the coffee
and pepper. They thought it went together — peppered coffee.
That was just the smallest part of the confusion existing between
his red brothers and himself. They thought pork was elephant
meat and would poison them. They burned it. They thought
rice was dried maggots and threw it away. Flour they played
with, tossing it on one another, painting their hands and faces,
marking horses' rumps with floured hand prints. They liked
sugar and did not waste it. He was not sure what happened to
all the white man's clothing that was distributed. Sometimes
he'd seen men's hats on the women. So much was wasted, lost,
not just in material things, but in the understanding between
the two peoples.

There was never time to teach them enough. And teaching
was itself another battle. He felt as if he were running to catch
a train that was pulling out of the station and picking up speed.
The harder he ran, the greater the distance became. Tatum's
head pounded.

Tatum — Old Bald Head, the Kiowas called him — walked
to the window of his office. A year ago he had been a farmer
in Ohio. He was then just a man, managing his farm and
family, active in his faith. He had read in the paper of his
appointment as United States Indian agent to the wild Kiowas
and Comanches and other tribes of the Fort Sill area. He had

15

had no training. He had only a trust that his God would accompany him and guide him as he sought to speak of that God to these wild men.

Today that faith seemed to him to border on the reckless. Had this whole policy that the Quakers and other religious groups proposed to President Grant been thoughtfully considered? Had the ease of its acceptance taken the Quakers off guard? Had they rushed headlong into the unexpected opportunity of implementation without the detailed plan that would insure success? They had come, willing to work, believing that the Indians must be treated as humans, not as vermin to be eliminated in the westward push. But they had known so little, so very little of these red men and their culture. Tatum's Quaker beliefs were greatly conflicted by the reality of the Indians. Perhaps the religious men had run where they should have walked. Now they were trying to build an agency with adequate facilities to feed, clothe, teach, and train the Indians. Tatum was trying to build buildings and a sawmill and hire farmers and carpenters. At the same time he was trying to understand these alien beings whom he loved so deeply in his faith.

He realized that, by and large, he was an object of ridicule to these people. They mocked farming, wanted only to kill or wound for sport the cows he brought to them for their herds. Tatum believed the herds and farms would make them self-sufficient people, not the white man's wards or victims. But the Kiowas already believed they were self-sufficient people. They had the land and the buffalo and the horse and their skills.

When he spoke of love and kindness, they laughed as warriors must laugh at weakness. There was no honor for them in the life Tatum proposed. Men did not farm. Men did not love their enemies; they killed them. There was only one way to overcome the white man for these Indian men. They had to drive him out, create such fear and misery in his life that he would abandon this encroachment on the land they claimed. They had done it before, successfully driving out the Mexicans and the Apaches.

Tatum could not tell them that the real defeat of this white enemy was self-sufficiency. He could not tell them that the white man could not be killed off or pushed back because it was his very nature to push forward, to deny the validity of any tradition that was not verified by his own. He could not tell them that, just as they drove others before them, the white man would drive them before him because he, too, was a warrior. He could not tell them that the Indian was already beaten, and he must take the poor offering the white men had given him and turn it against them. That was how this new game was played. He had tried to show the Indians the way to survive, but their hearts were full of the old ways. Perhaps they were, like Tatum himself, victims of their idealistic beliefs, unprepared for sudden confrontation with an unco-operative reality.

Tatum stood at the immaculately clean window and observed the Kiowa people camped in the broad flats east of Cache Creek in the two-mile space between the agency and Fort Sill. He could see the group at the warehouse commissary building. His clerk would turn them away and send them to the office, as Tatum had directed. Even as he watched with his hands clasped behind his back, the group of Kiowa leaders started away from the commissary.

Today he would ask the chiefs a question he had asked before when they disappeared for extended periods, then returned with horses and grizzly trophies they had not bothered to hide. Before they had run over him and his kindness. It would not happen this day. The Quaker had made up his mind.

On the 22nd of May, he had written to the Friends' Executive Committee:

I think the Indians do not intend to commit depredations here this summer, but from their actions and sayings they intend to continue their atrocities in Texas. Will the Committee sustain me in having the Indians arrested for murder, and turned over to the proper authorities of Texas for trial?

On the 23rd, Sherman had arrived at Fort Sill and had come to his office. Tatum had admitted candidly to the general that he could not control the Kiowas and Comanches. He had not denied the raiding into Texas, as Sherman had expected. Tatum had said simply: "I've not been able to accomplish anything in civilizing them. They pay no attention to my injunctions. The only tangible power I have with them is the issue of rations. In a few days they will be out of sugar and coffee. They will come to me, and I will ask them about the wagon train."

On the 25th, Tatum wrote again to Superintendent Hoag of the Quaker Committee.

When I ascertain who commits depredations in Texas will the Department approve of having the guilty parties arrested if they belong to the Indians of this Agency, and transfer them to the Governor of Texas for trial? Please, give me an explicit answer as soon as practicable.

Of course, any answer would take time.

When the absent chiefs returned to the reservation, Tatum had to make up his own mind. He stood at the window, watching them, coming toward him. The agency clerk, George

Conover, had turned the Indians away from the commissary and sent them for a counsel as the agent had ordered. Tatum's decision was made. If they committed crimes, they must be treated as white men who committed the same crimes. That was not kind or understanding; it was simply fair. His inner voice questioned his hardness again. *Perhaps they did not know they committed crimes. Perhaps they thought their actions were acts of war or games of honor.* Tatum's narrow lips set. He could not be responsible for that. His teachings had failed. Now the Kiowas must feel the consequences of their acts. That, too, was a teacher, a hard teacher.

"Friend Leeper," Tatum spoke softly to the interpreter Matthew Leeper, who waited in the room, "thou may ask the chiefs to come inside."

Tatum observed the leaders as they came into the simple room. Guipago was head chief since Tohausen's death in 1866. The bronze skin on his face was drawn tightly over the angular features. Guipago's eyes watched everything closely. Swaggering Satanta was his contender, eloquent, brave, but somehow not chosen as chief by his people. Tatum lightly focused his attention on Satanta. He was larger than most of the Kiowas, almost six feet, heavily muscled, strong enough to club a man or woman to death. He had been gone from the reservation for a month. Today he was back again for all to see and basking in the glory of activities while away.

Satank entered the room behind Satanta without fanfare. Satank was small, an old man with slivers of mustaches at the corners of his mouth. His eyes perpetually squinted against the prairie sun and the disguises of men's souls. For all Satanta's size and swagger, Satank was the giant among the Kiowa people. Tatum considered that. This fragile-looking old man who led his dead favorite son's sacred, bundled bones around on a horse was the most deadly and heroic of the Kiowa men.

The others, even the young men, deferred to him, moved out of his way quietly. Satank was *Koitsenko*, ranking member of the ten great warriors who wore the sash. With the sash, staked to the earth by an arrow, they would not retreat in any battle, especially desperate battles. They stood on foot, naked of the horse, an easy target for their enemies and a symbol of courage and hope for their people. Satank had earned the name of *Akia-ti-sumtau*, Admired One, but not needing it, he had given the name away. Satank spoke little, yet he was often eloquent when he spoke in a very quiet voice. He was famous for his generosity to the Cheyennes in the great peace making. Past seventy, he was the father of young children. Years of the Kiowa calendar were named for his exploits. Tatum caught himself admiring the old warrior and his integrity. Then he realized, again, this honorable man remained a killer of men.

The older Kiowa leaders took seats around the room. Benches had been built for just such meetings. Some of the younger men remained standing, as was fitting to honor the elders. Tatum could not restrain a small sigh. He drew himself to full height and waited for the men's silence. Slowly their attention turned to the bearded Quaker.

"A great general has come to Fort Sill," Tatum began. "He has brought word of an attack upon a wagon train in Texas. I would like to know who led this attack because he is guilty of a crime that will no longer be permitted." Tatum studied the faces of the Kiowas as young Matthew Leeper translated his words for them.

Satanta stood up and came closer to Tatum, standing almost in his face. "I led the raid in Texas. If anyone else said he did, he is a liar. I am the man who commanded." Satanta pounded his own chest with the fingers of his right hand, owning the act. He paused for the translation of his words by Leeper. "We know that you are stealing our annuity goods and giving them to the Texans."

Leeper translated this statement to Tatum who shook his head in disgust at the lie, but said nothing, waiting for Satanta's next affront.

"We have asked you many times for guns and ammunition, but you will not listen to us and give them to us. We have made many other requests that you have not given us. We must take for ourselves what you will not give." Satanta continued his attack, stopping at appropriate intervals for Leeper to make his words clear to the Quaker agent. As Leeper translated, Satanta sometimes watched the Quaker's face and sometimes checked the effect of his words on the other Kiowas.

"If we kill Texans, it is your fault. You took us by the hair and pulled us close to the Texans where we have to fight them. We are not going to stay here to be watched and tempted. We are going out with the Cheyennes in the Antelope Hills.

"Two and a half years ago, the dog, Custer, betrayed Guipago and I by arresting us under a white flag. He is no kind of man. He also killed our friend, Black Kettle, and his people on the Washita and betrayed his own men by abandoning them as he fled from the remaining warriors. Arresting Indians is played out now. That is what will not be permitted. You remember that.

"These are but some of the grievances I hold against the white men. We know also that you white eyes are planning to build a railroad across our land. That is what will not be permitted. Do not even consider it. Because of these things, I took more than one hundred warriors to Texas to show them how to deal with white men. Satank, Adoltay, Eagle Heart, Big Bow, Fast Bear, and Mamanti were with me." Satanta turned to the other chiefs, naming them, pointing them out for their honor. "There, in Texas, we met a wagon train. We killed seven men and took forty-one head of mules. Three of our own men and our Comanche friends were killed. We consider this issue even now. Remember this, if any other Indian comes here and says he led the raid, he will be lying, because I, Satanta, led it." Satanta waited after Leeper's translation for Tatum's response.

Tatum looked past Satanta at the seated chiefs. Satank, Adoltay, called Big Tree by the whites, and Eagle Heart were in the room. "Is this true, what Satanta said, that you and the others named joined him in leading the raid?"

After Leeper's words, the men nodded.

Satanta pushed again with an old and favored complaint of the Kiowas. "Why do you deny us guns and ammunition? You make us weak against white men and other Indians who have all the guns and ammunition they want. Why do you do this?"

Tatum wiped his forehead upward into the air above his head. Today he did not feel any words about the harmfulness of guns would have any point. "Perhaps you should take that up with General Sherman who is visiting up at the fort. Like you Kiowa chiefs, he is a man of war and knows such things well that I do not understand. We have talked enough. Your rations will be issued."

Some of the Kiowas started to rise and depart. "Wait," Satanta said. "The clerk said there was no sugar for us. You go to the fort and get Grierson to give us some of the soldiers' sugar. Don't take too long because many of us want to go home soon."

Tatum looked straight into Satanta's face. A momentary spark darted across his own blue eyes. So this was what the policy, the effort of trying to build a better life for this man came to, such complete contempt for the idea and the men who strove for it that he felt he could order them about, play with their leader in front of the others. Tatum glanced down and turned away from Satanta. "You are right. I should go to the fort immediately."

The Indians filed out toward the commissary building. Tatum watched them go, then went to his desk and wrote a note:

Fort Sill, Ind. Terr.,
Office Kiowa Agency.
5th Mo. 27, 1871

Colonel Grierson,
Post Commander,

Satanta, in the presence of Satank, Eagle Heart, Big Tree, and Woman's Heart, has, in a defiant manner, informed me that he led a party of about one hundred Indians into Texas and killed seven men and captured a train of mules. He further states that the chiefs, Satank, Eagle Heart, and Big Bow, were associated with him in the raid. Please arrest all of them.

Lawrie Tatum
Ind. Agent

He handed the message to Matthew Leeper and sent him to the fort. Tatum remained at his desk after the young interpreter had left. He spread his hands over the smooth boards and studied the sturdy fingers that had just ordered the arrest of his charges. He thought of Pontius Pilate who had washed his guilty hands, but could not rid himself of the guilt of turning over his responsibility to someone else, of betrayal of what was good and right. Tatum had betrayed his principles, had failed to make the Indians understand. They had gone on killing and killing and killing. He had not been able to stop them. He had not been able in his faith to stop the killing. His head pounded. "Dear God, dear God," he whispered. "Have I done the right thing?"

Tatum looked up at the squeak of the screen door. Guipago
— called Lone Wolf by the white men — was standing in the
doorway. "There is still no sugar. You said you would get sugar
from Grierson."

"You do not claim any part in this great massacre?" Tatum
said to the man.

"No," said the principal chief of the Kiowas. "This time I
was with Kicking Bird and Stumbling Bear. But you were right
about one of our young men. He is a great leader. You have
often remarked on Adoltay. He proved himself in the fighting.
He, not Satanta, led the young men. He cut off the wagons.
He counted first coup. You thought he would be a good leader,
and you were right." Guipago smiled and almost chuckled at
this jab at the Quaker who had thought he could teach the boy
peaceful ways. "We will leave soon and need the sugar before
we go." Guipago turned and left, letting the screen door bang
behind him.

Tatum rubbed his burning eyes. Adoltay . . . Big Tree. He
had forgotten to include the boy's name with those to be
arrested. Was it carelessness, or had he denied to himself that
the young man was as capable of murder as his elders? Once
more he must choose. Tatum reached for a sheet of paper.
Dipping the pen into the ink, he wrote starkly black letters on
the white paper:

**Big Tree was also in the raid with Satanta, I am
informed by Lone Wolf. Please arrest him also. But release him if found innocent.**

Tatum folded the note and held it in his hand. There was
no one to carry it up to the fort. He put the slip of paper into
his vest pocket, patting it into place. It was better, anyway, if

he went himself. It was his obligation to see the arrests. He could not hide here. He would have to see for himself. Calling out that he was going to the fort to his wife, Mary Ann, he walked to the door and took down his straw hat from the peg.

Guipago still leaned against the front gate, talking with another man. "I'm going to the fort now," the agent said, drawing his stirrup to him. "Please tell the other chiefs that the great Army chief at the fort will want to talk with them before they leave." He mounted his horse and rode off toward the fort.

From the commissary, Satanta watched Tatum trot toward the fort as he waited for the issue. The longer he waited, the greater his suspicions grew. Old Bald Head had never agreed with him before or done his bidding. Tatum moved the horse into a slow canter.

"Satanta," shouted out one of the warriors, "you have scared that old bald-headed man pretty good. See he is running away fast to get us sugar."

"Maybe so," the chief said. "Maybe I better go see that big general and talk to him, too."

The warriors laughed. Satanta's first wife nudged him. "Get me extra sugar," she said.

"Get my horse," he said.

Chapter Two

May 27, 1871
Fort Sill, Indian Territory

Colonel Grierson handed the arrest note sent by Tatum to William Sherman. The tall, thin, grizzle-bearded chief soldier read it and handed it back. "Mister Leeper, will you kindly inform the chiefs that I wish to see them here on this porch as soon as possible." Leeper went away. "Colonel, I want troopers ready for action. Have them saddled up and waiting in the corrals for whatever action may come up. Post men inside this building to cover the porch in the event it is necessary. None of these men . . . Satanta, Satank, Eagle Heart, Big Bow . . . is getting away from here. I want this porch completely secured. I want troops to close every side as necessary. Lieutenant Orleman, get some men down at the south end of the parade ground where they can watch what's going on in the Indian camps. If you encounter Satanta, Satank, Big Bow, or Eagle Heart arrest them on the spot." The soldiers went to their preparations.

The boy, Grant Hanby, was chewing a stem of hay, loitering about, watching the soldiers mucking out the loose stalls, when Sergeant Dutton came in, barking at the men who followed. "Double Quick. Get them nags saddled and be quiet about it, too. Hurry up now. We're going to a party." The boy watched as the men threw their saddles and tack on the fresh horses. "Mount up now, boys. Keep yer mouths shut and set real still till we get the signal." The black soldiers swung into the saddles and sat their horses behind the high stone walls of the corral.

The boy slipped quietly away.

Kicking Bird and Stumbling Bear sat beside Sitting Bear Creek, getting dressed for the meeting called by the great Washington soldier. Grant Hanby tied his pony and walked out of the dry creek toward them. "Don't go to the fort. You've got to leave," he said hurriedly. "The soldiers are waiting for you, hiding in the stone corrals. Take your people and go west toward Signal Mountain. I got to go 'fore I'm caught, or my pa'll thrash me sure." The boy slipped back toward the creek.

Stumbling Bear set down the moccasin he had been putting on. He looked at Kicking Bird who also rested from his dressing, thinking about the boy's words. "Maybe we get killed. But I think we better go, anyway. Maybe we can keep the talk peaceful."

Kicking Bird stood up. "Yes, we will go. I will tell the women to pack up everything and be ready to go if there is any shooting."

Satanta rode straight to the small house of Horace Jones, the interpreter at Fort Sill. The Kiowa trusted him. Jones spoke Kiowa pretty well, although he made many mistakes. When it was important, Satanta spoke for Jones in Comanche, one of the five languages the Indian knew. Jones was better at Comanche than Kiowa.

As the two rode toward Colonel Benjamin Grierson's house, the Indian saw Tatum's gray horse tied outside the picket fence. There were other men on the long, shaded porch. He could not see them all or recognize some he did see. The big general from Washington must be one of them. Satanta realized that he had only a pistol hidden beneath the ceremonial robe he wore. He looked closely to see if the officers had weapons.

Halfway to the house, Satanta realized he did not see anyone else in the quadrangle of stone buildings. The doors and windows were closed. No women or children were about. Glancing toward the Indian camp, he could see some of the families were already leaving. Others were still packing. None of them seemed to be aware of him. None of them was looking toward the fort. None of them was with him at the fort. Satanta was alone.

The Kiowa chief dismounted slowly. The men on the porch seemed unaware of him. They were involved in an intense discussion with Tatum. Satanta's moccasined foot came down firmly on the steps, leading up to the white men. Jones was behind him. One of them, a wiry, tall man in the civilian clothes like Tatum's came to the top of the steps.

"Are you the man who led the raid on the wagon train near Cox's Mountain?" asked Sherman.

Satanta eyed the abrupt, impatient man. He took another step, and, still on the steps, he stood level with the general. Jones asked the general's question in Comanche. Satanta answered, looking at the soldier, waiting for the translation. "Yes, I am the man."

Sherman did not know Indian ways. His experience with them was limited. But he did know that, among white men, sometimes a man will confess to a crime to make himself important. He had to be sure Satanta was not merely boasting. "Jones, you translate this for me. How many wagons were there?"

Jones repeated the question to Satanta. After the chief's answer, he said: "Ten."

"How did you get inside the circle?"

Jones gave the question to the Indian. Satanta smiled and spoke swiftly to Jones. "There was no circle. As the last wagon tried to close, Adoltay and some others killed the lead mules. They went down, and the driver was thrown out. He had to run very hard to get to the other wagons."

"How many men were killed?" Sherman pursued.

"Panse," said the Indian.

"Seven," said Jones to Sherman.

"How many mules were taken?" continued Sherman.

Again Jones conferred with Satanta. "Forty-one head."

As Jones spoke to Sherman, Satanta's attention was drawn to two of soldiers who moved into the stairway, blocking it. Each had a revolver stuck into his belt. Their hands rested on the banister close to the weapons' grips. He looked again about the yard of the large quadrangle formed by the buildings. There were no black soldiers about, no women and children.

"One of the teamsters was stretched over a wagon tongue and burned alive. Did you order that?" asked Sherman, drawing Satanta's mind from its own thoughts. Jones spoke the question to the Kiowa chief.

As he spoke, Satanta rolled his head against his shoulders, releasing the tension, trying to drive away the warning that something was wrong. He must consider his words carefully now. "I was present at the fight. But I did not kill anybody. One of our young men . . . Hau Tau . . . Gunshot . . . was mortally wounded by that driver. Burning him was the young men's choice. The young men wanted to have a fight. I together with some of the other older men just went along to show them how things are done. I myself stood back during the fight and only gave directions." He thought a moment. "You should know that we, too, lost men on this raid . . . three men killed. But we Kiowas are willing to call things even and start anew. You and I can negotiate any differences between us."

Sherman was not in a mood to negotiate. Somehow, seeing this large Indian, talking so calmly, assuming that the lives of the seven teamsters and all the other frontiersmen were negotiable, infuriated him. "You, sir, are a bunch of cowards. One hundred and fifty men against twelve is not much of a fight.

I certainly wouldn't call anyone who did that a *brave*."

Jones spoke to Satanta. The word *cowards* caused him to look sharply at Sherman. "You were a soldier in the great war in the East. Had you rather fight twelve men when you number a hundred and fifty or fight one hundred fifty when you were twelve?"

"A soldier fights other soldiers, not civilians. Those teamsters weren't fighting men. But, sir, the United States Cavalry are. And we will oblige you at any time, at any place you would care to name."

As Horace Jones made the translation, the general turned to Tatum. "I think, Agent Tatum, it's time to wait until some of the other chiefs get here to confirm or deny this man's story. I want to make it clear that the Army will not continue to stand by while United States citizens are slaughtered."

Satanta had been taken hostage by Custer under a white flag shortly after the massacre of Black Kettle and his village on the Washita. For him this situation was little different. He had come freely. He wanted to know if he could go freely. Seeing Kicking Bird and Stumbling Bear across the quadrangle, he started down the steps. The two soldiers at the bottom drew their revolvers. The Kiowa quickly queried the interpreter Jones: "What is this?"

Sherman did not need a translation. He spoke quietly. "You are not to try to leave. If you try to leave, you will be shot."

Jones gave the words to Satanta.

"I was a fool," Satanta said to Jones. "This *eck hobbits pah* . . . this red head . . . is no better than Custer. You go tell my people what is happening here. The other chiefs will not accept this treachery."

Horace Jones could see Satanta's anger and hear it in his voice. "Men have already gone to get them for a conference. Let's sit down and wait for them on the porch." He escorted the Indian to a pair of chairs near a table and sat down with him to wait. Satanta glanced at the pitcher on the table. In any Kiowa lodge a visitor was offered food and drink immediately. They had offered him nothing, and then betrayed his friendship. These white men had no honor.

General Sherman conferred with his officers along the railing of the porch for some time before Kicking Bird and Stumbling Bear reached the fence in front of Grierson's porch. Satanta noted, pessimistically, that neither of them had a weapon. Kicking Bird knew the soldiers well. Several of them slapped him on the back and shook hands with him. The Kiowa peacemaker approached Grierson quickly and began talking intently. Old Stumbling Bear, his cousin, moved deeper into the shade of the porch beside Satanta. He sat down heavily in an empty chair. The old Indian looked at the two soldiers at the bottom of the steps. He did not look at Satanta as he said softly: "We are going to get killed."

Satanta said nothing. He heard Jones tell Kicking Bird that the general wanted the other chiefs to come to meet with him. He watched Kicking Bird start to leave the porch. "I will go and get the others, " Satanta said. "Let me go."

Kicking Bird hesitated.

"No," Sherman said. "Satanta is not to leave."

Kicking Bird left the porch and mounted his pony.

"Tell everybody to come," Satanta called to him. He did not know what to make of Kicking Bird. He wanted to call him a traitor because he supported the white men and talked of peace, but he was afraid to do so, and Kicking Bird was no coward. They had tangled before, and Kicking Bird had not backed down. Among the Kiowas and Comanches, it was one thing to intimidate or question a weaker man and another to confront a strong man. They all knew the stakes. Insulting a warrior could be a fast trip to death. If he permitted your insult,

31

more would come. So the simple solution was to stop any insult immediately, with force. And besides Kicking Bird's courage there was the possibility that he might have some inside with the white man that would be useful when time for negotiations finally came.

"What have you done that the soldiers keep you here?" asked Stumbling Bear.

"They are not treating me right," answered Satanta stubbornly, slumping back in his chair.

The smoke from Sherman's cigar drifted across the dry air into Satanta's nostrils. It was a good smell. Satanta's eyes followed the general as he paced among the seated men. The general leaned back against the wall of the porch, drew one leg up against it, and crossed his arms, smoking intently. He listened to the others for a while. Finally he sat down on the porch rail and unbuttoned his coat. He smoked and listened and looked directly at Satanta.

A movement in the quadrangle drew Satanta's eyes away from the general. Kicking Bird was back. With him rode ten other Kiowa warriors, including the old *Koitsenko,* Satank. Seeing the old man made Satanta's heart lighter. Here was a man who could fight. As the warriors dismounted, the captive chief noted that they all had bows and quivers of arrows or carried Colt revolvers in their belts. He smiled to himself. Across the way, behind a building the soldiers were making, a group of Kiowa men on horseback briefly showed themselves and was gone. They were speaking to him, encouraging him. *We are here,* they were saying. Further away, in the trees, he thought he caught a glimpse of other warriors. This was, after all, going to be different from his meeting with Custer.

Kicking Bird and the others dismounted and tied their ponies at the picket fence. They came quickly down the short path and up onto the porch. As they assembled, Sherman spoke again to Mr. Jones. "Please tell these men exactly what I say. I want to know specifically who participated in the wagon train attack. I want to know if Satanta did, indeed, lead the party. I want to know who helped him. I want to know who killed those men. I want to know who burned that man over a wagon tongue."

Kicking Bird had been among white men enough to understand a great deal of what they said. Before Jones finished, he spoke quietly to the other men. "Say no more about this wagon train business. It is the issue here."

When Jones had finished, Satanta took the stage, loudly scorning Kicking Bird's advice. "I am the man. I have said I led the raid. It was for the young men. You know that. I did not kill anybody or burn anybody. How do I know anybody was burned?" He turned to the other chiefs for approval.

"I received a full report from Colonel Ranald Mackenzie that the men had all been scalped and eviscerated," said Sherman. "One of them had been laid over a wagon tongue and burned. Mackenzie found the body. It does not admit of dispute."

Assembled on the shaded porch of Grierson's headquarters were more than a dozen of the most important and bravest Kiowa men and the staff of soldiers that surrounded Sherman and Grierson. The general watched the Kiowas' faces as Jones spoke his words to them. Sherman continued: "I want to know which of you went on the Texas raid on the wagon train. Satanta and whoever else of the chiefs that took part in the attack are going back to Texas to stand trial for this crime."

Jones spoke to the expectant chiefs. "Satanta and whoever else led the raid are going to be taken back to Texas to stand trial for the attack on the wagon train."

Satanta spoke again. "What right do you have to do that?"

As Jones translated, Sherman rose from the railing. "I have

the right given by the treaty of Eighteen Sixty-Seven at Medicine Lodge. You know it as well as I know it. I believe you and Satank signed that treaty, knowing that it expressly prohibited raids in Texas."

"You have not kept that treaty!" snapped Satanta in reply. "Buffalo hunters are moving into the southern herd from Kansas every day. That was forbidden." The Kiowa stopped while Jones translated. "I am not going to Texas to be turned over to the Texans. I will die right here on this porch, among my people."

Before Jones had finished the last words, Kicking Bird was on his feet. He spoke in Kiowa to Colonel Grierson. "You know me, Grierson. I am for the peace road. I have led my people onto the good road. I have done many things to stop the raids. Sometimes I have caught young men and taken away their horses and whipped those young men. This has not made my people happy with me. But some of the wise ones have understood I did it to stop trouble. I have acted for peace. I have talked for peace. You know this well."

"Yes," replied Sherman to Jones's translation of the Kiowa's words, "I know of you, Kicking Bird. President Grant knows your name. We all appreciate what you have done. But today I will deal with that man." He pointed at Satanta with the cigar still between his fingers. "I am going to take him and whoever helped him to the place where they killed those boys. They're going to be tried in a public court and hung for their crimes."

"For the sake of what I have done," said Kicking Bird, "I now ask you to release these chiefs. In good faith, I will bring you the forty-one mules that were taken. I will continue to work for peace between our two peoples."

Satanta did not like this bargaining with the white men. He particularly did not like the influence their acceptance would give Kicking Bird and his peace efforts. Satanta had defied the white men. Now Kicking Bird would save him. The white men would make Kicking Bird a big man, the one who had saved their chiefs because of his influence among them. Satanta saw a change in the general's face as Jones expressed Kicking Bird's thoughts. *Why,* thought Satanta, *did I hold onto those ugly mules? I could have offered them when I said things were even. It was greedy not to offer the mules in good faith. Kicking Bird has made a graceful and grand gesture. Now he will either have to influence the others to return them or provide them himself by trading his fine horses for the worthless mules. Either way, this gesture makes Kicking Bird too important.*

"I will not go to Texas," shouted Satanta angrily. "I will die right here." He threw back his robe, revealing the pistol at his waist. As his hand closed over the grip, the shades on the porch windows were throw open. Twenty black soldiers pointed their rifles at Satanta and the Kiowas.

Too late! said Satanta to himself. He glanced at the other Kiowa chiefs on the porch. Several had leaned forward, hands gripping their feeble weapons. They had all waited too long to act. Now there were guns pointed at them.

Old Stumbling Bear slumped back. "They are going to kill us if we fight."

Suddenly all the chiefs were speaking, protesting the soldiers to Kicking Bird, to Jones who tried to translate the frustrated, angry words. — "Betrayer!" "No white man can be trusted!" "Men without honor!" "Council House." — Fragments of the shouting came to Sherman.

Satank, who sat on the porch floor, continued to smoke his pipe. He spoke quietly and calmly. "If you men want to crawl by telling pitiful stories, go ahead. I am sitting here, saying nothing. I am an old man surrounded by armed soldiers. Their guns are pointing at me. But if any soldier lays a hand on me,

I will fight. I will die right here."

Kicking Bird nudged Jones. "Say this," he said. "I have taken the white man by the hand. I have begun to walk in the good road. I have led my people in that road. I have been your friend. But if war comes of this, I will stand with my people, my blood."

In the midst of the turmoil on the porch, shots rang out across the quadrangle. The men's attention turned to the empty area beyond the buildings. Indians were riding about. Black soldiers were also riding about. More shots came from the trader's store beyond the walls in the other direction. "See what's going on," Sherman shouted to an aide. "These Indians are ready to bolt. Get some information."

The aide had barely left the porch when soldiers appeared with the young chief, Adoltay. He struggled in their grips, but two black soldiers held him fast, lifting him from the ground as he kicked and fell back, trying to free himself. They forced the young man up the steps. Dirty, his clothes torn, he breathed heavily from his extended exertion. Blood ran from a wound above his ear. He jerked himself free and found enough breath to curse the soldiers, pushing him. "Black dogs for the white men!" He spat at the soldiers.

While the other men's attention was drawn to the fighting warrior, Kicking Bird spoke softly to Satanta. "I can see Guipago with the men on horses. Should I motion for him to come?"

"If he is principal chief," said Satanta, "he belongs here."

Kicking Bird stood and moved from behind a porch post. Raising his arm with the long fringes of his sleeves rippling in the motion, he signaled to Guipago. "Come," he whispered.

In the distance, Guipago raised his rifle over his head and galloped toward the porch. He rode swiftly, a single rider, crossing the empty space. Sherman leaned on his forearm against the post. "By God, he's stony," he said. "Sergeant, keep those soldiers trained on the porch. Don't do any shooting."

Guipago skidded his war pony to a stop at the open fence gate. Throwing his left leg in front of the saddle, he dropped to his feet and looped his reins around the gate. Leaning a bow and quiver and two Spencer rifles against the fence, he methodically adjusted the blanket around his waist. Everyone on the porch watched his deliberate movements. He retrieved the weapons, laying the rifles in the crook of his left arm and grasping the bow and quiver with his right. He then shouldered through the two lines of soldiers, who had taken posts inside the fence, and walked to the porch. Seeing Stumbling Bear at the rail, he slapped the bow and quiver into his old hands. Stumbling Bear quickly strung the bow and set an arrow into the string. His bow hand held other arrows against the bent shaft.

Keeping one rifle, Guipago tossed one Spencer to Satanta. "If a fight starts, make it smoke," Guipago said. He walked down the porch and sat down on it near Sherman. He cocked his rifle, pointing it at the scruffy general. Without command every one of the black soldiers cocked their weapons. Sherman did not blink. Kicking Bird began speaking to him again.

Sherman could not know, but every Indian on the porch knew that Guipago had made a gift to Satanta and Satank and Adoltay. Knowing the hopeless situation, he had ridden to join them. Every Kiowa on the porch now made the same gift. The rebukes, the rivalries were put aside. They would all die together against the general and the soldiers.

Old Stumbling Bear began yelling at Kicking Bird. "Do not talk any more to these white men, Kicking Bird. I will only talk to my people."

Kicking Bird turned to see the old man.

"Listen to me, Kiowas. Kicking Bird is talking to the white men for you. He is a young man, but he has good judgment. He has tried hard to keep you out of trouble, but you have paid no attention. You have loved the old road. You have followed Satanta and Satank. See what you have gotten us into. Now before their guns you behave like women. Now I see you are afraid, whipped, beaten. I cannot stand this. Well, I am going to be the first to die. I do not know what it will be like after I die, but I'm about to find out." Stumbling Bear dropped his robe and raised his bow. "I only want to kill the soldier chief before I die."

As Stumbling Bear drew back the bow string, Adoltay grabbed his arm. The arrow flew into the ceiling of the porch and stuck above Sherman's head. Grierson leaped forward, forcing Guipago's rifle away from Sherman. The two rolled, struggling against each other into Kicking Bird, knocking him to the floor.

Satanta saw their faces before him, old rivals some, old friends some, Kiowas all. His heart leaped at the great courage. The Kiowas were men. *Great men!* he thought. Satank had stepped in front of him. *That old man will not give up,* Satanta thought quickly. *He laid down his life long ago. It has no meaning for him. He will see us all killed and not blink. But here are all the leaders, the strong and thoughtful men of the People. We will all die together. What will become of the People? I must make a gesture to match Kicking Bird and Guipago.*

"No! No!," he said. "No! Don't shoot. I am the man who led the raid. I will go to Texas!"

William Tecumseh Sherman relaxed visibly as Jones repeated Satanta's words. He scratched the stubble on his throat and said: "You damn' right you will. Now Kicking Bird, Guipago, the rest of you, a good beginning for settling this matter would be returning those forty-one mules."

Shots came from the direction of the agency. Soon a soldier rode around the corner of the house and shouted a report to Sherman who leaned over the rail. "What is he saying?" the men around Horace Jones asked.

"He says a soldier has been shot, and a warrior killed. The People are fleeing toward the west, the plains. The warriors are protecting their retreat." Jones turned to Kicking Bird and Guipago as he told the Kiowas the grim report.

"We will get the mules," said Kicking Bird. "I, Guipago, all of us will see that they are returned. Let us go now and see to our people."

Sherman rubbed the back of his neck as he turned to his officers. "Let's get this cleared away. Relax the guard here and prepare to let these men go. Get out word to your men that the Kiowas are not to be halted or harmed. Let them go wherever they wish on the reservation. Jones," he rasped, "all these men may go. Only Satanta, Satank, and Big Tree must stay."

Guipago and Kicking Bird quickly left the porch and went to their ponies. They forgot Satanta in their concern for the fleeing people. Satanta sighed. His gesture was lost for now, perhaps forever. Again the other two had shown their leadership of the People in their overriding concern for them. When he looked up, Guipago was riding away. Kicking Bird held Satanta's eyes for a moment, then dug his heels into his pony's side and whirled away.

A soldier closed iron cuffs over Satanta's unresisting wrists. Only Satank and Adoltay stood beside him now. He felt a rifle butt pushed against his back and moved down the stairs and across the empty ground toward the dungeon. He watched the Kiowa horsemen until they were gone and continued to watch where they had been. His heart filled with cold. He felt his own death. Satanta drew the colors of the sunset into him as the guard pushed his head beneath the low door of his prison. *Somewhere*, he thought in the sudden darkness, *the People are riding in the deep oranges and purples of the twilight.*

Chapter Three

Early June, 1871
Fort Sill, Indian Territory

"Drink this," Satanta said, offering Satank a cup of the coffee the soldiers had brought to the three jailed Kiowas.

The ancient warrior looked up into Satanta's face, placing him in a different time. "You were not as old as the young one," — he motioned in Adoltay's direction with his head — "when we made peace with the Cheyennes. Can you remember that time? The Cheyennes themselves had defiled the Sacred Arrows by shedding Cheyenne blood with Cheyenne hands. There was great danger for them in raiding. But their Bow String Society wanted to go out. The old Arrow Keeper told them they would all die. But they wanted to go out. The young men struck him with their quirts.

"They slipped out of their villages at night and came into the Kiowa country on foot. They thought to take many horses. They moved along the stream beds and waited. A man from my village went to water his horses. He saw their sign. He came back and told me. I was young and strong, then. An enemy had come among us. That made me very angry, an enemy slipping into my country. We went out to find them. They hid from us for many hours. Then, when we were tired of hunting and not finding the enemy and ready to go back to our camps, José, a Mexican herder, saw a barricade across a stream. We had found them.

"These Cheyenne Bow String warriors knew we had found them. They knew that the Arrow Keeper had said they would die. But they were men. They took mirrors and turned them into the sun's eye and flashed the light into our faces. They raised their beaded blankets over their heads, swinging them about, waving to us. 'Come and fight!' they yelled at us.

"We fought them in the streams and woods, all over the land. We fought them until we were tired. We fought them until they ran out of ammunition. When they could fight no more, we killed them. They were good fighters. But in the end we killed every one. We took their hair and their weapons, but did not take anything from their bodies. One does not pillage a brave man. We gathered and laid their bodies together in a line upon the prairie. We said for all to see . . . do not cross this line or you, too, will die. This is Kiowa land for Kiowa people."

"It was a great victory," agreed Satanta, speaking to Adoltay. "It was a great Indian fight. That was how warriors fought each other in the old time, the Indian time."

Adoltay drew his knees against his chest and watched Satank's eyes as they penetrated the gray stone wall behind the boy.

"There were forty-two bodies laid on the prairie." Satank gestured widely across the bodies laid out in his mind's eye. He stood again, looking at the slain. "We had defended our land and our families. We felt good. We had fought bravely against brave men. Every Kiowa had his own story to tell because there were so many Cheyennes. It was a great victory.

"As a result of our victory, we went to get ammunition for the Cheyennes' guns we had taken and to celebrate at Adobe Fort. We danced and sang and drank the white man's whiskey and waved the scalps of our enemies. An Arapaho man saw. He recognized two of the scalps we had . . . Red Tracks and Coyote Ear. He took what he saw to the Cheyenne people.

"All that summer and into the fall, the story spread through the Cheyenne lodges. They began to gather to talk and plan a revenge against us. But again they polluted their Sacred Arrows with Cheyenne blood. This time a chief called Porcupine Bear, who was getting up the revenge, got drunk as he was persuading others with his whiskey. His cousin called out for help, and Porcupine Bear and his men cut the attacker of his cousin so badly with their belt knives that he died. Porcupine Bear and the others became outlaws. They could not set up their tents within the Cheyenne circle of lodges. No one would have anything to do with them. But the outlaws, like the other Cheyennes, thought of nothing but revenge.

"The Cheyennes gathered themselves at last in a great camp circle. As every band came in, their women raised their lodges, and the men waited outside, preparing for war, painting their faces and their horses. Finally, there was a great parade of warriors, four abreast, riding back and forth through the village. Fathers and mothers came to give the warriors gifts so that they would avenge their dead children. The Cheyennes who grieved gashed their arms and legs. As they gave their gifts, their blood ran over the faces of the warriors who would bring them revenge.

"Snow caught the Cheyennes in their great camp. It was a very deep snow. They could not separate because they could not travel. There was not enough food for so many people. They killed and ate their starving horses and remembered the Kiowas who had brought about this sorrow. Finally they were able to separate into small camps, but all winter they remembered the killing of the Bow String warriors. Yellow Beard told me that in the spring, he said to the others . . . 'I want to see my son's bones. I want to go and get them and bring them home.' " — Satank considered the remembered words of Yellow Beard that he had just spoken. — "I did not then have a son of my own, so I did not understand all he told me."

Satank himself had recently gone to Texas to recover the bones of his favorite son. In his old age, he led the bones everywhere he went, tied to a fine pony. His women set up his son's lodge for the bones. The old warrior held feasts for the young men in the lodge just as if his son lived.

"In the spring, the buffalo came north again," Satank continued, "and the Cheyennes thought of what drove them north. And they knew it was the Kiowas and Comanches, hunting them, that pushed them north. They thought to themselves that our bellies were already full. The Cheyennes were still hungry after they ate because their hunger for revenge had not been satisfied."

"We learned these things from the Cheyennes later, on the Arkansas," Satanta clarified for the boy, "but we did not know these things that spring. We thought we had beaten the Cheyennes so badly that they would not dare to show their faces again in our country."

"But in the spring they gathered again," Satank resumed. "And they made a pact among themselves and with the Arapahoes that they would show no mercy, because we had shown no mercy to their warriors. They would kill anyone, old or young. They made this pact and did not turn from it.

"They came into our country and looked for us, but did not find us for many days. Then the outlaw, Porcupine Bear, discovered a hunting camp. Men and women went out early to find the herd. He rode his pony out of the creek bed, stuck his lance into the ground, and signaled as if he had seen buffalo. The Kiowas rode toward him, leading their buffalo ponies, laughing. When they were so near that the Cheyenne men, laying on their horses' necks in the stream bed heard the laughing, they rode out and killed them. They killed thirty Kiowas. Not one escaped to warn the other bands. The Cheyennes did not give Porcupine Bear and his outlaw band credit for counting first coup upon us, but the People knew who had done it.

"After many days of looking for us, they found our villages along Wolf Creek. Some women were digging roots in the mud flats. The Cheyennes killed them first, alarming the villages. We fought all that day from sun coming up till sun going down. There were great feats of bravery, many acts of individual combat. The women watched from the hills and called out to the warriors. When a Kiowa woman mistakenly went among the Cheyenne women, they killed her because they had made a pact to kill every Kiowa without mercy. We found her body. When the battle ended at sundown, we were very tired. We had fought since morning. We had had little time to think of our women and children or our friends. In the twilight we saw that many had died, more than the forty-two Cheyenne Bow String soldiers we had killed. That winter our hearts were dark. We talked in our sorrow. Some men wanted to make a winter raid and go and kill every Cheyenne we could find. Some men wanted to wait for spring. Other men said, no. There would be no end to killing if the tribes went back and forth in their revenge. No. There had been enough killing. It was even. One of our women married an Arapaho man, and together they took our talk to the Arapahoes and Cheyennes.

"In the spring seven of us men and one small boy rode north to talk with the Cheyennes. In the place of driftwood, where Two Buttes Creek flows into the Northern Canadian, we sat down together. The small boy we sat in an open space to see all that was done. All of us Kiowa men sat down, facing him. The Cheyennes came and sat down beside us, facing him. Eagle Feather, one of our men, lit his pipe and walked down this line, offering it to each man. If a man took it and puffed it, it meant he was for a peace. Every man took the pipe. The boy saw it. He was the witness for his generation to the peace made by our generation. The peace was recorded.

"Then we made a circle and talked to each other about the peace. We had brought back every head we had taken. They were wrapped carefully in a Navajo blanket. We treated them with care and wanted to give them back. Eagle Feather said . . . 'Friends, we have brought back the heads taken from your warriors. They are here.'

"High-Backed Wolf spoke for the Cheyennes. He lifted his hand to stop the bundle from being opened." — Satank made the gesture now. — " 'Friends, do not open this bundle. To show and talk about such things will make for new bad feelings. We know that our men were killed. You know that your villages were attacked. We have decided to put these thoughts aside. We have peace. Let us continue to have peace. If I saw my son's hair, I would forget peace. You take away these heads and use them as you think best, as our friends. But do not let us see them or hear of them. They would touch our hearts too deeply.'

"High-Backed Wolf stood up and spoke to his people who were waiting to hear what we had decided. 'We have smoked and made peace. We will not remember the wrongs we have done to each other any more. We are now friends. If you have presents for our friends, bring them and place them around the boy.' The Cheyennes piled so many blankets and presents around the boy that we could no longer see him.

"That summer our peoples gathered together to celebrate our friendship. The Cheyennes came from the north and camped on that side of the Arkansas, below Bent's Fort. We came from the south and camped on the south bank. It is a wide valley, big enough to hold the many horses we had brought with us to give the Cheyennes. They were going to give us presents, too, but no horses. We already had so many horses. We all had new moccasins for the new road.

"In the evening, we chiefs met together for a feast. In the morning we told the Cheyennes . . . 'You must come over to our camp. You must come on foot because each one of you will ride back on a fine horse.' In the morning, I took sticks and broke them and laid them in the bend of my arm." — Satank crooked his left arm and began laying imaginary sticks in the curve. — "I went out to the river bank where the Cheyenne people were coming up. I stood and gave each one, who passed by, a stick.

" 'Here,' I said." — The old warrior gestured, as if offering a stick from the imaginary bundle in the crook of his arm. — " 'This represents a horse. Take it to my herd. My herders will give you a horse for it.' "

Satank rubbed his palms on the knees of his buckskin leggings. "I gave away all the sticks to the Cheyennes. When they were gone, I cut more, and gave them away, also. No Cheyenne walked home. We gave them, every one, a horse, some as many as four or five, maybe more. I did this because I wanted peace. I did this because I had been guilty of wanting to kill all the Cheyenne Bow String warriors. It was too much to kill them all. What I thought would make the Cheyennes afraid and keep them out of our country had only made them angry because they are men, like us, who will not be intimidated. My misjudgment caused the Cheyennes to show no mercy to our people when they came south for their revenge. They knew they were not men to be made afraid. They thought we knew that, too. They thought we had made a war of annihilation, so they would do the same. We did not understand each other. It is good we talked before things went further between us."

Satanta had been watching closely Satank's face as he told the old story of the Cheyenne-Kiowa peace. *Why*, he wondered, *was Satank thinking of this story here in our prison?* The old man

47

was not given to idle reminiscences. "Do you think we have misjudged the white man?" he asked Satank.

Satank pulled a blanket over his chest and shoulders as he leaned against the wall. His eyes were closed. "Oh, yes," the old man said softly. "They are men like us. They will not be driven away by fear for long. I think, if we do not take a peace road, they will annihilate us because we cannot annihilate them. We are few. They are without number. The life of our people is a good reason for peace."

"You would be a farmer?" asked Satanta with contempt.

"No. I will not be a farmer. And these young men will never be warriors as we were warriors. There are too many people now. The land has filled up with people who do not understand a warrior's road. They do not like being killed for honor. When I was a young man, a warrior fought on foot. We did not have so many horses, then. To touch a man, trying to kill you, was as honorable as to kill him. You think that is old-fashioned. You must fight from horseback. You must kill your enemy. Times change for us, as they did for our fathers when the horse came."

"You think this brave young warrior should forget what the white man has done to us?" asked Satanta in disbelief. "You think Adoltay should be a farmer, even after you saw his bravery at the wagon train?"

Satank looked at the boy. A child-like innocence lingered on his young face. Like Satank's own dead son, Adoltay was born to be a leader. Unlike his dead son, Adoltay had stepped forward to lead. He had brought the young men off the hill and directed them around the circling wagons. He himself had taken the last wagon, drawing into the closing circle. And with his bow and an arrow taken from his cougar skin quiver, not a rifle or pistol, he had brought down the lead mule on the closing wagon. Adoltay had opened the train for them all. He

48

had ridden in the first display against the wagon men. He had struck first coup against the wagons.

Satank said: "I think Adoltay should count the cost of remembering too much. I think Adoltay should get to know the white men as we got to know the Cheyennes. It is not possible that they are all evil men and liars. I think Adoltay should not quit fighting for his honor and his people, but I think he must fight differently, just as you fought on the horse, and I fought on the ground." Satank rolled himself deeper in the blanket and stretched out along the stone floor. In a few moments he slept.

Satanta glanced at Adoltay in the deep shadows of the prison cell. "He is old and crazy," he said aloud. "You should not pay much attention to him. His time is past. You cannot fight white men tied to the ground by a black skin-sash. They will shoot you with a buffalo gun from a great distance. They know nothing of honor. We are unequally yoked with these white men. You cannot make peace with them as we did with the Cheyennes. They do not know our road. Indians who make peace with them are nothing to them. Those Indians dress in rags and push plows and go hungry because the white men forget to feed them." Satanta was quiet for a moment. "They do not forget us. We are always confronting them . . . stinging them like bees and wasps."

Adoltay said nothing, but settled into his blankets. *A bear,* he thought, *will rub his nose at the stings for a few minutes, but he will take the hive.* The young warrior moved restlessly on the stone floor. He twisted and turned on the thin blankets. He wanted to understand what was happening.

Adoltay was a prisoner of the white men because of the wagon train fight. He knew that. They were going to take him to Texas for a trial. He did not know what a trial was, for the concept of a legal trial did not exist among the Kiowas. There was a common understanding of what was acceptable and what was not. Killing a member of the tribe, for example, often meant being shunned or becoming an outcast. Incest likewise caused the People to turn away from an individual or a group that condoned such a thing. Adultery could be more complicated. A husband could disfigure, kill, or even give his erring wife to a group of men for gang rape. But this last was thought extreme, and the man would be outcast. But if the wife took up with a strong man, the husband was left no recourse. The other man gained place by taking what belonged to the husband. Killing a man's horse or dog also subjected an individual to judgment. Generally, whenever a man was wronged, he went to a strong man who took up the matter with the guilty party. If the strong man was strong enough, the guilty yielded. If the People were wronged, the great men gathered and considered a course of action. The Kiowas, like most Plains Indians, did not dally. They took action, individually or in the group. But the idea of a public trial based on a legal code, presided over by a judge and decided by a jury, was not something they understood. Justice was a matter of a man's acts in relation to a tribal understanding — attitude was as important as action. Even a great strong man was not accepted if he abused his strength and bullied others. A man must be generous and respectful of others.

The term — trial — for Adoltay had no meaning. *Perhaps,* he thought, *a trial could be the vision quest, the testing of a young man's courage as he sought his place in the scheme of things.* A testing was not something the boy feared. A testing was a good thing — a way of revealing one's character. A man sought to be tested, to be measured, to rise up.

One of the soldiers had said to a Mexican, in language the boy understood, that they were going to take the prisoners to Texas and hang them. Hanging, as opposed to simple killing,

50

the boy believed trapped a man's soul in his body. Adoltay did not want that.

Adoltay lay on the stone floor, listening to the sounds outside. Summer was on the land. The air was warm, almost empty of moisture. Even the faintest noises moved quickly through it — the sound of a fly buzzing, the sound of the soldiers, shouting orders, the sound of their feet on the hard-packed earth, the sound of their guns lifted, presented, the sound of hammers and saws on the new building, going up. The young warrior closed his eyes and listened. Listening, he fell asleep.

Chapter Four

Brazos Reserve
Spring, 1858

"Get those cows in there," one of the cowboys shouted. "Open that gate wider, yuh fool!"

The Indian boy watched the small herd of cattle pushed through the gate into the Brazos Agency corral. The cowboys were something to see for all the children. They stood together under the sparse shade of a mesquite where they had been playing and now drank in the cowboys. The oblivious white men shouted and spat and struck their legs with coiled ropes and moved the cattle with casual authority. Some of them sat a horse almost as well as a Kiowa. But it was the way they moved that struck the children. They moved so confidently, so sure of themselves, with just a dash of bravado that thrilled the children's hearts.

Robert Neighbors waited on the porch for the dust to settle and the men to come up to the frame house. The cowboy boss swung down and shook hands with the agent. Adoltay and some of the other boys darted to the corner of the building. He wanted to hear the men's heavy boots and the jingle of their spurs on the hollow floor. He did not understand the talk, but the words were strong and good-natured.

The cow boss went inside with the agent to get his money, but the five men with him dropped down in the shade to smoke and rest or work their saddle rigging into a better place.

Quietly the children emerged from around the corner, drawn by the fascinating men. One man looked up at them. "Mess of little ones, ain't there?" he said to the others.

52

"Nits make lice," another man observed, jerking on his saddle girt.

"Aw, shut up, Shorty," the first man replied. "You're always sour as a green persimmon. They're cute little boogers. Here . . . ," he offered a curious child a close-up view of his cigarette making. "Look here, here's how it's done. Yuh make a trough in the paper with your finger, then, tap in the tobac', close up your sack and put her away, then lift up the paper real careful and lick it, so." He slid his tongue along the thin paper. "Now close it shut and twist up the end. Ain't that simple? Stick it in yer mouth, strike a match to it, and you're in business." He started to stick the cigarette in the child's mouth.

"Don't do that, Smitty. He's just a little kid," John Wooten said. He was lean and hard and brown as an Indian, but he had blue eyes, and sandy hair stuck out from under his sweat-stained Stetson. A heavy, unkempt mustache bristled from beneath his nose.

The children looked up his length as Wooten took the cigarette and handed it back to the Smitty.

"I's smokin' regular, time I's his age," Smitty protested. "I never meant no harm."

"I know you never did," Wooten said, laying his hand on Smitty's shoulder. Then he turned his glance to the Indian children. "You kids know where there's any water to wash up in? ¿Agua para lavarse?"

The children stood and kept looking now at Wooten.

"Well, maybe around the building somewhere . . . ?" he continued and started around the side porch.

The children followed. A wash stand, soap, and a crumpled towel stood by the back door. Wooten slapped his hat over a peg and began to unbutton his frayed cuffs. He followed by untying his red neckerchief and dropping it over the hat crown. He proceeded to unbutton the front of the dusty denim shirt and tug it out of his jeans. He tossed it over the adjoining peg.

53

The children gasped. Underneath the shirt, where the Texas sun did not penetrate, the man was white as the flesh of a fish. Just his hands and neck and face were a deep red brown. He turned and looked at them, then turned back, and poured water into the bowl. Grabbing the cake of lye soap, he made a great lather in his brown hands. He whistled and sang softly as he scrubbed the back of his neck and ears and lathered his face before dipping it to the bowl and rinsing it with great scoops of water from his hands. He proceeded to his chest and arms with the soap, but rinsed with a rag that had been hanging on the stand. He was dry before he toweled off, but he ran the coarse cloth gingerly over his skin. He bent slightly, removing a gapped-tooth comb from a metal cup, and slicked down his cropped hair in the piece of mirror above the basin.

"Boys, there's nothing like cleaning the dust off to make a fella feel new made," Wooten said to the uncomprehending children. He reset his hat, retied the neckerchief, and finally pulled on his shirt again. He rebuttoned it as he clanked along the porch, followed by the children.

"Kids always follow you, Wooten?" asked Smitty.

"Mostly do," Wooten said.

The ranch foreman emerged from Neighbors's office, shook hands again, and turned to go. "Let's get on home."

The cowboys quickly remounted and started away. Before he left, John Wooten bent toward the Indian children. He touched the brim of his wide hat with a backward flip of his long fingers. "Seein' yuh."

Neighbors dropped his hands easily over the shoulders of the two biggest boys as they all watched the cowboys ride away.

The cowboys would bring cattle several times to the reservation while Adoltay was there with his mother. John Wooten would bring hard sugar candy in his shirt pockets for the children. One time there had been a card game between the white men and some of the warriors. Another time there was a horse race. Wooten's little horse

54

was a match for the Indian ponies when they rode straight down to the cedar tree and back to the agency porch. But when they rode an Indian race — no saddle, jumping over a rawhide rope at the cedar, turning quickly in the short space between it and a second rope, and jumping back out to race back — Wooten fell off. He laughed and laughed till tears ran out his eyes as the children tried to help him get back on his horse and catch the warriors, racing away. Adoltay rode back with him on the withers of the sweating horse.

Other white men also came to the Brazos. Some came with scowls on their angry faces and guns, lying across their laps. There was shouting between these men and Neighbors. The agent sometimes went with them. They thought the Indian people on the Brazos Reserve had stolen their horses, but checking the Indian ponies revealed no stolen horses. Yet, the white men were not satisfied. They were sure that the Indians had already gotten rid of them, and that the Indian-loving agent was protecting them. Indians, these men said, had no place in Texas.

Once when the angry men, coming in a group, became more strident, shouting more, demanding horses from the Penateka Comanche herds, Neighbors asked Wooten, who had recently brought cattle, to stay over for a few days at the agency. The cowboy worked on the corral during this time, resetting and strengthening the posts and ties. He tended the steers and watched gravely when the jubilant, shouting warriors tried to shoot them down like buffalo. But the old men were not good shots with rifles, and cattle did not run like buffalo. Wooten then walked methodically among the wounded, struggling steers, loading and firing his rifle, quickly finishing them for the women to butcher. Adoltay found him later, sitting on the steps, elbows against the higher step, holding the outstretched gun by the tip of the barrel. The cowboy's hat was pushed back on his thatch of hair.

"Candy?" the boy asked.

"Sorry, pard, I'm all out." Wooten turned his pockets inside out with his free hand. "I'll bring some more next time I come."

The boy sat beside Wooten, dangling his feet from the porch floor toward the ground.

"Looks like you've got a friend, Wooten," Neighbors said, also sitting on the steps.

The cowboy nodded.

"Tough going out there . . . having to kill all the wounded steers."

The cowboy nodded again. "There ought to be a better way to do that than to turn 'em loose and let everybody shoot at 'em. Runs the meat off 'em. Poisons what's left because of their fear. No wonder Indians ain't too fond of beef."

"The Indians always took their food by hunting in the old days before the reservation," Neighbors explained.

"This ain't exactly the old days."

"Killing the buffalo was sacred," Neighbors continued. "The Indian people respected them. They prayed to the buffalo spirit before they killed the buffalo."

"I don't think cows is sacred to 'em," the cowboy said softly. "I heard more sportin' than prayers. Cow killin' ain't meant for sport. Just kill 'em outright, 'cause it has to be done if we're goin' to eat. That's enough. Just kill 'em outright. Don't torment them. I mean, there ain't no respect for something in tormenting a living thing."

The days that followed passed calmly at the agency with the children flocking after Wooten. Neighbors began to think he had judged the threat falsely. Looking out his window, the agent saw the tall cowboy, carrying one of the little ones on his broad shoulders. Wooten set the tiny girl gently down as he began his work. A piercing scream drew the cowboy's head up. He rose and ran toward the new barn. Neighbors burst through the open agency door and followed him. The screams grew louder as the men ran.

56

Neighbors and Wooten stopped side by side, taking in the pandemonium. A group of masked riders was at the barn. Tossing loops over the newly reset posts, they tore the fence out and fanned the Indian cattle loose out onto the prairie. Two of the men cut off behind the cattle, yipping and shooting, killing the fleeing beasts. Others of the masked riders rode into the barn, tossing burning brands into the hay, igniting the entire structure as the agency man and Wooten watched.

Chief Double Mountain and others ran up beside the agent. The old chief drew back his bow to defend the barn.

Neighbors pushed it aside. "No," he said. "They want a fight."

"By God, the barn-burning bastards need a fight," John Wooten said, and started toward a rider emerging from the flaming building.

Neighbors caught the cowboy's arm. "No! Look!" He pointed up to the loft door where young Adoltay stood with the flames, rising around him.

Some of the malevolent riders gathered now under the child, taunting him.

"Come on, kid. Jump! I'll catch you . . . on the end of my knife," laughed one.

Wooten shrugged off Neighbors's heavy grip. He crossed the space to the barn in long steps.

"Tie the pulley rope around your waist," Wooten shouted at Adoltay.

One of the riders hit Wooten hard across the face with his quirt. The cowboy barely winced and dodged the next blow. "Your little Injun don't know what yer saying," the rider spat in Wooten's face. "Yuh Injun loving son-of-a-bitch!"

Wooten whirled on the rider, caught the quirt, and jerked him from the horse. He vaulted into the saddle and spurred the horse toward the barn. One of the arsonists rode in front of the cowboy, blocking him as another cut him off from the rear.

"You're goin' to watch the maggot burn!" the man in front

shouted into the cowboy's ear above the roar of the burning timbers and the child's frantic cries.

"The hell I am," Wooten answered. He drove a hard fist into the man's jaw, knocking him backwards onto the ground.

"Get the kid, Wooten," Neighbors shouted, slamming a shovel into the second rider's back. Chief Double Mountain and the other men swarmed over the grounded attackers.

Wooten spurred the horse toward the barn. He stood in the saddle and leaped for the loft opening. Pulling himself up, he took Adoltay by the waist, lifting him from the burning floor. He leaned out and caught the rope attached to the pulley. He set his boot in the heavy hook, hanging from the rope. "Hang on," he said to the child. "This'll be fun." But Wooten's face was serious when the boy looked.

From the vantage point of the roof, it was clear that the attackers had done their work and were leaving. Only two men were left, the ones Wooten and the agent had knocked from their horses. The Indians held them prisoners. Neighbors and some of the other men now were running toward the barn and stood, looking up at the grim cowboy and the Indian child.

"They're leaving," shouted Neighbors.

"Yeah, I see," Wooten said almost to himself. "Lower away," he called out.

The men on the ground took the lashed rope from its mooring and steadily lowered the two to the ground as the center of the barn crashed inward. A gust of fiery heat shot out the door into the men's faces.

Adoltay's mother took him from the cowboy almost as they touched the ground. She held him very close.

That night, Buffalo Going gathered her son and household and left the Brazos Reserve to return to her Kiowa people, free on the open plains. That day was the last Adoltay saw of John Wooten for many years.

* * * * *

The remnant of the decimated Penateka Comanches and Agent Robert Neighbors left the Brazos and Clear Fork Reserves in Texas and crossed the Red River into the jurisdiction of the United States on September 1, 1859. On September 2, 1859, Agent Neighbors was shot in the back and killed by a grief-stricken frontiersman at Fort Belknap, Texas. No one was brought to trial for the assassination.

Chapter Five

Early June, 1871
Weatherford, Texas

Even without a telegraphed message from Fort Sill, news moved rapidly among travelers on the frontier. Stagecoaches and wagon drivers usually brought the first reports from distant places, since men hesitated to travel alone during Indian trouble. The first report contained the barest minimum of information when it reached the office of Warren and DuBose, Freighters. According to Von Jordan, one of the freighters, the Yankee general, Sherman, had ordered the arrests of three Kiowa leaders involved in the massacre of the company's teamsters. The names were not well known, and the man did not remember anyone but Satanta. Still, three Kiowa Indians were to be returned to Texas to stand trial before a Texas jury. Also, the forty-one head of mules taken were to be returned. Von Jordan added that it was not, by God, hearsay. He'd heard it first-hand himself, at the fort.

Judge Charles Soward's clerk ran the news upstairs to the judge's chambers, overlooking the town square. Soward stood at the window, hands clasped behind his back, as the young man burst in. The clerk did not see the open letter, lying on Soward's desk.

"Judge, the Army has arrested three Indians involved in the Warren wagon train massacre. One of the freighters says they are to be tried in Texas. Judge, the trial will be in our district."

"Is that what all the rhubarb's about in the street?" asked Soward.

"Yes, sir, that's it. No damned Indian has ever been taken off the reservation and tried like a white man before," the clerk pronounced. "The people think it's something. Maybe things are changing . . . maybe the government's on our side at last. That's what they're saying."

The judge turned from the window and walked to his desk. He pushed the letter toward the young man. "We'll try the case in the regular July term at Jacksboro. The incident probably happened in Young County, but their records are in Jacksboro anyway, so we'll try it there."

"You knew?"

"Well, some preparations have to be made. The Army had to tell me." Soward rubbed his chin as he walked behind the desk.

The young man's eyes ran over the letter sent by General William Tecumseh Sherman to Fort Richardson and forwarded with other information to Judge Soward.

We now hold Satanta, Satank, and Adoltay, or Big Tree, three as influential and as bad Indians as ever infested any land — Let the Jacksboro people know of this — Remember this, these men must not be mobbed or lynched, but tried regularly for murder and as many crimes as the Attorney can prove; but the military authorities should see that these prisoners never escape alive, for they are the very impersonation of murder, robbery, arson, and all the capital crimes of the Statute Book.

"Tell me, Clerk Robinson, from what you know of the law and the community, do you think this can be a fair trial . . . I mean with an impartial jury, willing to consider both sides of the argument?"

James R. Robinson thought a minute. "Here, sir, there aren't two sides. I mean there can't be a side for attacking those twelve men on Salt Creek Prairie. There's no side for burning Samuel Elliott alive over a wagon tongue. How could there be?"

The judge sat in his chair and tilted it back against a squeaking spring. "No possibility, then, for a fair trial? This is our chance to nail those savages for all they've done to us for the last fifteen years?"

The earnest young man nodded. "Yes, sir, that's right."

"And who has been supporting the savages the last fifteen years?"

"Why, the bleeding-heart folks in the East and the Reconstruction government," the clerk answered. "People in safe places where there's no danger. They wiped out their Indians years ago, but are too good to let us handle ours."

"And how do you think those people in safe places are going to react to this trial if it's not fair and square? Won't they have made their point if we take those three Kiowas out and hang 'em from whatever tree we can find, or a wagon tongue if we can't find a tree?" queried Soward.

James Robinson dropped down without invitation in the fat leather chair in front of Soward's desk. "You mean we're the ones on trial?"

Soward nodded. "That's right, son. It's always the people who hold the trials and sit on the jury who are on trial. Lawyers tend to forget that in their absorption with winning. Judges tend to forget that in the fullness of their calendars. But it is always we who are on trial. If we are too harsh, something dies in the souls of the people. If we are too lenient, the fabric of civilization falls apart. If it's who a man is, for good or bad, rich or poor, and not the act he has done, then we've lost the thread of justice. If there is no fairness, no blind justice, we

62

are no more than the old kings of Europe who made one kind of justice for themselves and their friends and another for the rest of the people."

"But Judge, the people out on the street aren't going to think about that or give a damn if they do. What are we going to do? We can't let the Kiowas go. People won't stand for that . . . not after they've seen their families murdered and mutilated, their women and kids carried off. They'd burn the courthouse and lynch us."

"But such are the concerns of true justice, James. These are thoughts to ponder. We have a confession, but did the confessor know it was a condemning statement? We have a certainty that an atrocity was committed, but do we know, in fact, who committed it? Do we have condemning evidence on these particular men? We have a body of experience on this frontier that tells us the Indians' guilt is certain, but do we have a body of law that defines that guilt? Was the act murder in the first degree . . . premeditated, planned, and carried out in the midst of a robbery . . . or was it an act of some other sort, of war, say? Are two codes of jurisprudence in conflict here with one taking ascendancy over the other in this trial?"

"Judge," replied Robinson, "I don't think you'd better say such things outside this room."

"Perhaps not," said Soward, "but in here we must think them. We must find guilt and, at the same time, not forget justice."

"Aren't they the same thing, finding guilt and finding justice?"

"I'm not sure, son." Judge Soward swiveled his chair around toward the window and propped his dusty boots on the sill. "I'm not sure."

Chapter Six

Night of June 7, 1871
Fort Sill, Indian Territory

The soldier guard led Caddo George Washington across the dark quadrangle to the small stairway that led down into the subterranean room beneath the stone barrack building where the three prisoners waited. In the past several days the old Caddoan chief had made this journey several times. He was descended from the ancient Caddo people removed from Arkansas and the East. Farming was not alien or demeaning to his people. It had always as long as any man could remember been their way of life. The three sisters — corn, squash, and beans — had sustained the Caddos for centuries. They traded what they did not need to the wild tribes who became their friends, seeing the benefits of supplementing their buffalo diet with fresh watermelons and corn. And the Caddos, in turn, enjoyed their buffalo. Just as the wild tribes needed the buffalo, peace was something the agricultural people needed. They could not strike their lodges and move quickly like the Kiowas to fight or to avoid attack. They needed time for their crops to grow. They needed peace. Taking the white man's road was not so hard for them.

Caddo George was not, therefore, like the Kiowa chiefs in conflict with the government. He made no trouble, no disharmony with the song of peace. He walked the white road, sowed corn and beans, ran a little store. The Quakers pointed to his progress toward white civilization with humble pride. The Indians also trusted Caddo George. He was their friend and old

Satank's special friend and welcome at the prison. His little store supplied the Kiowas with many necessary things — beads and vermilion, metal arrow points and knives, the repeating rifles and ammunition used in the Warren wagon train raid. The man had nicely mastered, with native good sense, the elements of success. Since he was genuinely appreciated by both sides and also genuinely appreciated both sides, Caddo George could come and go without much fanfare. He became the prisoners' courier to their people. They gave him messages for their families. Sometimes he added a bit, softening Satanta's words about war, encouraging the return of the mules. He also softened the Kiowas' thoughts for the white man's benefit when he talked with them. No need to make things worse. He told the chiefs, in turn, what was happening with the People and the white men. Caddo George had a deep well of understanding. He knew that all men were, after all, just men. A few things were very important, but most things were not and could be softened for the sake of civility and profit.

The black soldier, a good man, talked easily with the affable Caddo chief as they walked. "Satank has been asking for you. That old man's got a bug in his ear for sure. He's asked twice for you. That's the most he's done since he's been in here. Mostly he jest sets and looks at the far wall like it ain't there, like he's seeing the prairies or watching the years played out on it." He held the lantern high to show Caddo George the descending stairs. "I can't give you the lantern to take inside. Something happened . . . the building might get burnt down. Then where'd I be? In trouble sure. But I can hang it here by the door, and it'll give some light."

At the soldier's nod, the guard, standing beside the door, bent and inserted a key into the lock. "Move back," he said to the chiefs inside. "Move away from the door." Satisfied with their response, he twisted the key and swung the door open

65

into the cell. Caddo George passed into the low room. The door closed. The key turned again in the lock.

Having been ten days in this room, the chiefs were tired and disheveled. Caddo George observed their altered appearance. Satanta, usually boastful and arrogant, was quiet and sullen. The boy, Adoltay, rested his chin on his arm as he looked out the narrow slit of a barred window at the land beyond. Satank alone seemed full of energy and determination. The People had always believed in his power. Tonight again, Caddo George saw it in the old man.

"You have told Stumbling Bear's wife about my children?" asked Satank without rising. "I want her to see to them. They are just babies. They must develop their power in the white man's world as I developed mine in the old world of our people. I have seen the power in them. It must be nurtured . . . both the boy and the girl. Ahvoty knows the way. She will raise them right."

"I have spoken with Ahvoty," Caddo George said. "She will see to your small children. It is good you have made these arrangements. Tomorrow the soldiers are carrying you to Texas."

The three chiefs straightened. Satanta walked into the light. "You are sure it is tomorrow?"

Caddo George nodded. "They will bring wagons for you in the morning."

Satank was on his feet now. He moved toward the door, glanced out at the oblivious guard. "Tomorrow you must go to the school and get the children. Take them to a place by the side of the road where they can see the pecan tree beside the creek. You will tell my son to wait somewhere near the tree for me. You will tell our families we are leaving." Satank turned to the other men. "Do you have words to send?"

"Please tell my mother," said Adoltay. "Tell her that I will go to Texas for a trial. I will remember her. I will do my best to take this trial just as she taught me when I was a child, crying from hunger."

Caddo George turned to Satanta whose face was obscured by the shadows. He did not speak at once to the chief, but waited. "Tell my family I will come back. I will talk to these white men. We will negotiate. I do not intend to die."

Satank led the Caddo chief toward the door. He spoke quietly. "Tomorrow you will bring something for me, my friend. We will embrace after I am checked for weapons, and you will give it to me. Do not forget the children. They must see . . . with their own eyes. Then they will see the future more clearly."

Caddo George Washington nodded and shook the bars of the door. By the time the soldier opened it, Satank was in the far dark corner.

"We can negotiate with these white men. The time has come," Satanta said to the old man. "Don't you agree that we should negotiate in Texas?"

"I am not going to Texas," came the answer from the deep shadows. "I am *Koitsenko*."

Chapter Seven

June 8, 1871
Fort Sill, Indian Territory

The three Kiowa prisoners blinked at the brightness of the early morning sun. Around them members of the officer corps and enlisted men of the 4th and 10th Cavalry formed a passageway to the waiting wagons. They shuffled forward, struggling with the leg irons joined to their handcuffs. Old Caddo George Washington forced himself suddenly between the soldiers and embraced his old friend, Satank. They looked at each other for a long moment before the soldiers forced the Caddo chief away. Satank pulled his blanket closer and straightened before walking on. Satanta and Adoltay followed.

Colonel Benjamin Grierson and Colonel Ranald Mackenzie observed the passing. For a moment old Satank moved toward them. They thought he wanted to shake hands in parting, as he had done with the commissioners at Medicine Lodge. Adoltay and Satanta quickly grabbed him and hobbled with him toward the first wagon. The old man struggled in their grip, saying words unknown to the white bystanders. He did not look back as Satanta and Adoltay struggled aboard the second wagon, grasping the single wagon hoop to which all the canvas top had been gathered. Their escort waited, then mounted beside them. Corporal John Charlton seated himself beside Adoltay on the right side of the wagon, facing forward. A private sat down beside Satanta with his back to the front. Antonio Burrel — called Tony Bordello by the soldiers — held the reins of the three span of mules and waited for

Mackenzie's command to move out.

Satank stood stoically beside the forward wagon, refusing to climb up onto the sacks of corn that made the wagon's seats. The sergeant conferred quickly with the lieutenant and rode forward. At his order, four men lifted the Kiowa chief into the wagon. Two climbed in beside the old warrior — Corporal Robinson sat next to him; a private faced him. Mackenzie nodded to Lieutenant Thurston, I Company, 4th Cavalry, officer of the day.

"Sergeant Varily," the young officer said, "move the party out."

"Move out," shouted Miles Varily, throwing his gloved hand in the direction the wagons would take.

As the first wagon pulled forward, an eerie sound drifted softly back over the creak of leather and wood, of horses and men. Satank was singing. "Going away to die. . . ."

Horace Jones, the interpreter, stepped closer to Mackenzie. "Colonel, you'd better watch that old man. He's singing his death song."

Mackenzie said nothing for a moment, but looked at the ground and brushed the dust with the tip of his boot. "What can he do, Mister Jones? He's seventy years old. He's shackled hand and foot. And there are two armed guards with him, not counting the escort."

"He means trouble," said the interpreter.

"If there is trouble, from any of them or any other warriors, we will kill them. Those were Sherman's orders." Mackenzie contemplated the orders and the scene before him. "That old man can't make much trouble the way he's trussed up."

Jones said no more, but walked away from Mackenzie. When Corporal John Charlton and the second wagon passed, he said: "Watch that old Indian. He means trouble." Charlton nodded.

Jones's eyes followed the departing wagons as they flowed through the quadrangle and down toward the agency buildings and the creek. He stood beside the 10th Cavalry's officer of the day, Lieutenant Richard H. Pratt. As they watched, Caddo George Washington drove a wagon, filled with agency school children, alongside Satank's wagon. He had told the teacher, Josiah Butler, that the children had been sent for. He did not say by whom.

"*Akia-ti-sumtu,* Admired One," the Caddo said. "Here are the children from the school. All the Kiowa children have fled away."

The old chief looked at the children. "They will do. Take this message to my people. Tell them I died beside the road. My bones will be there. Tell my people to gather them up and carry them away." He rode in silence for a moment, watching the road ahead. "Do you see that tree, old friend?" The Caddo nodded, following the direction of Satank's look. "When I reach that tree, I shall be dead."

One of the Tonkawah scouts, Captain Charley, rode between the two wagons, purposefully breaking the connection between the two old friends. He grinned, enjoying the sorry situation that the Kiowa chief was in. Satank knew his old enemy. All his long life he had despised the cannibalistic tribesmen. "You foul vermin, crawling over the white man's testicles, you may have my scalp. I, Satank, who killed every Tonkawah he could, give it to you, because you could not take it honorably. The hair is poor, thin, and gray now. It is not worth much, or I would not give it to such a nothing as you are. Still it is the best scalp you will ever get."

Satank turned away from the rider and began to sing again:

Iha hyo oya iya o iha yaya yoyo.

70

[Going away to die.]

Aheyo aheyo uaheyo ya eya heyo e heyo,
Ko-eet-senko ana oba hema haa ipai degi oba ika,
Ko-eet-senko ana oba hema hadamagagi oba ika.

[Oh, sun, you will live forever.
But we, *Koitsenko*, must die.
Oh, moon, you will live forever.
But we, *Koitsenko*, must die.
Oh, earth, you will live forever.
But we, *Koitsenko*, must die.]

Caddo George slowed his team, letting the wagon, carrying Satank, pull ahead. As the other chiefs passed by, Satanta called to the Caddo trader. "Old man, tell my people not to raid while I am in the hands of the Texans. Tell them to bring in the mules. Tell them, Satanta himself said this."

Washington nodded as he turned out the children's wagon and drove toward a rise that looked down on the road leading to East Cache Creek and the big pecan tree beyond. The children stood solemnly, holding the rough board sides of the complaining wagon as it rocked and swayed across the land. They were silent.

Horace Jones and Lieutenant Pratt walked out behind the wagons, keeping them in sight as they pulled through the quadrangle and down past the forge and stone corral. The interpreter watched closely the distant movements. The few buildings of the Kiowa-Comanche Agency lay ahead. Jones could almost hear the rocky bottom of the creek, grinding under the iron wheels as the teams crossed and headed up the grade toward the wide-spreading pecan tree. The children's wagon had come to a stop on the eastern rise.

"He's singing his death song, Pratt. He means to die where the People will see. If he has a chance, he'll do anything he

71

can to provoke his death. He's going to kill himself by our hands."

Lieutenant Pratt glanced thoughtfully at the dapper little interpreter with his trimmed mustache, brushed hat, white shirt, tie, and coat even in the June heat. Together they turned and walked back toward the main buildings of the fort. Grierson and Mackenzie still spoke near the prison.

"Damn, that noise is irritating," said the private in front of Satank. "Shut up!" He spit a stream of tobacco juice at the old man.

Sergeant Varily rode hastily forward. "That's enough of that! You will treat this man as a prisoner of the United States government. Is that clear, soldier?"

"Yes, sir," the black man said quickly. To his companion, he muttered, "I didn't hit him or nothing."

Satank pulled his head beneath his blanket, and the singing stopped. The soldiers laid their loaded guns in the bed of the wagon within easy reach. "Well, that's a relief," the private said.

Satank's head popped out of the blanket again. "Going away to die. Going away to die. Oh, sun, you will live forever. But we, *Koitsenko*, must die. Oh, earth, you will live forever. But we, *Koitsenko*, must die. My son, I will see you soon. I am coming to you. Make a little feast for me." He withdrew again to silence beneath the blanket.

The soldiers rocked in the heat of the June sun. Their eyes searched the land toward the horizon. They had been told to expect an attack, a rescue attempt.

"Bet it's hot under that blanket," the talkative private said. "But he's quiet under there."

Satank pulled the blanket from his head.

Corporal Robinson, sitting next to the old warrior, glanced at his companion opposite and grimaced. The private stared at the old man. "Looks like there's blood on his mouth and teeth," he said.

Robinson leaned forward to see. Suddenly the old one plunged a knife to the hilt in the man's thigh. The soldier grabbed the wound and howled. Standing up, staggering away from his attacker, he somersaulted backward out of the Indian's reach. The private rolled out the opposite side as Satank rose to his feet. He drove the knife he still clutched into the end of the black sash tied across his chest fastening it to the wood floor. He snatched one of the carbines from beside it. The warrior chief tried to lever a round into the chamber of the gun, but it jammed as an already loaded shell was poorly ejected. Satank fought the gun, trying to jerk it into action.

Lieutenant Thurston stood in his stirrups. "Shoot him! Shoot him!" Soldiers in the escort grabbed for their carbines, searching the far horizon for attack. "Fire!" the lieutenant yelled.

Corporal John Charlton, who saw the action in front of him, raised his carbine, aimed. Tony Bordello swung into his sights. He waited, found the Kiowa chief again. His index finger circled over the trigger.

Satank suddenly stood erect, throwing the betraying weapon from him, allowing Charlton's first bullet to strike him in the chest. Charlton fired again. The impact of the shots knocked the old man backward against the driver's seat. He reached for the second weapon, lying on the floor, and raised it over the side of the wagon.

"Fire!" yelled the lieutenant. More shots, now from other soldiers, pounded into the ancient warrior until he fell from the wagon to the road a few yards from the pecan tree.

Charlton felt a weight on his arm as he cocked the carbine again and stepped to stand above the fallen warrior. He looked down. Adoltay had placed his hand on his arm. "*Por favor. Por favor*. You have killed him enough."

The thought fleeted across Charlton's mind: *Why had the young Indian not done that before? Why had he not tried to take the gun?* He glanced at the private, facing him, to see if he had the young Indian covered. The private had slipped onto the wagon floor with his gun raised toward the front over the wagon's side. Satanta sat quietly as before, looking backward. Their eyes met for a moment, and Charlton knew that he had done exactly what the three chiefs intended.

Thurston was shouting as he turned his horse, looking for other enemies. "Hold your fire!" He rode quickly forward to the sergeant who already sat his horse above Satank. "Check him, Sergeant."

The sergeant dismounted and kneeled above the stricken Indian. "God A'mighty," he said softly to himself. "He's breathin'." Just as he spoke a moan came from Tony Bordello, up near the mules. The sergeant moved to him. Blood ran from the driver's head. "He's been hit, Lieutenant. Don't look too bad. Just a crease on his head. No vitals."

Back at the fort Mackenzie at the first shots had thrown himself into his saddle and dashed toward the sound of the guns. The colonel skidded into the confused escort party, shouting: "Deploy for the main attack. Where is the main force? Get ready." He drew to a halt over the lieutenant and sergeant whose bodies hid Satank. "What the hell's going on here?"

Lieutenant Thurston stood, revealing the warrior, propped against the wagon's front wheel. "He tried to escape, sir. He had a knife, seized a gun. I ordered the men to fire."

"Escape, hell," said Mackenzie, dismounting. "Get some flankers out, Lieutenant. This is no place to stop. You're wide open. Surgeon. Patzki, where are you?" Mackenzie was kneeling over Satank as he shouted. Patzki was forward beside the driver, Bordello. Mackenzie glanced up. "Surgeon!"

74

Patzki turned. "This man is badly wounded." He meant Bordello.

"*This* man is a prisoner of the United States government, Doctor Patzki! I want a full report on his condition . . . now!"

Patzki walked over and squatted beside the chief. "Well," he said, wiping his hands on his handkerchief, "he's shot to hell."

"Could you be more specific, please? Shot to hell is not an appropriate summary of the situation." Mackenzie kept looking about, expecting an attack to come from somewhere, feeling vulnerable and insecure in the open position. "Do this right, Patzki. Examine the man."

The surgeon felt the carotid artery in Satank's neck. "His pulse is very weak." He checked the dying man's eyes. "Pupils dilated." He moved down Satank's body, pulling the blanket and clothing away from the wounds. "He has at least five fatal wounds, Colonel, and a number of others that could together prove fatal."

Mackenzie glared at the arrogant surgeon. "Can this man live?"

"No," Patzki said.

Satank blinked and opened his eyelids slowly, lifting his gnawed hand weakly. The men followed his gesture toward the rise beyond the pecan tree. A mounted warrior, naked of all clothing, sat his mount beside another horse, carrying a small, carefully wrapped bundle on its back. "My son, I am coming to you. Make a little feast for me." Satank sank back.

"Dead?" asked Mackenzie.

"Dead," answered the surgeon.

"All right, let's get this outfit firmed up. Lieutenant, what's wrong with that soldier?" asked the colonel, noticing Corporal Robinson at last.

"The old man stabbed him, after he slipped his cuffs, sir."

"Slipped his cuffs?" asked Mackenzie incredulously.

"Yes, sir." Lieutenant Thurston spoke, looking straight ahead. "He chewed his hands to the bone so he could slip off the cuffs."

Patzki lifted one of Satank's gnarled, bloody hands, revealing the lacerations.

Mackenzie studied the old Indian. Somewhere in his analytical mind the wily colonel catalogued the willingness of the old Kiowa to mutilate and destroy himself rather than die in the white man's prison. He was writing there, in his mind, the field manual on fighting the American Indian. Mackenzie observed. Mackenzie learned. He did not make the same mistake twice. Already he had his men carry any extra ammunition on their persons. Leaving it in saddlebags only provided it to the Indians when the horses were stolen. More chapters were to be written in the coming campaigns.

"That soldier has a deep wound to his thigh and cannot ride," Patzki broke into Mackenzie's thoughts.

"We'll need an ambulance down here from the fort, Lieutenant. Get these men up to the hospital." Then Mackenzie asked: "Where'd that Indian go that was on the hill?"

The others looked about, but the man and the horses were gone. Mackenzie walked back along the side of the wagon, hastily checking the horizon. He stopped beside Satanta and Adoltay. Corporal Charlton stood with his back against the wagon hoop with his gun trained on the remaining chiefs. Both men sat emotionless, still, unseeing. "Everything under control here, Corporal?"

"Yes, sir," Charlton answered.

Mackenzie walked back along the wagons, retrieved his hat that had blown off as he hurried to join his men. "What the hell are you doing?" he asked the Tonkawah, Captain Charley, who had drawn his knife and kneeled beside Satank's body.

76

The scout looked startled, but grinned and gestured toward the scalp. Mackenzie kicked Satank's bloody, bullet-riddled blanket toward the scout. "Take that and get out of here." Mackenzie shoved his foot into the iron stirrup and remounted his horse. "Post a guard over the wounded men and Satank's body until Grierson sends an ambulance. Move this party out of here, Lieutenant. We're sitting ducks."

The colonel trotted ahead to examine his thoughts in the clear air of the rolling land.

Chapter Eight

June 10, 1871
Between Fort Sill and Jacksboro

Corporal John Charlton stood looking at the bodies of Satanta and Adoltay. Stakes had been driven into the prairie at their hands and feet, and the manacled men were lashed to them. A mosquito stung the soldier's sunburned neck, and he slapped it. Satanta groaned and twisted in his bonds. Charlton looked closer at the savage. Like all the men he was suffering from the continual attack of the insects that thrived after the spring rains. The soldiers had built fires of green wood and were trying to keep themselves within the smoke for protection. Some had rigged a kind of bonnet made from a portion of a woman's hoop skirt and cloth over their faces. Still they could not rest because of swarming, blood-sucking insects that pierced their heavy clothing. The air was alive with the high-pitched whine of insect wings. Unlike their captors, neither Satanta nor Adoltay could even attempt to defend themselves. They were stretched in torment.

Charlton squinted his whole face as he watched them. He walked away and stood with his back to the struggling Indians. "Shit!" he said to himself. He walked out into the brushes and broke two leafed limbs and returned to the suffering Kiowas. Loosening one of Satanta's manacled hands roughly from the leather thong that tied him to the stake, the soldier shoved a branch into it. "You make any trouble for me, and I'll . . . by God . . . shoot you dead. But I ain't goin' to watch you et by skeeters. You got that?" He looked straight into the Indian's

78

black eyes as he spoke. Satanta did not understand the words, but the gesture and the tone were plain. Charlton moved to the other man, released a hand from the thong, and gave him the other leaf fan. He repeated his injunction.

On the evening of June 15th the six units of the 4th Cavalry under Colonel Ranald Mackenzie arrived at Jacksboro, Jack County, Texas. As the now closely covered wagons rolled through the town square, the two chiefs were already securely inside the stone morgue, their prison at Fort Richardson. They had been sent ahead on horseback with a heavy guard. Not knowing this, the frontier town's citizens silently focused their hatred on the passing wagons.

June 16, 1871
Weatherford, Texas

Judge Charles Soward stood, watching at his window two stories above the street. A rider sat on his horse, surrounded by citizens of the county seat town. Other men were pouring out of the stores and saloons and off the board sidewalks to get closer to the messenger from Fort Richardson. James Robinson stood beneath the large window. He yelled up. "They brought the Kiowas in to Fort Richardson last night."

Soward turned to the young attorney who stood beside him. "Look at their faces, Joe. That's honest emotion. All the bitterness and hatred of your fellow man is right there for anyone to see. There's no effort at disguise out there tonight. Do you see it?"

The attorney nodded.

"There's something else there, too . . . the stunned look that comes from an unexpectedly realized hope. They are like the common folk who just heard that King John had signed a

79

document called the Magna Carta after all the years of fear and despair, after all the grim acceptance of tyranny. They never expected to see the Kiowas who killed their friends and family brought before a court of justice. They hoped it perhaps, but they gave it up. They are frontiersmen. They expect to be knocked down over and over. And they expect to get up and keep going without anyone else's support or approval. They settled for a killing here and there. They never thought the world would give them the chance to put their enemy before a true public court of law and display his heinous nature. There's an innocence in that. Look closely at them, Joe. They are your friends and neighbors." The judge clasped his hands behind his back as he walked to his chair. He gestured the younger man to another. "Have a seat, Joe. I want to talk to you."

Joseph A. Woolfolk limped around the spacious old desk and sat down. He was not a large man, but what was there was hard and tough as a frontiersman had to be. Woolfolk had survived the war and the Ohio State Penitentiary to make his way, finally, back through Kentucky to the frontier town he'd left. He had returned with his young wife. They were expecting their first child. The ex-soldier eased his war-injured leg out and leaned back.

Soward still stood beside his own chair. "We are going to have a trial in a few days. You and I know it can't be a fair trial. I've been talking informally to members of the bar here in Weatherford. I can give you a rough consensus up to now. We are going to try this case before a jury in Jacksboro at the next, regular session of the Thirteenth District Court of the State of Texas. That'll be July Third. Satanta and Adoltay will be found guilty and sentenced to hang. There won't be any detailed records. There won't be any appeals. S. W. T. Lanham will prosecute. I want you to defend."

Joe Woolfolk's head came up from the close study of his outstretched boot. "Defend?" he said incredulously.

"That's right. Defend the Kiowa chiefs." Soward nodded at the amazed younger man.

Woolfolk drew a deep breath and leaned his head against his hand. Soward studied the lawyer. Woolfolk opened his mouth, then closed it again. He had started to say — "Judge, I've got a family . . ." — but didn't. He had started to say — "Are you trying to destroy my life, my future?" — but didn't.

"Joe, you were in the Frontier Regiment. Every man out there knows you've ridden down raiding parties that killed settlers. Every man out there knows you've seen what raiders do. You were at the Mason and Cambren place. You saw. You know. Nobody would think less of you or call you an Indian lover for defending the Kiowas. They'll know it's just a job you're stuck with, and you're keeping up appearances for all of us. You might even win a point now and again. Defending the Indians won't hurt you like it would most of the other lawyers."

"You're going to try the Kiowa chiefs in a court of law . . . find 'em guilty . . . sentence 'em to hang . . . there won't be a real record anybody can go over and see I didn't do my job . . . there won't be an appeal, so there's no danger of a reversal for the court . . . and you want me to defend them because nobody else will, and maybe it won't ruin my future because of my past with the Frontier Regiment?" Joe Woolfolk framed the facts as he understood them into a long question.

"That's right, Joe." Soward nodded.

Woolfolk sat with his face resting against his hand. He did not move for long moments as the judge waited above him. Finally he reached over and removed his Stetson from Judge Soward's desk. He rose and walked slowly to the door before he set the wide-brimmed hat thoughtfully on his head. He paused with his hand on the doorknob. As he left, Soward heard him say: "I'll defend the Kiowas."

Chapter Nine

Joe Woolfolk walked through the crowd in the street, unseen and unseeing. The sign, hanging beside the stairway that led up to his small office, read: **Joseph A. Woolfolk, Attorney-at-Law.** He stopped and looked at the sign, then walked past it toward home.

Jinny Woolfolk heard the front door open and left the kitchen. "Joe? Joe?" she called. She found her husband, placing his hat flat on the hall table with just the front brim hanging off. He sat a small vase on the back edge of the brim. This, she had learned, was Joe's one vanity. He could not stand a hat with the brim bent up in back. His good hat had to be placed right and not carelessly moved. "What's wrong, Joe? You look terrible."

"I'm fine," he said, and went to his rocker.

Jinny stood, watching him, wiping her hands on the cup towel. "You don't look fine."

He sat. She moved to light the lamp beside him. He caught her hand and held it, looking at it, at the simple, gold band on her finger. She settled onto his lap. "Joe?"

His fingers closed over her hand and drew it to rest over their baby. "Judge Soward wants me to defend the Kiowa chiefs." Jinny pulled away in anticipated outrage at the judge's audacity. "I said I would."

Jinny Woolfolk came to her feet. "You said you would? Joe, what have you done to us?"

Joe looked up into her gentle face. "I don't know," he said, shaking his head. "I was walking out, and I heard myself say

. . . I'll defend the Kiowas. It really won't be a defense, the way the judge put it. Lanham will prosecute. The jury will find them guilty. They'll be sentenced to hang. There won't be a record of the trial. There won't be an appeal. He thinks, because I was in the Frontier Regiment, people won't hold it against me that I defended them."

"He thinks!" Jinny exclaimed. "He thinks! Well, I think he's playing a very unfair game with our lives."

"Well, Jinny, that's so. But I was thinking, coming home, about my sign. Joseph A. Woolfolk, Attorney-at-Law, it says. That means me, my name, Joe Woolfolk. But what does Attorney-at-Law mean? Is it just a job, like cleaning the stable? Freddie Boone doesn't complain about mucking out the stalls. He doesn't say, well, I'll tote the hay and sweep out, feed and water and saddle and harness and clean the tack, but I ain't wading in that horse manure. Freddie may not like it, but he does it without complaining. He doesn't expect that privilege of choice. And he doesn't get paid as much as I do."

"Freddie didn't put as much into his education as you have," said Jinny. "It isn't the same."

"That, dear Jinny, depends on how you look at it. I've worked myself out of the stable. I wear clean white shirts and work at a desk in my office or in the courtroom. Most of the time things are mighty pleasant . . . no heavy lifting . . . contracts and property, seeing my client gets a good fit, seeing I make a good living. Other times I'm called on to defend somebody the state says has committed a crime. I like to think I'm protecting innocent people from the injustices of the state. Sometimes I am. Sometimes I don't know. Sometimes I know that my client is guilty and a menace to his fellow man. In that case, am I just keeping Freddie Boone, or in this case S. W. T. Lanham, from hauling out the manure because I can, because I'm good? Now, if I

84

succeed often enough, because I can and for my own gratification, manure will pile up until it ruins the barn and kills the animals. On the other hand, I might catch Freddie or Lanham hauling manure into the barn."

"Why on earth would Freddie haul manure into the barn?" asked Jinny, smiling.

Joe looked at her pretty face. "I don't know. We haven't established his motives. Maybe somebody down the street is paying him to get rid of theirs without anybody knowing. Maybe he's trying to impress his boss. Look at all the manure I'm hauling out! Anyway, let's say Freddie's trying to put manure in the barn, even with the good intention of later hauling it out again. It'll still destroy the barn and kill the animals just the same as manure left naturally in the barn. Now what do I do? Keep it in or keep it out?"

"Oh, Joe," the woman smiled. "Are you toying with my mind?"

"I am not." He spoke seriously. "This is a crucial question . . . in or out. Answer the question."

"Well," said Jinny, "you'd better think about what's important. Why are you hauling manure to start with? In or out doesn't matter. You're trying to make the barn a clean, wholesome place where things can live good lives. That's what you've got to keep foremost in your thinking. Don't get your mind on the manure. Think about the barn and the life in it."

"Thank you, Missus Woolfolk. You've seen with the clear, profound eyes of innocence." Joe drew in a deep breath and stood up. He put his arm around Jinny and walked her toward the kitchen.

"By the way, Joe, whichever way Freddie is hauling that manure, I need some to improve my garden." Jinny Woolfolk suddenly stopped and looked into her husband's face. She realized he had again turned her thoughts from their needs to something larger, using of all things manure. "Manure," she added softly.

"I'll see Freddie in the morning. What's for supper, Missus Woolfolk?"

Chapter Ten

Mid-June, 1871
Fort Richardson, Texas
The Prison

"Do you hear women singing?" asked young Adoltay.

Satanta listened. "I hear women's voices, but they are not singing. They are laughing and talking."

"Are there women in prison here?" wondered the young Kiowa.

"Perhaps," speculated the older man. "But I think they are the women who wash the soldiers' clothes. When we came in, we were brought through the room with tubs for washing. I can see women out this window. They are hanging up soldier clothes."

Adoltay went to the window and looked where Satanta pointed. Women with big baskets of wet clothes were hanging them quickly and turning back to the baskets for the next shirt or pants. The wind lifted the heavy garments and walked beneath. The women were laughing and talking, oblivious to the watching men.

"They seem good-natured," ventured the young man. "That one with the scarf in her hair is good to look at."

"Do not look too hard, Adoltay. It will be a long time before we know women again." Satanta sat down with his words. "I guess it is usual for young men to think of women. I myself do not think of them much. If I have a need, I take one. I do not care much what woman it is any more. It is just my need. My mind is more on other things. Right now, I wonder how

I am to get out of this place."

"Will we try an escape?" asked Adoltay, turning his face from the window.

"No," Satanta stated. "I do not see how. My legs and arms are always in chains. The walls are stone, many inches thick. The bars on the window are iron. My people are far away, maybe still running from the white men. No, I cannot escape this prison. I must use my head now. I advise you to do so also. Be amiable. Tell them what they wish to hear. When I am a free man again, I shall do as I wish. I told the old Caddo to tell the People not to raid as long as I am held captive. I told them to return the mules. The white men will negotiate. They are too weak to hold a course for very long. I know that Kicking Bird is even now trying to make himself big by bringing those mules in for me." Satanta laughed. "It will cost him a lot to get those mules for me."

The Kiowa Camp

"Do you not care that Satanta and Adoltay are in the white man's prison in Texas?" asked Kicking Bird.

Pacer nodded. "Yes, I am concerned."

"Then why will you not return the Texas mule?" pursued Kicking Bird.

The little Kiowa-Apache warrior looked at the ground. "It is a very good mule. My wife likes that mule very much. She says it is the best mule she has ever had."

Kicking Bird settled against the log backrest and studied Pacer. "Then give me another mule. The Texans only want forty-one mules. They will not know which forty-one."

"I don't have another mule," Pacer said softly. "If I had another mule, I would need it, too."

Kicking Bird continued gazing at the other man. "Satanta

is not my friend. I do not care what happens to him. I am not concerned about him. I am concerned about the People. We have too many old and too many young to fight the white man. Satanta does not think about that when he takes men to Texas to raid. You do not think about that either, Pacer, when you slip away with him. You have been my friend. I believed you understood."

"I could not stop the young men. They wanted to go against the Texans. Mamanti told them they would have a good fight with many coups." Pacer scratched the belly of one of his innumerable dogs.

"Well, you are no help," said Kicking Bird. "You cannot stop your young men from raiding, and you will not return the Texas mule."

"My wife prefers that mule," Pacer protested.

Kicking Bird tapped the stick he held lightly against the ground. "I want you to pick this up and hold it close, Pacer. When the white man tires of dallying, he will come on us hard. Do not play with this tiger. He will kill you and all your people. You must stop the young men from raiding. Kill their horses and break their weapons but stop them."

"Why do you say such things, Kicking Bird? You are not afraid of white men. I know you. We have ridden many times together. You are a true Kiowa. Remember when we chased the soldiers all day, and they hid between their ponies?" Pacer relished the story. His hands gestured rapidly as he recalled what the white men called the Battle of the North Fork of the Little Wichita. "It was almost exactly a year ago. You divided us into groups. We came from every side . . . this way and that way. While one group hit them, another would rest. We never even got tired, fighting all day. Satank and Guipago could say nothing. It was a great victory."

Kicking Bird listened to Pacer's excited tale of his victory

89

against the soldiers from Fort Richardson. Pacer's recollection would remind him of the peace chief's power for war. Kicking Bird had had to go against the whites to prove that he had chosen the peace road from strength not fear. Satank and Guipago had been ridiculing him to the other chiefs. The Kiowas were not listening any more to his council. He had thought a long time about fighting before he had proposed it to the others. It was to be a fight. There would be no stealing, only fighting. Rather than sneaking into Texas to kill and loot the settlers, he had picked a worthy opponent, the United States Cavalry at Fort Richardson.

Several of his young men bolted, going off on their own to hit the mail stage at Rock Creek Station. This pulled Captain Curwin McClellan and fifty-three troopers of the 6th Cavalry into the field. Kicking Bird capitalized on the premature venture of his men. Little by little, with a sign left here and another farther on, he drew the soldiers through the spring rains toward him. McClellan found the whip of the stage driver on the banks of South Fork of the Little Wichita. He crossed. More sign lured him over the Middle Fork. When he crossed the North Fork, he was forced into camp by heavy rains.

On the morning of July 12, 1870, Captain McClellan spotted what he believed to be the main party of Kicking Bird's Kiowas. The veteran commander formed the men into ranks, unfurled the flag and regimental guidons. With sabers drawn, the troopers advanced at a trot. The white men could see the Indians clearly dressed in their finery, their ponies dancing in anticipation.

With the Kiowas only five hundred yards ahead, McClellan learned of his mistake. Two bands, equal in number to the one in front, appeared on his flanks. The captain called a halt, formed a living barricade of his horses — one man holding and three firing for each group of mounts — and began a slow retreat back toward the river. Kicking Bird kept up a galling fire throughout the morning and afternoon, pushing the troopers, sending three-fourths of his two hundred and fifty men at a time, resting the other fourth. Kicking Bird broke off the action about nightfall, after driving the soldiers over the South Fork. He had made his point. His honor and prestige were restored.

The Indians said Kicking Bird led the first charge against the soldiers himself, sweeping past the front ranks to impale a soldier on his lance. Army records made no mention of that action. When McClellan and his weary, exhausted soldiers finally returned to Richardson, they counted two men dead and twelve wounded. Eight horses were killed and twenty-one wounded. Thirteen soldiers received Medals of Honor for gallantry in action at the North Fork of the Little Wichita.

Captain McClellan himself reported the mission was a "perfect success." He wrote that he had "taught them a lesson they will not soon forget." Dr. Julius Patzki, post surgeon, noted in his "Record for the Month of July, 1870":

The systematic strategy displayed by the savages, exhibiting an almost <u>civilized</u> mode of skirmish fighting, struck the officers and men engaged.

Kicking Bird never led another war party. He had made his point to both red and white men.

"It was a great victory," Kicking Bird repeated quietly after Pacer finished. "Ask yourself, old friend, are there fewer white men? Have they run away in fear of us?"

Pacer shook his head. "No, there are still white men."

"But there are not so many Kiowas," said Kicking Bird. "My wife has died. I have only my daughter left. My life is gone. I would like now only to see the People survive."

"You have spoken well, Kicking Bird. I will talk to my young men."

Pacer followed Kicking Bird toward his horse.

The peace chief swung into his saddle. "Perhaps tomorrow your wife would like to bring her exceptional mule and exchange it for two good horses from my herd."

"I will talk to her," Pacer said.

Kicking Bird rode away toward his camp.

Chapter Eleven

Weatherford, Texas

Before Joe Woolfolk hit the stairs to his office, a heavily-mustached cowboy, John Wooten, said from under the shadows of his weathered Stetson: "Hey, Woolfolk, I hear you've turned Injun lover."

"Shut up, John," Joe said. "You know better than that. Judge Soward just assigned me to the defense. I didn't have a choice."

As Joe climbed the stairs, he knew the words were a lie. He had made the choice to defend the chiefs. At least some part of him had made the choice and spoken out to the judge. He had lain in his bed all night without sleeping, examining the words he had spoken. He'd agreed to defend men he personally loathed. What he probably hated worse was that he'd agreed to an essentially rigged trial, a kangaroo court. Moreover, he may have agreed to ruin the best chance at a life he and Jinny had. In the morning light his decision only irritated him — the high ideal of keeping manure out of the great barn called justice didn't seem so clear any more.

He opened the unlocked door, asking himself where his character had gone, where his good sense was? He stopped short in the doorway. Feathers on a Kiowa lance, driven deeply into the wooden top of his desk, fluttered in the draft. From the lance dangled three blonde scalps. On the wall behind someone had painted in foot high letters: **Injun Lover!**

Without thinking, Joe ran, almost sliding, down the wooden stairway. He collided with John Wooten, who still loitered below, talking with friends. John caught him and staggered back. Joe slammed his fist into the hard belly of the other man.

Wooten grunted — "What the hell, Joe!" — but he drove back into the little lawyer with a hard fist.

Joe closed his eyes and fell back, but regained himself, and swung again at the bigger man.

John Wooten absorbed the blow and pressed heavy knuckles into the lawyer's jaw. "By God, Joe," he said as the lawyer hit the rough boards of the sidewalk in front of Teezer's General Mercantile.

Joe strove for his knees, but, before he could rise, Wooten clipped him under the chin and sent him out into the street. "Quit fightin' me, Joe," Wooten insisted, shaking the pain out of his own hand.

Joe picked himself up from the dirt. He brushed himself deceptively, then plunged again into Wooten.

Both men fell back over the chairs beneath the store's glass window. They rolled and tumbled, pulling each other up, pushing each other down, until Mrs. Teezer emerged with a new broom and began pounding both of them.

"Get up from there!" she cried. "What's the matter with you, Joe Woolfolk, and you, John Wooten? Why you're friends forever. Stop this foolishness right now."

Under the woman's hard blows the men were quick to come to a settlement. They moved swiftly apart. Mrs. Teezer managed a last thrust at each man.

Woolfolk was still steaming, "You bastard, you called me an Injun lover."

"Well, I done it a long time 'fore you came down them stairs. Did you have to think about it 'fore you got mad?" queried the lean cowboy.

"Hell, no," Woolfolk shouted. "You wrote it on my wall

94

and stuck that damned scalp lance in my desk. That ain't funny, John."

"Watch your language," Mrs. Teezer said and slapped the broom at the attorney.

John Wooten bent and picked up the crushed Stetson of his friend. He handed it over. Joe smoothed his hair back and reset the hat. "I never wrote nothin', Joe. Did any of you fellas write on Joe's wall?"

Nobody in the crowd stepped forward. Wooten turned and started up the stairs.

"Just a damn' minute, " Joe said, shouldering past. "It's my office."

"Lead the way, then," yielded Wooten. "I hope you're feelin' better after that fist swingin', 'cause I ain't your problem. You're just short fused 'cause you got yourself into this mess in the first place. Charlie Soward didn't hold you down."

"Shut up," said Woolfolk, knowing the truth of his friend's words. He stepped aside, revealing the desk, lance, and painted wall to the other man.

John Wooten walked to the desk and jerked out the lance. He ran his long fingers over the gash in the wood. "Don't fix that. Your kids'll want to point to it someday when we're civilized." The cowboy leaned back against the desk and examined the weapon, turning it in his hands.

Woolfolk came and stood beside him. "Didn't old Isaac Lynn pick that up when we chased that bunch of raiders from Willis Jordan's place?" he recalled.

The cowboy's hand touched the scalps gently. They were graduated down the shaft from small to large. The first two were short with hair no longer than five or six inches. The fineness of the hair had made the cowboys think at the time that maybe one or both had belonged to children. The other was long and silky, a woman's hair. "This could be Isaac Lynn's daughter's, her husband's, and the Cambren child's hair. The old man thinks these are their scalps."

"Maybe he's wrong," said Joe, sitting in the chair in front of his desk.

"Don't matter," responded the cowboy. "They belonged to some white people. We might as well let the old fella have it his way."

"God A'mighty, John," protested Woolfolk, "I'm not trying to mess with that old man. I know as well as you do what he's been through. I just don't want him coming in here and planting that lance in my desktop and writing Injun lover on my wall."

"Well, he thinks you are."

"Well, I'm not. You know that. You know me, John. I'm not some stupid back East Indian lover." Woolfolk leaned into the words.

"Then what are you worried about? If you ain't, you ain't."

"I don't like being called names," the lawyer said.

"If you're that thin-skinned, why'd you go for the defense?" asked the cowboy, setting the lance on its butt and looking at the lawyer.

Woolfolk tossed his crushed Stetson at the desk. "I don't know. I just heard myself say I'd do it."

The cowboy was not impressed with this answer. He waited.

"Hell, I've been there . . . put in prison without a fair trial. No trial really. Left to rot. Treated like I didn't exist as a man."

"It was war, Joe," the cowboy said softly. "You was way up in Ohio with Morgan's Raiders, and you got cut off and caught and put in prison. It was war."

The jurist came to his feet and paced away. He turned. "Well, maybe those damned Indians think it's war, too."

"Now you've stepped over it, Joe. Anybody on the street hear you say that and they'd swear to God you'd lost your mind and were sure enough an Indian lover. We've made peace after peace with the Indians. Every raid has broken that peace."

"Listen to what you just said, Wooten," Woolfolk countered the cowboy. "People don't make peace with crooks or killers. They make peace with sovereign nations. They make peace with people they are at war with. Besides, you know from experience there's white men who have broken the peace as often as the Indians."

"Is that your defense?" asked Wooten.

"I don't have a defense yet," Woolfolk said.

"Well, that one sure won't play. Anybody whose family's been butchered and their children carried off or who know friends and neighbors where it's happened ain't goin' for that deal. I've heard Satanta's bugle myself. I don't think he was making war. I think he was killing and stealing because he wanted to, because he enjoyed it."

"It's their way of living," Woolfolk spoke slowly. "The men gain status by acts of bravery against their enemies. They're no different than I was, riding with Morgan."

"You don't mean that, Joe."

"I mean all men like to risk themselves, prove themselves. We're alike in that."

"You didn't butcher women and children," Wooten insisted. "Fighting men is one thing. Fighting women and children is another. The Kiowas crammed a lance down the Cambren child's throat because he was crying."

"Chivington killed Indian women and children during the war. Custer slaughtered Black Kettle's people on the Washita. Hell, he and Sheridan took Satanta hostage under a white flag and pretended they didn't know what a white flag meant." The lawyer struggled with his words. "Those were white men, the product of thousands of years of civilization, John. They're Christians in name, if not in fact. By all we hold right and fair, they knew better. They knew better. A man is responsible for what he knows. And I know somehow that everything I believe in won't be worth a drink at Tiny's if I don't defend these men, *really* defend them. This whole sham of a trial is trying to put manure in the barn. And I'm not going to let anybody put shit in the barn."

"What?" asked the cowboy.

"Oh, it's just something I was talking to Jinny about. Anyway, as civilized people, we put away revenge for justice, and justice means I ain't laying down in this farce of a trial."

The cowboy sat in the chair opposite his friend. He sighed and then rested, without words for some time. "Guess you've counted the cost?" he asked finally. "Not just to you, but to Jinny and the baby?"

"I think so," said the ex-soldier hoarsely.

"Joe, there won't even be a record or an appeal," John Wooten reminded his friend. "Nobody will ever really know what you're doin', except the folks here, who'll hate your guts. I mean, you're pissin' in the wind, and you're goin' to get wet, dirty wet."

Joe looked up into his friend's face and nodded. "Yeah," he said. "But I can't just do what Soward wants, take it easy, take the verdict, and go home without a backward glance. I don't know why I can't. I can't put the why in words exactly. But it's something to do with all the little steps men have ever made against the darkness that wants to overcome us. Hell, maybe it's no more than my cussed nature not wantin' to do what I'm told."

The cowboy was quiet and thoughtful, then he spoke softly. "Well, pard, if you can't lay down, then you've got to fight and take the consequences, for good or bad. Shoot, I knew what you'd do 'fore the tale-teller got it out of his mouth. If you weren't goin' to put up the best defense you can, then I

98

would be amazed. Reckon that contrary streak in you is what's made us friends these many years." John Wooten stood up, took the Kiowa lance across his knee, broke it, and tossed the pieces in the corner. "Things like that shouldn't be kept for reminders. I'm headin' out in the morning, takin' cattle for Missus Chastain to her spread west of Belknap. If the Indians don't get me, I'll have you on my mind. Seein' yuh, Joe." He stopped at the door and turned around. "You might ride along, maybe look around out on the Salt Creek Prairie, before you go back to Jacksboro. You haven't forgot how to ride a horse, have you?"

Jinny Woolfolk packed her husband's traveling bag. She smoothed the collars of the well-ironed, white shirt he would wear in court. She had scrubbed it on the metal ribs of the rub board with lye soap she had made last spring on a fire she had built in the yard. She had dunked it again and again in the cold starch she'd made and twisted it damp dry in her slim hands. She'd snapped it out and hung it neatly by the tail in the hot Texas sun to dry. She had ironed it last night with flat irons she'd heated on the stove in the airless, hot kitchen. *Women are silly,* she thought, *putting so much time and effort into ironing a shirt that will get wrinkled and dusty before a man even puts it on. Why does a woman do that?* she wondered. And she knew. *Because to her it's not a shirt. It's her honor and her pledge, kept to remember all her hopes and dreams.*

"I asked Judge Soward again to hold the trial here in Weatherford," Joe Woolfolk said as he entered the small, immaculate bedroom.

Jinny closed the satchel as he continued.

"There's an outside chance that here we might find a juror or two who would listen before he made up his mind." He sat on the bed, facing her. "By the time I got to his office this morning, he had a petition signed by every other lawyer in town, asking him not to make them go to Jacksboro this term. Too dangerous for them and the jurors and the witnesses. But even in the face of grave danger, the noble judge won't change the venue from Jacksboro. Civilization can't back up in the face of adversity, he says. So now he's got a signed document from all the local lawyers, saying there's a terrible Indian danger. And he's got the trial right where he wants it because of his stand on high moral principle."

Jinny handed the bag to her husband as he stood up. "You've got your two best white shirts. Take them out of your bag and hang them up to get some of the wrinkles out if you have a chance. There's plenty of underwear and socks and your razor and cup. I bought a scented soap at Teezer's and a new comb." She looked at the man before her with tears in her eyes. "Oh, Joe!" She put her arms around his neck.

He dropped the small carpetbag. He held her tighter and tighter, drawing her strength into him. Joe Woolfolk could not let go.

Finally, Jinny snuffled and straightened. She smoothed the lapel of his coat and patted it She looked into his face. "You'll do just fine. I'd never want you to do less than your best, Joe. I don't believe we could live with that."

Chapter Twelve

The stage carrying the officials of the Thirteenth District Court arrived in Jacksboro late in the afternoon. Judge Charles Soward stretched as he stepped down.

"James, you go on over to the courthouse and start getting things prettied up," the judge said to his clerk. "Lanham and I will walk out to the fort to talk with Mackenzie." To the driver he said: "Just set the bags in the hotel lobby. Missus Maurice will know what to do with them. Ready, Lanham?"

The clerk watched the judge and district attorney walk along the south side of the square and disappear into the road, leading across Lost Creek to Fort Richardson. "Are folks stirred up about the trial?" the clerk asked the driver who set the men's bags on the porch of the hotel.

"Let's put it this way," the surly man said, "if it weren't for the blue belly provost guard and the rest of the soldiers, those Indians would already have found justice at the end of a rope."

"Oh," said the clerk, "there must be a trial. That's important. A trial will show the world we're civilized, and it will show the Indians they can't get away unpunished any more."

"There's folks think a rope would make that point. You tell Missus Maurice who these bags belong to now." The driver climbed back onto the high box, overlooking his team. "Hehyup," he called and clicked to the horses, popping the reins lightly on their rumps. He never looked back at the court clerk or the baggage left sitting on the porch. He drove slowly toward the stable.

Soward walked contentedly in the late afternoon air. "Cooling off now," he said to Lanham.

"Yes, Judge, the day is coming to rest all around us." Lanham walked thoughtfully for a while. "You can almost feel the change coming. The sweet breath of civilization is in the wind."

Soward grunted and cast a sideways glance at the young lawyer. Lanham was apt to get eloquent, but that wouldn't hurt the trial any. Frontier people expected lawyers and politicians to put on a good show. Elocution was a form of social recreation. Young men formed debating societies. School children rehearsed great speeches and practiced the grand gestures of famous orators. Parents took pride in the medals won for declamation. People would expect the trial to be something, especially coming so close to the Fourth of July. Folks would be coming to town just for the trial. Wagons and buggies and visitors would jam the square of streets around the courthouse. Country people would bring their meals and talk to their children about the great event that was about to take place. They'd eat their dinner on the sparse courthouse lawn. Town folks would close their shops and businesses. School would be let out. By seven in the morning the court would be packed.

Soward mused about that. Only about two hundred could get inside — that was with some standing and parents holding their children. The sheriff would have to keep the rowdies out. The court officers could just say to these undesirables, and be telling the truth, that places had to be saved for high ranking officials and their guests. The court would get soldiers from Mackenzie, of course, and post them around the room to make sure no harm came to the Kiowas. A lot of people had old grudges, just grudges, against Indians. *God,* he thought, *we've got to take care of those Indians. They can't be killed in the courthouse.* For a moment Soward was thankful that the Reconstruction forces were still around.

What about the crowd outside? They'd be peeved at not getting in. They'd be milling about, wanting to know what was happening. Rumors could run like wildfire. If the crowd thought things weren't going right, there could be trouble out there. More soldiers, thought Soward. He relaxed a little. *There really was no chance that the folks outside would not know what was going on inside. It was July. All the windows in the second-floor courtroom would be open. Some Texans could be counted on to report the proceedings in a timely manner out the big windows to the crowds outside.*

Yes, the people would come, and the people would want to know what was going on. A trial this important would sure draw a crowd. Soward enjoyed the thought. *That's American democracy proved out — open trial for everybody to see, for the children to see and know that justice was the way. Oh, yes, this would be a show, a parade. Folks on the frontier took a lot of pride in the way things got done. Lanham would do just fine. He was young, barely twenty-five, handsome enough, and sharp as a tack. For some he might be a bit windy, but he'd be eloquent. He'd say things right and probably say the right things. After all, Daniel Webster and Lincoln and those boys back East didn't own grand words or grand ideas. Texas has its own greatness.*

Mackenzie's office was orderly and spare. There were not personal mementos. Everything was Army. When the judge and attorney were shown in, the young colonel came to his feet. He shook hands with the two officers of the court.

"Well, Colonel," said Soward, "it looks as if we are to have a trial."

Mackenzie nodded. "We've done our best, sir. My orders are to see that no harm comes to these Indians. I have done

103

that and will do that throughout the process. Now it's your turn."

"You've planned for security in my courtroom and on the way to it?"

"Oh, yes," said Mackenzie. "We try not to make errors that we can plan for. There will be soldiers inside and outside. The prisoners will be screened from public view by a column of soldiers as they are loaded into the wagon. Three armed soldiers will sit in front of them, and three behind. Cavalry will ride in close formation on either side of the wagon. Nobody is going to get a shot at these men."

"Fine, that's just fine." Soward nodded. "What about evidence and witnesses?"

"I think you should send some citizens up to Fort Sill to gather the evidence. This is, after all, a civil trial. The Army is happy to co-operate, but the burden should be on civil authorities."

"Does that preclude you from testifying?" asked Lanham.

"I don't think my testimony will be necessary." Mackenzie drummed the top of his desk with his good left hand. The crippled hand he kept always in his pocket or lap.

Lanham seemed disappointed. "Colonel, we may know the men committed the crime, and we may have a pool of citizens eager to convict, but we'll need more. So far all we've seen are some arrows taken from the site of the killing. The state will need more evidence and expert witnesses, if we are to make a credible case."

"I have a sergeant, Miles Varily, that knows far more than I do about the Kiowas and Indians in general. He was at the scene on the Nineteenth. He buried the freighters. He can tell you about those arrows in great detail . . . about the site . . . how it looked after the attack . . . about the condition of the men's bodies." Mackenzie looked out the window. "I've been in several high casualty battles, with heavy artillery, but I never saw anything like that before. There's also Doctor Patzki's official report."

"What about the confessions of Satanta?" queried the District Attorney.

"If I were conducting the prosecution, Mister Lanham, I'd send someone up to Fort Sill. Any written documents, regarding Tatum's knowledge and his subsequent request for the men's arrest, will be there. Matthew Leeper, the agency interpreter, heard and could testify to the statement of Satanta to Tatum. The post interpreter, Horace Jones, was present on Colonel Grierson's porch when Satanta confessed to General Sherman. He can tell you all the nuances of that confrontation."

"Will Tatum appear in court?" asked Soward.

"I wouldn't count on that. He took a big step in asking for the arrests. I don't think he would want to appear in a capital trial. Frankly, we don't want Tatum harassed or compromised with his church or his charges. He's the first agent who ever admitted that there was an element among the tribes that he could not control and that needed control. We hope to have his help to end the raiding. Get his note to Grierson. That will say all that's necessary."

"A note won't be very dramatic before a jury," noted Lanham.

"It will be if it's presented right in the light of Tatum's knowledge of the Kiowas, his history among them, and his very difficult personal decision to ask for arrest, Mister Lanham. I can write him to send Leeper, if you think that will add drama." Mackenzie spoke flatly. He did not think this trial needed any drama. His great task was keeping it from becoming so dramatic that a mob of citizens would try to take the prisoners from the Army and lynch them.

"Was anything taken from the wagons found in the chiefs'

possession?" Lanham was carefully constructing his points.

"The forty-one mules." Mackenzie rubbed his eyelid with the forefinger of his left hand.

"Nothing identifiable as belonging to one of the men?" pursued Lanham.

Mackenzie rocked back in the chair. "I'm not aware of anything. You or your agents can pursue that at Fort Sill. That would be telling, wouldn't it . . . something from one of the teamsters in Satanta's possession, say? I'm not aware of it. He was wearing an Army bugle across his shoulder when arrested. That's an interesting story. Lots of ranchers claim to have heard that bugle on raids at their places." Mackenzie looked down as he thought. "There was a woman when the citizens petitioned General Sherman. A Missus Fontaine, no Chastain. Elm Creek raid. She said she heard a bugle, like the cavalry was coming to help."

Lanham made a mental note of Mrs. Chastain. He knew the name and the story. Probably no white person knew as much about Satanta as the former woman captive. Her testimony, though not directly related to the Salt Creek massacre, could still be useful. Getting her to town, though, might be difficult. Then he remembered, she had come to Fort Richardson to present the affidavits listing the Indians' outrages to Sherman. She wanted her granddaughter back. That might draw her again to town.

"She wasn't an eye witness to the Warren massacre," stated the prosecutor.

"No," said Mackenzie, "but there are survivors. Thomas Brazeal was in the hospital here until a few days ago. He may still be in Jacksboro."

"Um," Lanham made the notation, "we'll get him."

"Any chance the Kiowas could testify, be cross-examined?" asked Soward.

"They don't speak English," Mackenzie stated. "An interpreter could be used, of course, Judge Soward. If their attorney is worth anything, he probably won't want them on the stand."

"Probably not," agreed Soward. "Are they in good shape to appear?"

Mackenzie looked up quickly. "They are prisoners of the United States Army, sir. Aside from a few mosquito bites and the chaffing of their wrist and leg irons, they should be suitable for presentation. We'll provide baths and fatigues for them before the trial. Would you care to see the Kiowas, gentlemen?" Mackenzie was already on his feet.

Soward and Lanham followed him across the open fort toward the laundry. He walked quickly, and the jurists hastened to keep up. "They'll be having their dinner about now," Mackenzie observed. "They really have been model prisoners. No trouble, not even when Satank was killed. They could have made a great deal of trouble, but they were both very subdued."

Satanta continued to eat as Mackenzie and his guests appeared at the door. He sopped a biscuit with gravy and lifted it to his mouth. As he chewed, he observed his observers. Both the judge and the district attorney seemed pale and very straight up. "Kenzie," Satanta saluted the officer. In Kiowa he added: "Have some dinner. The Army cooks good."

Young Adoltay sat very still, holding his plate on his knees. He never knew what the white men were doing, what their coming here meant — some visits were routine, like meals and lights out, others random like this one. When was the trial? The boy felt disoriented, away from the land and the People. "Who do you think they are?" he asked Satanta.

"White men." Satanta took another warm biscuit.

Soward cleared his throat. Standing before the Kiowas gave him the same feeling as watching a rattlesnake in a glass box. He was safe, but his heart raced within his chest. He took a handkerchief from his pocket and wiped his forehead and hands. "I know they are very securely incarcerated. And, here and now, they are just men, but anywhere else, anytime else. . . ." the Judge's words trailed off. "What they have done. What they can do."

Lanham was quiet as he followed the judge and Mackenzie away from the cell door. He stopped for a moment and turned back to see the chiefs, sitting in the circle of lantern light in the dark interior. He moved his jaw side to side, allowing the tension to drain away. The Judge had said it — "Here and now, they are just men, but anywhere else, anytime else. . . ." *They are blood-thirsty killers,* the prosecutor added in his mind. He moved ahead to catch up with the others.

Chapter Thirteen

West of Fort Richardson

"Thank you, John," Joe Woolfolk said, shifting in his saddle, "for bringing me out here behind these cattle. It's been nothing less than misery. I thought I had a rotten job, defending the Kiowas, but it isn't nearly as bad as pushing cows. You've made a grateful man of me."

Wooten smiled. "No use lyin', Joe. I can see you take to the cattle business."

"Yes, when I retire, which may be right after this trial, I want to be a cowman."

"There's worse lives, Joe," the cowboy said.

The two friends pulled their ponies to a stop and watched the wranglers turn the cattle south toward a shallow creek.

"Is he still there?" the lawyer asked.

John Wooten lifted and turned in his saddle, resting his hand on the cantle. He nodded. "He's there. He's doggin' yuh, Joe. Started with that spear in your desk, now you've got him tied to you like an albatross."

"Wonder why he never rides a horse?" the lawyer queried. "I've never seen that old man on a horse long as I've lived here. He raises good ones, but never rides, always walks. Damn, he must have walked a million miles."

The wrangler turned back in his saddle. He and Woolfolk slowly moved their ponies west, each thinking his own thoughts.

**It is an ancient Mariner,
And he stoppeth one of three.**

109

"By thy long gray beard and glittering eye,
Now wherefore stopp'st thou me?

The Bridegroom's doors are opened wide,
And I am next of kin;
The guests are met, the feast is set;
May'st hear the merry din."

He holds him with his skinny hand;
"There was a ship," quoth he.

Wooten intoned the poem.
Joe Woolfolk joyfully took up the ballad at a later stanza.

"O shrieve me, shrieve me, holy man!"
The Hermit crossed his brow.
"Say quick," quoth he, "I bid thee say –
What manner of man art thou?"

Forthwith this frame of mine was wrenched
with woeful agony,
Which forced me to begin my tale;
And then it left me free.

Since then, at an uncertain hour,
That agony returns;
And till my ghastly tale is told,
This heart within me burns.

I pass like night, from land to land;
I have strange power of speech;
The moment that his face I see
I know the man that must hear me:

To him my tale I teach.

"By God, we're good." The lawyer reined in and offered his hand to his friend.

"Sure we are," the cowboy said, ignoring the offered hand of departure. "I told Frank, I'd ride on with you a ways. That's a good bunch of hands. They will keep the herd movin' easy on. I'll catch up to 'em 'fore they reach Missus Chastain's place. We can ride back a ways together, then you can find your way to Rock Creek and Jacksboro, can't you?"

"Sure I can. I've only ridden all over this country in my primitive days," Joe Woolfolk agreed. "You don't have to ride with me any farther."

"What are you tryin' to do, counselor, keep me from seein' what I come to see for myself?"

"I'd never do that, John."

The lawyer kicked his pony into an easy trot. The cowboy squeezed his pony forward. Both men fixed their eyes ahead. Neither spoke. They moved steadily toward the loaf-like hill, called Cox's Mountain, that rose from the sun-parched plain. They rode over a small rocky hump in the land.

"There, Joe. I can see the grass burned off past the hill." John Wooten pointed.

"I see it," the lawyer said, drawing in his reins. His pony slowed to a walk. "Let's go in slow. I want to think it through. The wagons came just the way we have along the road. They left Jacksboro early. They made Rock Creek Station before it got hot and watered the mules in the tank. That took some time. It was hot and sticky. Black clouds rolled behind the mountain as the men drove toward it. They could see lightning in the clouds and hear the distant thunder. It was still. They nooned quickly and pushed on because of the coming storm. They'd want to get on to Belknap

111

or maybe Murphy's Station before the rain hit."

"It must have been tough going through here with loaded wagons," observed Wooten, as the riders followed the rutted road around the wooded north side of Cox's Mountain and came in full view of the Salt Creek Prairie. In the distance a conical hill with sandstone outcroppings, protruding from its sloped sides, sat on the flat expanse of prairie. Both men stopped. Spread before them on the empty plain lay the burned out wagons of the Warren train.

At last, Joe Woolfolk clucked and nudged his horse toward the site. "Ten wagons. Twelve men. Corn for Fort Griffin." He spoke almost absently as Wooten rode beside him.

The men observed the sight before them closely, slowly absorbing the facts from sign and the terror from their natural instincts as men.

"They got well out onto this flat before the Indians came from behind the hill, before they saw the Indians," speculated Woolfolk.

"They tried to circle," said the cowboy. "Look how the wagons are spaced out. They couldn't close up. See, there's the carcasses of the dead mules. That left 'em open."

The friends rode among the remnants of the murder scene. Only the heavy burned-out boxes of the wagons were as they had been on May 18th. The wolves and vultures had eaten the dead, bloated mules. The bare rib cages and white long bones lay close to where the animals had fallen. Here and there, pieces of corn sacks or clothing stuck in the grass and clung to brush. A pile of full sacks had once made a barricade for a fighter, but the sacks had been split, and grain had flowed out like the men's lives. Wheels from the wagons had been ripped off and rolled out far onto the prairie.

"Looks like boys was playing with those wheels." Wooten could almost see the wheels flying out, staggering, and falling victim on the land. His eyes narrowed against the sun.

"When the Indians began dismounting to pillage the train, Brazeal and the others that lived ran out that way toward the timber on Cox's Mountain." The lawyer tried to decide the shortest distance to the hill. He knew the men were running for their lives when they left the broken wagon circle. "Brazeal said about a dozen Indians kept after them. They ran down two of the drivers and scalped them as they fought and retreated. Five made it to the hill, all wounded. They had some luck, then. The Indians were afraid they'd miss their share of the loot, so they went back to the wagons. That's when the rain began."

Woolfolk guided his horse around the corn pile toward a low stone, sitting up on its end and wedged into the loose mound of dirt. A second stone marked the other end of the common grave of the teamsters. Seven notches had been filed into the stones. He sat quietly for a few minutes.

"At Tiny's I heard a sergeant say that they buried them in one of the wagon boxes. Had a terrible time digging that big of a hole in the rain. Had to keep bailing it out. He said by the time his men crawled out they looked like mud men. The dead men, he said, was washed white and clean by the rain. No blood on their wounds, all washed away, just white and clean."

Joe Woolfolk sighed audibly and looked about. "Well, they won't be lonely. There's more than twenty other graves on this little spot of God's good earth."

"Hell, why can't the cavalry patrol this stretch?" asked his companion. "The Indians have used that mountain for cover anytime they felt like it. Let a party drive off Cox's Mountain, commit to the prairie, and hit 'em two or three miles from cover. Sitting damn' ducks."

Joe Woolfolk turned his horse away from the grave and

headed him toward a wagon. The cowboy took a last look and caught up. By the time he reached his friend, Joe Woolfolk was on the ground. He squatted near the wagon tongue. A fire had been built under it and had burned the wood into a black, cracked charcoal ready to crack through. Chains still hung from the front wheels. Woolfolk squatted and touched the ground with the tips of his fingers. He brushed aside the dead embers, revealing the white enamel of a human tooth. Both men knew that Sam Elliott had been lashed to the tongue, his arms stretched to the wheels. His head had been laid over that fire, and he'd been burned alive, screaming until his teeth were smashed and his tongue was cut out.

Woolfolk stood up at last and returned to his horse. "I want to see where the Indians came from, where they waited for these men."

The men jogged their horses toward the sandstone hill. The grave of Ordlee — the only Comanche among the Indian raiders who had died on the field — had been opened and his bones scattered about by men and animals.

They rode slowly, trying to see if anything was left after the rain, after the soldiers, after the curious, after the wind and sun of Texas. They let the ponies follow their noses up a path against the hill. When it ended, the animals stopped. The men sat looking at the panorama before them.

"What a spot?" said Wooten. "No general could want a better position to call a battle."

"They are not stupid, John. They are old in this country, and they know how to use it." The lawyer sat a long time, looking at the field of battle. "I talked to one of the freighters at Warren and DuBose. He said, when the wind of the storm hit, he heard a bugle, clear and fragile and distant."

The cowboy looked closely at his friend whose eyes never left the scene.

The long twilight was at their backs as the men rode again down the road toward Rock Creek Station and Fort Richardson. "Why do you reckon men do things like that to other men?" asked Wooten. "Did you ever want to burn anybody alive or cut his tongue out?"

Joe Woolfolk's voice was hoarse as he answered. "Not so long ago, the civilized people of England used to draw and quarter men for punishment. Flay them alive of their skin. Disembowel them as they yet lived, and then pull them apart by tying their arms and legs to horses and sending the horses in different directions."

"God A'mighty," Wooten whispered. "I wish you'd quit countering one horror with another. If I say the Indians did somethin', you tell me about Chivington or the Englishmen, like one thing justifies the other. You're makin' me crazy."

"What will it be, John, the horror of your white brothers or your red enemies? That's how you choose. You have to take a side, knowing that both are guilty as sin," said Woolfolk.

"The hell I do," muttered the cowboy. "I don't care who done what. I don't want nobody getting killed that way. It ain't the color of the men, killed or killing. It's the act that turns my stomach."

"Lawyers don't have weak stomachs, John. We have lost our innocence and know the human heart in all its vileness. So we hold up the unattainable ideal of justice, of giving both sides a fair hearing, an honest defense, washing our own hands of decision, hoping if both sides are told, justice will somehow reach out and take the matter from us, relieving us of guilt, yet knowing that justice is in the hands of men as fragile as ourselves."

"Shoot fire," said the cowboy.

They rode on without speaking any more into the darkness.

Chapter Fourteen

The two friends sat around the embers of their small fire. Their food lay untouched. Only the coffee had satisfied. Wooten rolled onto his stomach. "I see his fire," he said. "Way out there, just a little speck of flames."

Woolfolk turned to see the distant flame of Isaac Lynn's fire. "Why doesn't he come in?"

"He ain't ready," answered Wooten.

"Why doesn't he kill me?" Joe Woolfolk asked the cowboy.

"They'd just get somebody else," came the reply. Wooten rolled over onto his back and looked at the canopy of stars. "I sometimes think, if the world was empty but for two men, and everything was available to them two, that in the great emptiness when the stars looked down, they'd see one of those men killing the other."

"That's a horrible thought, coming from you, John," said the lawyer.

"Yes, it is . . . a senseless, horrible scene I see in my mind." The cowboy's thoughts wandered in a dark reverie.

The cabin was old-fashioned — a double pen log house with a passage of ten or twelve feet between, and a porch running along one side of the thick walls. It was just daylight when John Wooten's boots struck the passageway. He noticed the door of the right hand cabin was partially open. He pushed it wide. Isaac Lynn was sitting before a large log fire as the young cattleman entered. He held a long forked dogwood stick in the old stone fireplace. Wooten looked closely at the object held over the fire. It was an Indian scalp, thoroughly salted, the hair tucked inside. Lynn turned it carefully over the fire. Grease ran out. The flames spit and fussed and consumed it. The scalp had drawn up until it looked as thick as a buffalo bull's scalp.

Lynn glanced over his shoulder. "Morning, son," he said.

Wooten stared at the face in the half light of fire and darkness. He had never seen such sadness. The man turned back to the task of roasting the scalp.

"What are you doin' with that infernal scalp?" the younger man asked.

"The weather's so damp, I'm afeared the damn thing will spoil."

"Where'd it come from?" The cowboy did not have to ask why Lynn had it. He knew. Since the killing of his daughter and son-in-law, the old settler had had a craving for Indian scalps. All the boys in the neighborhood brought him the scalps of Indians they killed.

"Up northwest of here," the quiet voice answered. "It's a whole head scalp. Must 'a' been an important damned Indian." He pulled the dripping mass from the fire, shook it, and turned it inside out in his leathery fingers. "Look-a here, there's three silver bells tied to the hair." The man's sad eyes glanced up into the younger man's face. "They're here in the Keechi Valley now, ain't they?"

Wooten nodded. "The neighbors are meeting at your place to go after them."

"Who has been kilt?"

"Sherman and his wife," Wooten said. "He didn't even have a gun."

"What about the baby?" the settler asked, looking through the younger man.

Wooten sat on the bed and took off his hat, holding it in his hands. "It's dead, too. They staked Missus Sherman to the ground, raped her, and shot her with arrows. But she was still alive, lived till the next day, giving birth to the baby. It come out dead."

Joe's words broke his thoughts. "You remember that time just before the war when a bunch of raiders came into the Keechi Valley and killed twenty-three people?"

"Sure I do," spoke the cowboy softly.

"After Ross found that Comanche camp on the Pease, and took back the white woman captive and her child, Cureton wasn't satisfied because he missed the fight. You and I cut sign of two scouts, riding away. 'Take ten men and scout it out,' Cureton told you. Hell, it's a miracle we're not dead ourselves, John, riding up on that main camp with ten men."

"We'd be dead if we hadn't hid in that undercut till past dark. You know, I never believed that Bible story about the sun standing still for Joshua's battle. But since that long day, I have doubted my doubts. The sun did poke along that day. I sure had had enough of Indian fightin' for some time."

"Old man Lynn hadn't," said the lawyer. "When John R. Baylor took up the trail after the first of the year, he followed him to the spot where we had left that big camp. Mister Lynn walked along behind with his gun across his shoulders. The horses got poor as hounds because the buffalo had grazed off all the grass. There was only alkali water to drink. And they began to drop. By the time Baylor came back down the Wichita half the men were on foot. All of them nearly starved to death. Mister Lynn walked on up to the mouth of the Pease, scouted the plains to the breaks of the Colorado. With a zeal born of blood and nurtured by hate the indomitable frontiersman" — Joe Woolfolk made the words sound like high oratory — "walked on. After we'd given him up for dead, he finally came home with a bag full of scalps."

"Don't make fun of the old man," Wooten said softly. "I don't know how I'd act if my family was butchered?"

Joe Woolfolk watched the small fire. "I'm not making fun.

My lawyer ways are just coming out. It's a long time since I believed in more than you and Jinny and I. This trial has brought all the anger and old hurt back again. I'm stuck, John." Joe was speaking quietly. "I can't get out of this. I don't want to lie down and roll over for Soward. But I can't give my heart to any more lost causes. I've had enough of that."

"Lots of soldiers feel that way, Joe."

"You're not bitter at all about the war?"

The cowboy shook his head

"That damned hog that cut your leg saved you from going East to fight."

"Maybe so that's right. By the time my leg had healed, I knew I'd do my fightin' right here on the frontier. Didn't seem I could leave what needed doin' here to go off somewhere else to fight. Nobody much was looking after the folks left in Texas. Maybe, fightin' at home, I was just tryin' to stay alive and mind my own business. I didn't have any great ideas, like saving the Union or defending the rights of the States. No big ideas, no big disappointments . . . just day to day with the land and tryin' to keep it long enough to make a life. I never expected nothing more. No, the Frontier Regiment was as big as I could see, Joe. You was lieutenant. Why'd you leave?"

"Obenchain, that Virginia windbag, I guess. He made fighting for the right of people to set their own course sound like the only honorable thing to do. You never liked him," the lawyer said.

"No, I did not," the cowman agreed. "I think it was that dumb-assed bugle for roll call even when you could look around and see everybody was right there. Where else could they be in the middle of the plains? And there was that French Melish's map he stood by with the North and South Canadian showed as the Red and the Brazos. Hell, he never knew where he was."

"Still, he carried the flag," the lawyer said.

The cowboy tapped the toes of his boots together. "Did he? I always figured he'd get somebody else to carry it and get killed while he sat in the shade. Remember that little tent he had set up away from the men . . . us fightin', us without hardly a shirt on our backs, and him too good to be with us?"

"That's the way armies are, John. At least, that was the way I thought they should be back then. But by the time I'd stayed in the saddle twenty hours a day for two weeks, rotted in the Ohio Penitentiary, and seen Morgan humiliated by the staff officers in Richmond, I didn't have much use for desk soldiers or their politics."

"You had a good lesson then," the cowboy quipped. "You ain't near as prissy as you were before the war. But you know things didn't go the way I expected, either. I figured I knew this part of the country, and it was sorely neglected, so I tried to hold it. After I mustered out and I went home, I found my neighbors had mavericked my cattle. The stay-at-homes got my cattle increase, and I got the experience.

"Even the fighting here didn't turn out just right. Belknap ain't what it was when we were first there. Before you left, we was out after Indians so much you couldn't tend to your court clerk business. After you left, the Comanches and Kiowas pushed us back all the way to Jacksboro. Our records are still at Jacksboro. I was talkin' to Newt Gram the other day. He's still holdin' out at Belknap. He said Sherman stayed there overnight on his way to Fort Richardson. Sherman asked him what happened to the town, just two families left. Newt told him, Indians and the fear they carry. He didn't think the general believed him. I guess he does now. The Warren wagon train massacre made a believer out of him."

"John, what did you do with that bugle Obenchain gave you for roll call when he took over the Frontier Regiment?"

"I threw it in the lake where we was camped."

" 'Dismiss what offends thy soul,' eh?" the lawyer quoted the line from Henry Thoreau.

"I found that horn again about a year ago. I guess the rains washed it out onto the prairie. This country don't let nothing rest . . . not a bugle in a pond, or a man and his thoughts about himself. 'Night, Joe."

Joe Woolfolk broke a small limb across his knee and laid the pieces on the fire. He looked across the prairie night at the speck of fire where Isaac Lynn kept his vigil.

Chapter Fifteen

Fort Sill, Indian Territory
June 28, 1871

The Jacksboro citizens' committee sat patiently in Lawrie Tatum's office, waiting for his return. W. M. McConnell tapped the paper in his hand against the side of his chair. "This won't do," he said. "The way it's written, we can't use it as evidence against Big Tree." The other four men with him nodded. "Tatum's got to make this right."

"Make what right?" the agent asked, as he entered through the house door, dusting the bread crumbs from his dinner off his dark coat.

"We've been at the fort, like Mackenzie suggested, to get evidence for the trial. Colonel Grierson gave us the file and the letter you wrote, asking for the arrests of the chiefs. Here it is." In two steps, McConnell was at the Quaker's desk. He spread the letter open. The Quaker studied his own writing. "Is that what you meant to say?"

Friend Tatum rocked back in his chair and looked at the man, standing before him. "It says that Satanta in the presence of Satank, Eagle Heart, Big Tree, and Woman's Heart admitted he led the raid on the wagon train, killed seven people, and took the mules. I said Satank, Eagle Heart, and Big Bow also participated in the raid. I asked the colonel to arrest three men."

"That's right," agreed McConnell, "but you left out Big Tree. We're holding Big Tree for trial in Jacksboro, but the letter doesn't ask for his arrest. Should he have been arrested, based on what you know?"

The Quaker rubbed his lips as he considered the question. The flavors of his dinner were still in his mouth. "Adoltay . . . Big Tree, thou calls him . . . took part in the raid in Texas. Guipago told me after I had sent the first message. I wrote a second, put it in my pocket, and took it to Colonel Grierson. Finding Sherman with him, I just told them about Big Tree. In the confusion of the arrest, I never gave him the note. I later threw it away."

McConnell sat in a chair and drew it to the desk. "The letter has to say that Big Tree must be arrested also."

Tatum spoke softly. "Guipago is not always truthful with me. Sometimes he tells me what I want to hear. Sometimes he tells me what I do not want to hear. I have thought that Big Tree shows much promise. I believe he may take the peace road. Guipago may have told me of the young man's part in the raid for spite. When I wrote Grierson, I asked him to let the boy go if he found him innocent."

McConnell leaned on the desk. "Mister Tatum, as far as I'm concerned, there is not one innocent Indian on this entire reservation. If they didn't raid, they knew about it and enjoyed the fruits of it. Give me a letter I can use in the trial. You said that Big Tree was in the room and heard what Satanta said and did not object to being implicated. That means he was part of it, proud of it, and should be arrested. Guipago confirmed his guilt. That's two witnesses, Mister Tatum, the boy himself and the principal chief."

"The solution to this is simple," the voice of another member of the Jacksboro citizens' committee said. "Mister Tatum obviously meant to include Big Tree among those to be arrested. It was an oversight in haste. All that is necessary is for him to correct the letter. He can rewrite it to include Big Tree's name."

Tatum considered the words briefly and reached for his pen and paper. He began to copy the earlier letter.

Col. Grierson
Post Comd.

Satanta, in the presence of Satank, Eagle Heart, Big Tree, and Woman's Heart, in a defiant manner, has informed me that he led a party of about one hundred Indians into Texas, and killed seven men and captured a train of mules. He further states that the chiefs Satank, Eagle Heart, Big Bow, and Big Tree were associated with him in the raid. Please arrest all of them.

Lawrie Tatum
Ind. Agent.

He handed the note to McConnell for approval. The committeeman nodded. "Thank you, Mister Tatum. This will about finish our business before we leave in the morning. I think Mister Leeper and Mister Jones will ride back with us for the trial. We'll certainly need their testimony if we want this case to stick. This trial could change everything, put an end to the trouble. Colonel Mackenzie says we could not have made the case without your help. We want to thank you, all of us want to thank you."

The Quaker's mouth set into a firm line. "The time has come for the Kiowas and the others to face the same consequences for their actions as white men. But they do not yet see their actions as culpable. To them the Texans are their enemies, not their victims. To themselves, the Kiowa chiefs are brave men, not murderers. Can thou consider that?" He looked at the men's faces and read nothing for his hope there. "Will thou take a letter from me to the prosecutor? I will send it to thee before thy party leaves in the morning."

W. M. McConnell patted the copied letter from Lawrie Tatum in his coat pocket. "I reckon there is space enough for two letters in here," he said.

As the five citizens of Jacksboro walked down the path and out the gate of the picket fence, Lawrie Tatum, Quaker agent to the Comanches, Kiowas, Kiowa-Apaches, and other tribes, wadded the original request for the chiefs' arrests and threw it into the waste paper basket. He picked up his pen and dipped it again into the ink and began to write:

To S. W. T. Lanham, Esq; District Attorney
6th Month, 29th day, 1871. . . .

Chapter Sixteen

Joe Woolfolk stepped quietly into the small circle of light thrown by Isaac Lynn's fire. The old frontiersman sat, looking into the flames.

"Figured you'd come," said Lynn. "The man you used to be would come."

Woolfolk sat down across the fire. "What do you want with me, Mister Lynn?"

"I want to tell you a story I've never told," the older man stated, "that I've carried for more than thirteen years." He fell silent.

That moment that his face I see
I know the man that must hear me:
To him my tale I teach.

The words of the Coleridge ballad ran unwanted through Joe Woolfolk's brain. "I know what happened to Mary and Tom," the lawyer said, breaking his own thoughts and the silence.

"Do you, now?"

Joe cleared his throat and spoke without emotion. "Raiders hit their place and the Cambren place about noon. At the Cambren place they killed James Cambren and his sons, Junior and Luther, in the field. At the cabin, they took Missus Cambren and the other children into the yard while they robbed the house. About that time another group of Indians went over to Tom and Mary Mason's place. They killed Tom as he was trying to keep them from stealing his horse. They killed Mary as she tried to bring him a rifle. The group at Tom's and Mary's place left the children and the house unrobbed. The other took Missus Cambren and her four young children captive. She and one of the children were killed away from the home place where the raiders joined with the other group. They took the oldest boy with them. They left the other two Cambren children."

Isaac Lynn listened to Joe with eyes glittering from the fire light. He made no comment on the lawyer's recounting of the known facts. He began to speak to the fire, the night, God maybe. Joe watched the old man's face sink into sorrow as he told his tale.

" 'Wife,' I says when I got up that morning, 'I'm thinkin' I'll go over and see how Mary and Tom are.' I had a restlessness in my spirit about the girl and her young 'uns, but I never said such a thing to my wife, because she's a practical thing who don't hold to notions. But she answered me right back . . . 'Isaac, I think that's the thing to do.' She fixed me a sack of food.

"Takin' my old rifle across my shoulders I set out for Lost Valley. This land is rich in April . . . warm and full of life. There was flowers bloomin' here and there, like yellow blankets on the hill. I thinks to myself, it's an early spring, and May still to come. This country . . ." — his eyes looked out into the darkness — "this country is a shallow stream for fragile beauties. It favors strength mostly. But for a few weeks there is mercy. The new grass sweets the antelope's milk as the baby finds its legs and starts to nudge. Men drive their plows into the moist earth and dream again before the summer heat and the winds blow dreams away. That day was a dream time. I ate my lunch, lookin' up at the new, green, mouse-ear leaves of the mesquite, and I knew the winter was past for another year. A pair of gentle doves fed their young above me. Between the leaves, beyond the doves, far away, I saw a pair of eagles, riding the warm air. They are hunting, I thought. They have young, too. For a minute I was sad, thinking that a rabbit or the doves would die to feed the young eagles.

" 'Doth the eagle mount up at thy command, and make her nest on high? She dwelleth and abideth on the rock, upon the crag of the rock, and the strong place. From thence she seeketh the prey, and her eyes behold afar off. Her young ones also suck up blood; and where the slain are, there is she.' God told Job that. 'Who hath given to me that I should repay him? Whatever is under the whole heaven is mine.' God says that, and on a spring day a man knows the truth of that.

"The earth renews itself, the eaters and the eaten, and it goes on as it has gone on before man's foot stepped onto this place we call Texas. And it will go on after man's foot no longer falls on the new grass. I was content with the endless ebb and flow of it, the mystery that my small mind cannot know or even question. I could not deny that God had done it all without my small skill or guidance. None of it was of my doing. None of it was for me to question. I thought that then.

"It was past noon when I saw the house in the distance. I figured Tom would be plowing, but I did not see him in the new-turned field. The wind was still and quiet at that moment when I stood on the hill, looking down at their place. No human sound touched the great quietness. I listened and, finally, I heard the wind again, and the barn door slam. I started toward it, figuring Tom was there working. But he was not. He was laying dead on the path I come up to the house. Sure they had scalped him, flies black all over the wound. My daughter, Mary, lay between him and the house, lifeless as a shell. Her hair was long and yellow and spread out around her on the ground. There was just a little red circle, not more than two inches, over her forehead. That was all he took of her scalp, like maybe more would have been too much, even for an Injun, like maybe it was something he had to do, but did not like to do. Well, my Mary's baby sat on the ground against her side. He had blood on his face, ear to ear. But he were not wounded. My daughter's blood had painted him like a savage beast. The innocent child had nursed her as her life blood flowed from her wounds. The older boy, Tom, was playin' quietly up by the porch, pushing a toy wagon in the dirt."

Isaac Lynn sat quietly. "I do not have educated words for what I felt. I did not fall and weep for my daughter or her husband. It was too late. That time had passed, and I had missed it. They were not there. They had been gone a long time. I saw her children alone, abandoned, among the dead. I saw that they did not dwell on death, but unaware of their own soon-coming death, played on the footstool earth. Children do not dread death or life. For them, any experience is taken as it is, unquestioned. The children were healthy, living, living in the sliver of time before they, too, would die. And I had come in that sliver, and they would not die. I had no feeling, only understanding that I had come in time. I did not hate. I did not question. I picked up the baby, Lynn, and walked up to young Tom. The three of us sat on the porch together and rocked for a long time in their father's chair.

"After a while, I went in the house and found some corn-bread and gave it to them, made a sugar sack for the baby to suck. Carrying the baby in one arm and the gun in the other, I walked with little Tom over to the Cambren place. Jim and his boys were dead in the field . . . arrows shot so close and with such force they were driven through their chests. I thought how direct their deaths, all their deaths, had been. The killers had not been feared, had had plenty of time to use their weapons without resistance. It had been that way at Mary's place. But the Cambren place had been torn apart. The yard was littered with the furniture and dishes the Indians had no use for. But the door was closed. I went up on the porch with my grandchildren and called out . . . 'Is anyone yet living?' After no answer came, I started off, was down the steps and out in the yard, when I stopped. I went back and called out louder . . . 'Is anyone yet living?'

" 'There's me and Witt,' the little girl's voice said, so soft and gentle I barely heard it.

"She lifted the bar from across the door and stood in the light, looking up at me. I believe the little girl was five and her brother two. She was holding his hand. 'Where is your mama?' I asked.

'Over yonder,' she said, pointing toward a distant peak, 'where the Injuns left us. When it got late, I come on home with Witt.'

"The children and I started walking back toward my place on Lynn Creek. There was no horse to ride or pull a wagon. The Indians had taken them all. You see, they only wanted the horses. We made slow progress. The little children did not complain. Finally, we came to the peak where the little girl said she had left her mother. I found Missus Cambren and her son on the mountain. It looked like the two gangs of Indians had joined up again there. There were a lot of horse tracks around. Missus Cambren had been shot in her chest. The little boy, about three years old, had had a spear rammed down his throat. There were two more spear wounds in his side. The little girl said her mother had cried out when the Injuns began to tie her older brother on a wild mule. The mother's fear-filled words started the little boy crying. An Injun stopped the crying with the spear and killed him. I guess they killed the mother, too, because she could not be shut up any other way. They'd both been roughly scalped. The little girl had waited till almost

130

sunset, then doin' all she knew to do took her brother's hand, and led him home. She barred the door and put him in the underbed and covered him with a ratty quilt and lay down beside him. They did not see or hear anyone until I came the next afternoon.

"We walked almost all night across the rolling land. There was a raiders' moon, 'most light as day. I could not carry the gun, the baby, and the little boys, so I made a sling out of my shirt. I knew I did not need that gun, anyway. I would make it home with no trouble. I carried Lynn in the sling. Mary . . . the little girl was named for my Mary . . . led the little boys, Tom and Witt, by turns. I'd let one of them sleep a spell on my shoulder, and then set him down for Mary to lead. I could not put the baby down. He was too small to walk." Lynn thought in silence for a few moments. "That Mary was a fine little girl."

Joe Woolfolk set his jaw, then spoke quietly. "You said you did not hate. I do not understand, Mister Lynn, with what you've said, I would have been consumed with hate."

"You were not there," the old settler said. "The grief and goodness was greater than hate."

"Goodness?"

"Oh, yes, great goodness was there. The dead had not suffered. None of them seemed to have feared their death or resisted it, except Missus Cambren and her son who had been carried off from Lost Valley. And the rest of the children were alive. The children were not just breathing, but living, accepting without a judgment against their fate. I expect that will come as they grow up and folks talk about the killings. But then, they did not fret or complain against their Maker, then both life and death belonged to His mind."

"Mister Lynn, it sounds to me like the killings touched you different, like you forgave the killings. But I know you took scalps off every cowboy that killed an Indian and hunted Indians down yourself. And you did stick that scalp-dangling spear in my desk when you knew I was going to defend Satanta and Adoltay. Somehow that doesn't seem like acceptance or forgiveness to me."

"That spear, son, was a test to see if you could be driven away easy. But, as I expected, you are a dogged man, after something."

"What something?"

"I do not know that," the elder said. "I expect you ain't sure, either."

Woolfolk slumped. "Why did you follow me out here?"

"To see what you'd do, of course."

"Well, did I do what I was supposed to do, Mister Lynn? Did I pass your crazy test?" The lawyer had lost all patience with the other man. "Hell's bells, Satanta and Adoltay are guilty . . . bloody-red guilty. I know that. Everybody knows that. A few years ago, if I'd caught them red-handed, I'd have taken their scalps myself. Hell, if I caught them now, I'd do it."

Isaac Lynn's eyes looked up into the black sky dotted with the thousand small lights of stars. "Men think that those lights are stars. I think they are witnesses. Not that they see what we do so much, as that they bear witness to light in the great darkness."

The lawyer signed audibly. "Mister Lynn. . . ."

"What's your hurry, son? My tale is just begun. I once wore pants with Injun scalps in a row down the side of the legs. I took scalps from the cowboys, and I took 'em myself. I kept them in bags and took them out and looked at them. Folks said I'd gone crazy because I found my daughter and her husband killed, because I saw the Cambrens and the little scalped baby with a spear run down his throat. Folks was more

132

than helpful to me. But I never took a scalp because of Mary, or Tom, or what I seen. I took them because of what *I* done." Isaac Lynn cleared his throat quickly and continued.

"Everyone figured Injuns from the Clear Fork Reserve came up on the cabins. That's why the Cambrens and the Masons didn't resist. They didn't expect trouble from the Injuns."

"That's what the oldest Cambren boy said." Joe Woolfolk remembered the little blue-eyed, ten year old telling his story. Hunters from an emigrant train had spotted the raiders and their stolen horses the day following the massacre. Securing the train, they had returned with more men to pursue the Indians. The Cambren boy had been tied to a wild mule after his mother and brother were killed. The Indians had left him at the mercy of the beast with the Indian herd the rest of that day and night. The next day, one of the raiders had taken the exhausted child off the mule and had put him up behind himself on a horse. During the pursuit by the emigrant men, the rider had pushed the boy off to lighten his load and facilitate his own escape. Coming back from their futile chase, the white men had found the Cambren boy in the tall grass. "I am here yet," he had said, thinking his deadly captors had returned.

"Do you remember who the child said claimed him among the Injuns?" asked Lynn.

Woolfolk sorted the memories from thirteen years before. "A red-headed white man," he answered. "That's right, the boy said a red-headed white man was with the raiders and had him up behind him on the horse."

"I found that red-headed white man, and I executed him," the old man said hoarsely. "Except it turned out not to be a white man. It was near a month later. I was hunting for some of my dead son-in-law's cows to drive over to my place. I come on a party of Injuns. They was leaving the reserve about eight miles north of Lost Valley. I seen that red hair. I stood on the

133

hill and sighted on that man, and I killed him. The Injuns with him started jumping around, trying to figure out what was going on. I walked up on 'em. There was not a red-haired man among 'em. It was just friendly old Caddo Jake and his wives and a young fella riding with 'em. The young fella was dead, and Jake's little wife was kneeling beside him, holding a bright red, fox-skin cap the boy had been wearing. I raised my rifle again and killed her. I killed them all, steady and quick, with Jake runnin' around the whole time, giving the grand hailing sign of the Free Masons. That was all he knew of white men. I reckon somebody showed it to him and told him it would show he was a friend. Finally, I killed him, too. Then I walked among them and took every scalp. You must embrace a man to take his scalp . . . draw him against your body and hold him there by his hair while your other hand does the cutting. You can smell the cedar smoke in his hair and the blood as it flows over your knife."

Joe Woolfolk drew in air. "Damn," he swore in shock.

"Why did I do that, young Joe?" the frontiersman continued. "Justice. I thought I had caught the culprit, and I executed him. Guilt. I had killed a man wrongly, and I could not bear the innocence of those people. They had done nothing wrong, had nothing to do with the killings of a month earlier. But I had to kill them. After that, I would wake up in the night, seeing the old Injun making the hailing sign, hearing my gun. I would get up and set out right then to find and kill Injuns. Maybe I hoped one would kill me. But they didn't. I've stood in the open and never been near touched. Folks made it easy for me to tell myself that Injuns was all alike . . . guilty and deserved killin'. But I knew that they was not. Nobody said once . . . 'Don't do it.' One time I heard your friend, Wooten, fought a man going to make a quirt handle out of Jake's little squaw's arm bone. The story was Caddo Jake was a friend of

134

his. I think Wooten knows that there is innocence, and it is wrong to kill it in man or beast. It is to spit in the eye of God. Innocence, you see, is trust before it's been tricked and flindered with. And trust is the prime thing between men and before God. Faith some calls it."

"Mister Lynn . . . ," Joe Woolfolk began and kicked an ember back into the fire. "What is it you want from me?"

"I wanted you to hear my story. I ain't ever told no one before, and I expect you won't pass it on. Folks thinks they knows what happened and why, and they take comfort in their knowing. If I swore on ten Bibles I killed Caddo Jake and all the others because I could not stand myself, they'd not believe. Revenge they understand. Guilt is not universally accepted. But, boy, it is real as sand in your teeth. I could not swallow it, and I could not spit it out. I walked clear to Colorado, looking for Indians, and I killed some, too. Many times I walked all day and all night because I could not sit down or lie down with myself. One morning, in the company of dead men, I walked up on a great panorama. As far as I could see there was nothing but emptiness. I was the only human there was . . . there was only me.

"I sat down against the rock ledge and closed my eyes. When I awoke, a tawny golden mouse was sitting on my knee. With his front feet drawn up, he considered me as I considered him. I have never seen such a beautiful little creature, more beautiful than all the great creation behind him, and more perfect because of the extreme smallness of his making. Each whisker vibrated his contemplation of my smell. Eyes black and bright took me in. His flesh was full and firm from feeding on the bounty of the land. The pattern of his hair ran into a seamless, shining whole. My heart leaped up in pure love for that speculative mouse. He washed his face and groomed his tail and lay down to nap in the scalp tied to my knee. I stayed

135

so still. I barely breathed lest I disturb his sleep and trust in me. From that time I was free and whole again."

Woolfolk sat, looking at his hands, folded in his lap. "The Kiowas are guilty. The jury is going to find them guilty whether I put up a defense or not. There is nothing I can do about the verdict. There is nothing I want to do about the verdict."

Isaac Lynn nodded his head against his chest. "A bitter, lost war can kill a man's innocence. Sometimes he can find it again. A man, I think, can kill his own innocence as I killed Caddo Jack and his wives. Would be a shame, Joe Woolfolk."

The lawyer rose to his feet and brushed the dead grass and soil from his pants. He walked away across the fading night from old Isaac Lynn, back toward his own fire.

"Folks think guilt is from God. It is not. Guilt and the bondage it brings is the great instrument of evil, causing a man to hold himself in contempt and to drive himself from his true home. This is the lost principle of Christ . . . unmerited and undeserved reconciliation with God for any man who will take it, the end of guilt and self-destruction. Good behavior and good works may come from reconciliation, but they cannot substitute for it or bring freedom from the bondage of evil."

Woolfolk did not hear these words of Isaac Lynn who had lived with guilt and escaped. The old man did not intend for him to hear them. He spoke to himself.

Chapter Seventeen

Saturday, July 1, 1871
Jacksboro, Texas

Joe Woolfolk returned alone to Jacksboro. Wooten was with his
herd, and Isaac Lynn remained somewhere on the prairie. The
term of the circuit court usually brought a crowd to the little
Texas town. Unneighborly disputes normally occupied the
court's attention as they did the first few days of this term. But
everyone knew what lay ahead. Even as the insignificant personal cases were quickly handled, the town began to fill with
those whose curiosity could not be satisfied with less than
first-hand knowledge, with those who wanted a fair vengeance
for the murder of family and friends and close-held dreams,
and with those who came to see that moment in history where
they perceived change.

Joe left his horse at the livery. He took his usual room and
parked his gear, including his clean white shirts, at the Wichita
Hotel. Passing the busy, commodious bar, he made his way
along the crowded walk and across the teeming street to the
courthouse in the center of the square. The newly completed
court building was made of yellow limestone quarried from the
surrounding land. It was a square, angular building with no
pretense at architecture or ornamentation. Its chief attributes
were the large windows that opened to let in the wind and cool
the courtroom. The first floor consisted of business offices for
the judge and county clerk and important records. A wide
hallway ran through the building and could be opened on each
end to create a kind of dog-trot similar to those of the fron-

tiersmen's cabins. A staircase large enough for horse-drawn vehicles, it seemed to Joe, ran up to the second-floor courtroom.

"Hey, Joe," a man in the hallway called out to the lawyer as he entered the shaded comfort of the building. "When are we going home to Belknap?"

"Beats me, Ira," Joe responded. "Maybe it won't be too long now."

The man laughed. "That's what I thought. Soon as you see these damned Kiowas get their *fair* trial, we'll get our homes back." He joked with the men around him as Joe went toward the small office of Judge Soward. "That's Joe Woolfolk. I rode with him many the time in the Frontier Regiment. He knows how to treat an Injun." The man made a gun with his thumb and index finger and squeezed off a shot. "Boom!"

Joe heard the words and knew the sentiment. He stepped inside the office and closed the door. He stood a moment, looking at the floor, thinking about the man's words, about their common past. During the War Between The States, Kiowa and Comanche raiders had managed nearly to depopulate Young County. Things became so bad that many frontier folks retreated to safety farther east. Those that stayed formed central fortified places, like Fort Murrah and Fort Bragg, where all the near neighbors could run in the event of attacks. Belknap, in spite of becoming headquarters for the Frontier Regiment, could not maintain its function as the county seat. Trying to keep up a front seemed pointless with so little population and almost no one to run the offices. The county could not even keep a sheriff. Its records, including those Joe Woolfolk wrote as county clerk, were now stored here in Jacksboro, waiting for peace, waiting for the people to come home.

The greeting from James Robinson, Soward's clerk, interrupted Joe's thoughts. "Go on back, Mister Woolfolk. The judge has been wondering what happened to you."

"Thanks, Jim." Joe removed his hat and hung it on a waiting peg.

"Well," Soward said as the still dusty attorney entered the small room, "I was beginning to think you did run off to get away from this case."

"Can't run that far, Judge," Joe said.

"Good," the judge agreed and gestured to a chair. "Grand jury's meeting right now, upstairs. Should have the indictment pretty soon. You have any chance to talk with Lanham before you left Weatherford?"

"Briefly," the defense lawyer nodded as he sat.

"You two straight on the evidence and such?"

"Well, it isn't too complicated, Judge Soward. Lanham has some arrows he said were taken from the wagon fight. He has the testimony of Brazeal about the fight. Maybe Tatum and Mackenzie will confirm Satanta's confession and arrest."

"Tatum isn't coming." S. W. T. Lanham closed the door behind him as he entered. "He sent a copy of his note, ordering the arrests of Satanta and the others. Leeper and Jones, the interpreters, witnessed the confession and arrest. They'll be here. Mackenzie won't testify, either. I'll put on his sergeant, Miles Varily."

"Indictment ready yet?" queried Judge Soward about the grand jury upstairs.

"Not quite," the prosecutor responded. "Pretty much finished, but the wording and details have to be worked out. We're just taking a break. I heard Joe was here and thought we'd get the preliminaries finished. Who are you going to call, Joe?"

"Brazeal, Jones, Leeper, and Varily on cross, I guess."

"Are you going to put the Kiowas on the stand?" asked the prosecutor.

"Don't know that, Lanham," Woolfolk answered. "Haven't had a chance to talk to them."

"They are woolly boogers," Lanham said, now opening the door. "You want anything else from me, Joe?"

Woolfolk shook his head.

"I'd better get back upstairs. See you in court, counselor."

"Yeah," Woolfolk said. "See you in court." He rose slowly to his feet. "Guess I'll go out and visit with my clients unless there's something else, Judge."

"How you doing, Joe?" the judge asked out of concern.

"I'm fine, sir, just fine." The defense attorney opened the door and closed it quietly behind him.

Jim Robinson entered and lingered in the doorway. Both he and the judge watched Woolfolk remove his hat from the peg and place it on his head before going into the hall. "Is Thomas Ball still here?" Soward asked from his desk.

Robinson turned his attention quickly to the judge. "I think he's over at the Wichita Hotel."

"Good. Send word I want to see him and Woolfolk at four o'clock."

"Right," said Robinson, closing the door as he left.

Joe Woolfolk covered half the twenty-seven saloons in Jacksboro before he found Jim Donat, the greasy half-breed who spoke a half dozen Indian languages besides English and Spanish. Fortunately it was early, and Donat was not yet deeply inebriated. They walked together to the post and made the necessary arrangements to confer with the prisoners. Walking through the laundry, back to the guarded morgue where the prisoners waited, Donat smacked a fanny or two of the laundresses before Woolfolk's stare returned him to business. He shrugged and sighed to the women and went on.

"Damn it, Donat," the lawyer said, "get your mind off

women. I'm already out of patience, and you're pushing me."

"I can go back to the warmth and fellowship at Mollie McCabe's Palace of Beautiful Sin if you get surly, chief," said the 'breed.

"Don't call me chief," Woolfolk snapped. "You've got a gold eagle in your pocket and another coming when your work is done. That should buy you *mucho* fellowship later."

"Mucho," smiled Donat, as they walked. He allowed Woolfolk to lead and continued the conversation with himself. "But you ain't an easy man to like, chief. Reckon you're goin' to need my help more than you know."

Woolfolk stood at the heavy door, looking at the Kiowa chiefs. Chained to the walls by their ankles, they were naked except for their dirty breechcloths. Sweat stood on each man's body in the July heat. The defense counsel observed that there were no fresh marks or abrasions on the men. Neither the Army nor the vengeful citizens of Texas had treated them roughly. They had been fed regularly and a tin pitcher on the window sill held drinking water.

"These men need to be able to bathe," Woolfolk told the guard.

"Oh, sir, they'll be havin' a lovely bath before the parade," the Irish soldier said.

"The older one is Satanta," Jim Donat pointed out.

Woolfolk nodded. "Open the door, soldier."

The soldier hesitated.

"Give him your gun and boot knife, Donat."

The 'breed complied, but the soldier continued to hesitate.

"Open the door. I am the defense counsel for these men, and I have a right to talk with them in private."

"Right ya are, sir," the soldier agreed and put key into the heavy lock. "Call me when ya need out now. I'll just step away and leave ya to the lovely Injuns."

141

"That man don't like you, either," Donat said, as the door closed and locked behind them.

Neither Satanta nor Big Tree rose to greet the attorney.

"Give my greetings to them," Woolfolk instructed the 'breed.

The Kiowas listened attentively. Satanta stood slowly. His figure was massive beside Woolfolk. The lawyer looked at the broad naked chest marked with white scars from Satanta's battles. The muscles on the Indian's arms and legs were lean and hard. Satanta was very dark compared to his young companion, Adoltay. His face was broad. Looking into his eyes, Woolfolk was not sure of his intelligence or of how much he understood of the events whirling around him. Woolfolk stroked his graying beard. "He doesn't have to stand up. Tell him he can sit back down."

"*Sientese, jefe,*" said the interpreter. "You going to stand up, or you want me to call for a chair?" he asked the lawyer.

"Just sit down." Woolfolk watched as the 'breed hunkered. "Does he understand that I am here to help him? Hell, Donat, I want to know if they understand what's happening to them. Do they know what a trial is?"

Jim Donat talked intensely with the two men. "Chief, they ain't sure, and I ain't sure how to explain it exactly."

"Tell them they have been accused of murder . . . intentionally killing other men . . . an extremely serious crime among white men. They will be taken before a council of white men who will decide whether they are guilty of the act. I will act on their behalf. Another man will talk against them." Woolfolk waited for the translation.

The 'breed chewed his jaw and looked at Satanta, then began a discussion with the Indian. Finally he turned back to the lawyer. "I told him you were a mighty man among the whites, and you would act as his champion among them.

Kiowas understand that . . . weak man getting the strong man to take his part. He says he ain't weak and wants to talk for himself. But I says you was the man to talk fer him. He ain't sure you are a strong man. You look kind of weak and puny to him. And he ain't sure you're honest or trustworthy. How come you're standing up for him, he wants to know. I said, according to the ways of white men, you have to take his part. It's your job. You have to do it. And you have to do it right. If you don't, you'll lose face. You'll lose your honor."

"He accepts that?" asked Woolfolk.

"He trusts you, chief," answered Donat. "More or less, since there ain't a thing he can do about it, so to speak."

The defense counsel began a slow circuit of the room under the steady gazes of the other men.

"Tell them that if they are found guilty by the white men's council, which is extremely likely since many of the men on the council know Indian trouble, they will be sentenced to hang for their actions against the Warren wagon train." Woolfolk watched the Indians intently as Donat conveyed his deadly message.

"The soldiers have been saying the white men are going to hang 'em," said Donat.

"Yes, but do they understand that everything comes from their attack on the wagon train?"

"Chief, that wagon train was fair game to them. Kicking Bird made a successful raid last year about the same time. The Kiowa men were still talking about fighting the soldiers. Satanta and Satank and Mamanti wanted to do something to look good themselves. The killings were part of that to them." Donat rubbed his eyes.

"All right. Ask Satanta if he understood that he would be put in chains and brought to Texas to be tried, hanged, or put in prison when he said he led the raid?"

Jim Donat conferred with their client. "No, chief, he did not. He was purely talkin' to intimidate Tatum who he refers to as Old Bald Head. He wanted Sherman to know what men the Kiowas are so that they could talk as men of war, as equals."

"He told Sherman that he led the raid, then later he said that he was just one of the leaders, that he merely observed the young men to see that they did things right. Which is the truth?" asked Woolfolk.

Jim Donat talked with Satanta. "He was one of the leaders. The older men were there to direct the young men."

Woolfolk stopped at the window and looked out at the laundry, blowing in the wind. The same wind blew through the fragments of clothing and sacks on Salt Creek Prairie, lifting the bloody rags like flags or prayers for the victims. "What were the raiders after? Why did they go out . . . to make war, to take things? Did they plan to kill anyone they met?"

"Well, that's a lot of asking?" said the 'breed.

"I've got time," Woolfolk stated softly.

As the 'breed and Satanta talked intently, Woolfolk watched the young man, Adoltay. There was a softness about the boy's face. He followed the other men's words, but did not interject any of his own thoughts. *That would have been bad form,* thought Woolfolk. A young man on his way up had to defer to the older men. Be brave. Talk strong to the young men, but listen to the old men.

Adoltay felt the intensity of the lawyer's eyes and looked up. His look had no defiance in it. It was frank and observant. There was uncertainty, perhaps, but not self-doubt or personal fear. The boy had no guilt. By his standards, he had fought bravely. He had acted honorably as a Kiowa. And this was the problem Woolfolk faced. These men would be tried, found guilty, and hung without any understanding of what crime they had committed.

"There was good grass. The ponies were sleek. It was time to go out and fight," explained the 'breed. "Some men went for vengeance, to kill, because the Texans had killed someone in their family. Some men went to get horses and mules to trade for better guns and cartridges. Some men went for glory against their enemies."

Woolfolk looked now at Satanta. He realized that the quizzical expression did not reflect a lack of intelligence, but a reading of situations and men. Satanta had had his days of ideals and glory. Now he wanted power. He wanted to be principal chief, to speak with the voice of the Kiowas. Power came from giving other men what they wanted. Murder for those who sought vengeance. Loot for those who wished guns. Glory for the innocent who fought for honor. Satanta was reading them all, trying to discover what they wanted. What could he give the white men who only wanted his death and the death of his people?

Chapter Eighteen

The grand jury papers were lying on the desk in front of Soward when Woolfolk returned from the fort a little before four o'clock. S. W. T. Lanham was in attendance. The judge lifted the top document and handed it to Woolfolk. "That's the jury call. See if it suits you."

Joe Woolfolk accepted the paper and read from it:

THE STATE OF TEXAS
224 vs.
SATANTA AND BIG TREE

It is ordered that a special venire issue herein for fifty good and lawful men to appear before this court on Monday next at half past 8 o'clock A.M. to serve as jurors herein.

The defense counsel looked up. "The sheriff will have to be in the saddle day and night to serve fifty jury summonses in time to get a pool by Monday. Pretty dangerous riding, too, I expect, with the distance between places and the Kiowas and Comanches about."

"Ah, Tom," the judge said, ignoring Woolfolk to greet the man who had just entered his chambers. "You know Tom, don't you, Joe?"

"Sure." Woolfolk extended his hand to his fellow lawyer. "How are you, Tom."

Tom Ball shook Joe's outstretched hand and sat down next to him with a nod and smile. Both lawyers turned to the judge.

"Joe was just reading the special venire, Tom," Soward explained. "I've asked you both here because, after consideration, I don't think one man should bear the burden of the Indian trial alone. The strain could be too great, both now and later. I want you to act as co-counsels." Woolfolk straightened in his chair. "I'd consider it a personal favor, Tom," pursued Soward, "if you would join the defense. What do you say?"

"I didn't expect this, sir," Tom Ball said. "I haven't even considered the case. I mean, I know what folks are saying, but not much more." Ball shifted in his seat to look at Joe Woolfolk. "What about it, Joe? I'd do what I could, but you're way ahead of me on this."

Woolfolk looked at the judge and then at Ball. "Well, Tom," he said softly, "I think Judge Soward is way ahead of both of us. Isn't that so, sir?"

"I believe I made myself quite clear to both of you, to all the lawyers in Weatherford. We can expect a guilty verdict in this trial. But I don't want a lynching. The law and its proper decorum will be observed. Put up the best defense you can, under the circumstances. Don't draw things out or stir people up. What's your answer, Tom?"

Ball checked Joe, but did not find his answer there. Woolfolk's eyes were on the judge. Tom Ball considered his hands. "As a personal favor, Judge Soward, I would do it."

"Fine, that's settled," the judge said. "Now, Joe was just questioning the venire. He doesn't think it's possible to call in fifty good and lawful citizens by Monday next . . . too much riding through too much territory and danger. He's right. It's not possible. I've decided to impanel men from around Jacksboro. I believe we can come up with as many capable men here as anywhere around. They won't be unduly exposed to danger. They are likely to be as fair or fairer than the men we would round up anyway."

Joe Woolfolk felt the muscles in his face tighten. He flexed his jaw. "Whatever you say, Judge Soward," he said hoarsely. "We'll just have to do the best we can with what you give us. Right, Tom?"

"Right," said the new counselor, slightly thrown by Joe Woolfolk's tone.

"Can we look at the indictment now, sir?" Woolfolk's words were polite and formal, but Soward knew that the man was angry.

"Here, Joe." The judge handed a copy to Woolfolk. "Mister Lanham, do you have another copy so they can both read one?"

"Here, Tom," S. W. T. Lanham at the window said, offering the copy he had been holding.

The defense attorneys began to read:

Now comes the grand jurors for the State of Texas: — S. W. Eastin, Foreman. N. Atkinson, J. W. Brummett, C. W. Cooper, J. A. Dean, Joseph Fowler, Moses Dameron, A. L. Henson, William Hood, U. M. Johnson, J. R. Reagon, James Garrison, D. W. Patton, E. M. Callis. Being duly elected, impaneled and sworn for the County of Jack, and return into open court through their foreman the following bill of indictment endorsed by their foreman, S. W. Eastin, as a true bill which is entered and numbered as follows:

THE STATE OF TEXAS
224 Vs. Murder
SATANTA & BIG TREE

CASE 224

In the name and by the authority of the State of Texas

the grand jury for the County of Jack, and also for the County of Young, in the State of Texas, which said Young County is attached to said County of Jack, in the State of Texas for judicial purposes, duly elected, tried, impaneled and sworn to inquire in and for the bodies of the County of Jack and the County of Young aforesaid and true presentment made of all offences committed cognizeable by the District Court of the said County of Jack, State of Texas upon their oath in District Court do say and present that to wit the 18th day of May, in the year of our Lord, Eighteen Hundred Seventy-One, in the County of Young, in the State of Texas, Satanta and Big Tree, late of the County and State aforesaid, with force and malice not having the fear of God before their eyes, but being moved by and seduced by the instigation of the devil in and upon the person of S. Long, James Elliott, N. J. Baxter, James Williams, Samuel Elliott, John Mullins, and James Bowman, in the peace of God the State of Texas then and there being willfully, unlawfully, feloniously and of their malice aforethought made an assault, and that they, the said Satanta and Big Tree, have certain guns and pistols, each of the value of five dollars, then and there charged with gunpowder and leaden bullets and then and there being deadly weapons which said guns and pistols the said Satanta and Big Tree have in their hands, then and there held them and there willfully, unlawfully, and feloniously and of their malice aforethought did discharge and shoot off to, against, and upon the said S. Long, James Elliott, N. J. Baxter, James Williams, Samuel Elliott, John Mullins and James Bowman, then and there with the leaden bullets, aforesaid so as aforesaid discharge and shoot out of the guns and pistols aforesaid by the said Satanta and

Big Tree in and upon the heads of them, the said S. Long, James Elliott, and N. J. Baxter, and in and upon the head and sundry parts aforesaid of the bodies of them, the aforesaid James Williams, Samuel Elliott, John Mullins, and James Bowman, each one mortal wounds each one of the depth of four inches and of the breadth of half an inch; of which said mortal wound the said S. Long, James Elliott, N. J. Baxter, James Williams, Samuel Elliott, John Mullins and James Bowman, then and there instantly died.

And so the grand jurors aforesaid upon their oaths aforesaid do say and present that they, the said Satanta and Big Tree on their manner and by the means aforesaid then the said S. Long, James Elliott, N. J. Baxter, James Williams, Samuel Elliott, John Mullins, and James Bowman willfully, unlawfully, feloniously and by their malice aforethought did kill and murder contrary to the form of the statute on such case made and provided, and against the peace and dignity of the State of Texas.

> S. W. Eastin, Foreman of the Grand Jury
> S. W. T. Lanham, District Attorney

"What does 'with force and malice not having the fear of God before their eyes, but being moved by and seduced by the instigation of the devil' mean?" asked Woolfolk incredulously.

"It means folks are damned mad after hearing the evidence presented today," said Lanham.

"I want to know if this is a religious trial, an inquisition?" Woolfolk continued.

"It is a trial for murder in the first degree," Lanham blurted. "The statute says, 'all murder committed in the perpetration, or in the attempt at the perpetration, of robbery is murder in the first degree.' "

"Are you going to try it that way or by jelly bean rhetoric?" Woolfolk was on his feet, facing Lanham.

"I'll try it for the people on this frontier as the people on this frontier demand of their prosecuting attorney." Lanham stepped forward toward Woolfolk.

Chapter Nineteen

"Joe," called out Thomas Ball, as he tried to catch up with the man who strode out of the courthouse toward the Wichita Hotel.

Woolfolk finally halted and waited in the street for his co-counsel to catch up.

"Joe, you're squaring off with Lanham way too soon."

Woolfolk began to walk again.

"Look, Joe, the essence of the indictment is that Satanta and Big Tree attacked the freighters and, being in possession of loaded firearms, discharged the weapons against and upon the victims, causing mortal wounds from which the victims died. They willfully, unlawfully, feloniously and by their malice aforethought did kill and murder contrary to the form of the statute on such cases and against the peace and dignity of the State of Texas. That's all, Joe."

"Lanham let in that crap about God and the devil," said Woolfolk.

"That's just . . ." — Ball searched for the word — "just blow, rhetoric for the electorate."

"Look, Tom." Woolfolk stopped. "We are going into a trial that we know is fixed. Lanham doesn't have to rub our faces in it or make political hay."

"Come on," Ball pacified the angry little lawyer. "It isn't personal. It's just the way things are. Sure, Lanham's ambitious. Hell, who isn't in Texas? Let's get a drink and talk about our case."

"Let's go out to the fort," Woolfolk substituted. "I want

you to meet our clients before we talk about the case."

After gathering Jim Donat again, the lawyers returned to the prison.

"Look at 'em close, Tom," Woolfolk urged as they entered the cell. "These are the bastards that killed your neighbors. Donat, when we were here before, Satanta said he confessed the attack to Sherman to show that he, too, was a great warrior, an equal to negotiate with. In fact, he said, he was just one of the leaders. He and the others were there to show the young men how to fight. My question is . . . could he have stopped the killing at any time after it began? Could he have prevented the torture of Sam Elliott?"

The 'breed and Satanta exchanged information with gestures and words. Then Donat said: "No, he could not. Once a fight starts, the men get crazy, like dogs . . . can't stop them. Taste blood, like it. Want more. Want to win honor."

"What about Elliott?"

"Elliott made everyone very mad," Donat explained. "He shot a boy named Gunshot in the face, blew the side of his head off so that you could see the inside of his mouth. This was very bad, chief. The Indians knew the boy was going to die pretty soon. He was kind of their pet, an innocent boy on his first raid. Killing him that way was bad. They could not save the boy, so they let him go wild, revenge himself, make his name before he died. They all just went crazy because they were so mad about the white man, killing that young boy."

Woolfolk posed another question. "The survivors of the wagon train say they heard a bugle. Lots of white folks have heard that Satanta blows a bugle to direct his men and to deceive his victims and the cavalry. That's a good story, isn't it, Tom, a real frontier myth? Does Satanta even have a bugle?"

Donat conferred with the Indian. "The soldiers took it when he was arrested."

Woolfolk looked at Tom Ball. "So much for that," he shrugged. "I want to know what part Adoltay played in the raid," the lawyer then told Donat.

Donat spoke quietly with Satanta and the boy. "Well, chief, Adoltay is a fine young man by Kiowa standards. He is a leader of the young men. He cut off the wagon closing the circle by killing one of the lead mules. He counted first coup on the wagon drivers."

"He killed the driver of the closing team?" asked Thomas Ball.

"No," said Donat. "He killed the mule. He counted first coup by touching the man as he ran. Tapped him with his bow. That's big stuff . . . touching the enemy. The old Kiowa warriors did that. It is considered very dangerous and very honorable."

"Did he kill anyone during the raid?" pursued Ball.

Donat asked the question directly and listened to the answer. "No, sir, he did not. There were not enough freighters for all the young men to get a coup. Adoltay already had first coup, so mostly he left the killing to the others, so they could get honors. This boy knows how to be chief . . . be brave, take some honor, leave some for somebody else."

"Whether he killed anyone or not," Woolfolk reminded his colleague, "killings were committed in the course of a robbery. That makes him guilty of murder."

Over dinner at the Wichita Hotel, Joe Woolfolk and Thomas Ball began the preparation of their case. It was clear to them that the prosecution held all the cards. Neither lawyer could think of a single character witness to call for the defense. Woolfolk looked about the dining room. He knew most of the men. They were men he had known a long time, ridden with against the Indians. Time was when he would have said they were fair men, all fair men, except for a few with mean, narrow streaks. But now he knew that was not true. All of them had been tainted by their experience. Whatever case he and Ball made would be judged against that experience, against knowing the men killed or the women and children carried off by Kiowa and Comanche raiders. *Still,* he thought, *most of them could separate things enough not to want to kill the innocent. On the whole, they are not blood-thirsty men who have killed any red man because he was red and would make no exceptions for women and children and old people. A lot of them were disgusted with Custer's attack on Black Kettle's village. Most would not choose to drink sociably with Chivington or his men. They would tolerate them, even accept them in company and in business, knowing the ruthlessness of Indian raiding parties and the widely felt need to stop it, but they would not think of themselves as their companions or friends. The question is, can they separate guilt in the murders of the teamsters from guilt in a hundred other incidents? Can I differentiate the defendants from other Kiowas and the deeds of their own past?*

Woolfolk's thoughts were so intense, he did not notice that the room had become silent. Tom Ball touched his arm. Across the dining room, standing in the doorway, was Adrianne Chastain.

She waited for the stares, for the whispers, to recede as coolly as a marble goddess. She did not avert her azure eyes from the curious, the shocked. She raised her chin very slightly and walked alone toward a table behind Woolfolk and Ball. As she passed, Joe caught the sweet smell of violets. He sat a moment, staring at his plate, then rose quickly to his feet and gallantly pulled out her chair. She nodded. Joe wanted to stare, too, because Mrs. Chastain was a beautiful woman. Even the long, white scar, running from her eye to her chin only added to her beauty and mystery. Joe swallowed and returned to his table.

"What's she come for?" asked Ball quietly.

"Church tomorrow, most likely," Woolfolk speculated innocently.

"Church, hell," muttered Ball. "We're dead. She's here to see Satanta hangs."

"Think so?" asked Joe, chewing the last bite of his steak, feeling it grow in his jaw with each stroke. "Lanham can't call her, can he? She wasn't on his list."

"She'll be there, Joe," noted Tom. "Her presence will be enough."

Joe Woolfolk sat up and laid his knife on the table. "Hell fire! Everybody knows she heard a bugle at Elm Creek. That damn' Lanham will put her down front, and every time the jury looks up, they'll see that beautiful woman with that terrible scar and remember Satanta led the raid. This just ain't fair. Lanham's out of hand."

"He hasn't done anything yet," cautioned Tom Ball.

"He will," grudged Woolfolk. "If you're finished, let's adjourn to the bar while we can still get in. By the time this trial is over, we'll be drinkin' alone in dark hotel rooms."

Rising with him, Tom Ball smiled. "Everything is a crisis with you, Joe." He caught a good look at Adrianne Chastain behind his partner. "We'd better buy the bottles tonight."

Chapter Twenty

Sunday, July 2, 1871

Joe Woolfolk's head pounded the next morning as the waiter at the Wichita Hotel poured black coffee into his cup. The aroma rose in his nostrils and energized the sleeping cells of his troubled brain.

"You look like hell," observed John Wooten, throwing a long leg over the chair back and settling in beside his friend.

"Come to see me fall on my face, John?" asked the lawyer, lifting his cup with both hands and holding it beneath his nose.

"You give up already?"

"Might as well," snorted the irritable lawyer. "The final straw is Adrianne Chastain, the beautiful Missus Chastain, victim of my honorable client, Satanta. Why'd she come? Didn't you just take a herd of cattle out to her place? Didn't I help you drive them? She ought to be at home, tending her cattle."

"What are you eatin', Joe?" The cowboy studied the lawyer's untouched plate. "That bacon looks good."

"Take it." Woolfolk pushed the hot plate toward him. "Take all of it."

The cowboy pushed it back. "You've got to eat, Joe. Jinny would be mad if I ate your breakfast and you didn't." Wooten signaled the waiter. "Same as Joe's havin' for me, Fritz."

"Did you ever try to chew an egg you don't want?" asked Woolfolk.

"If you can't even chew your eggs, how are you goin' to chew this case you bit off?" the cowboy questioned.

Woolfolk looked up. "Don't be smart with me, John. I ain't in the mood."

Fritz sat a plate of eggs and bacon in front of the cowboy who tucked his napkin in his shirt front. " 'Course, you ain't in the mood to chew these lovely eggs," he said. "You're too full of self-pity to swallow anything else."

"You want to go outside, Wooten?" flared the attorney.

The cowboy cut another bite. "Certainly not. You know, Woolfolk, you are a very belligerent man, like all good lawyers."

"Hell, I ain't a good lawyer," said Woolfolk. "All I can think about is losing."

"That ain't up to you, Joe," the cowboy spoke as he chewed. "Jury decides that."

"Right, jury decides impartially, on the basis of evidence presented in the trial as they sit there and look at that beautiful scar running down Missus Chastain's beautiful face. Why in the hell would anybody cut her like that?" the lawyer asked.

"Kiowa women cut her." The cowboy continued to eat as he talked. "That's what she said."

"Why?"

"She didn't say. But I reckon, if I was a woman and she was brought in, I'd try to lower her value." The cowboy pushed his plate away and turned to his coffee.

"It didn't work," noted the lawyer grumpily.

"No," said Wooten. "It kind of looks right on her."

"So, you sweet on her?" The lawyer was suddenly alert.

"Since Britt Johnson was killed, I'm the cow boss. That's all I am. She's a smart woman about cows and business."

"Must have learned it from one of her husbands," observed Woolfolk.

"I reckon she's just smart," said the unruffled cowboy.

"Don't you get interested in that woman, John. She's hell

on men, three dead already and who knows. . . . even that Negro, Britt Johnson."

"Don't speculate on Missus Chastain's character, Joe," the cowboy said calmly. "She may ruin your trial for you, but she ain't a bad woman."

"And how would you know that? You ain't exactly a man of the world."

"She's an honorable woman. I seen her business dealings. I seen the way she treats her men and their families. I seen the way she loves that little granddaughter of hers, Lottie."

"She's worldly, John. And she's old."

"Shut up, Joe." The cowboy smiled, refusing to take the bait.

"She wasn't a fit mother. Her own daughter, Susan, sued to keep her from having guardianship of her little brother, Joe Carter."

The cowboy looked up into the lawyer's face.

"And she won, John. The daughter won." The lawyer gouged the table top with his forefinger as he spoke. "She won."

"How you goin' to win *this* case?" asked the cowboy, ignoring the provocation.

Joe Woolfolk sighed. "I wish you'd let me get my mind off this damn' Indian trial."

"Court opens tomorrow morning at eight-thirty. I heard they're looking for fifty good and lawful men for the jury."

"They're not looking very hard," the lawyer said sourly. "According to the judge, they are going to take whoever is in town." He brightened suddenly. "You're in town, John. You're a good and lawful man. I'd accept you without hesitation."

"I might vote against you, Joe."

"You'd listen first. Hell, you believe Adrianne Chastain is an honorable woman."

* * * * *

Sunday afternoon Woolfolk and Ball went over their case again in Woolfolk's hotel room, turning it and twisting it, anticipating Lanham's evidence and witnesses.

"Good God Almighty," swore Woolfolk. "I wish we had one good witness who'd say these Indians are not just Indians, but men. And maybe as men, Adoltay and Satanta are not too different from the rest of us."

"Even at that," Ball said, "they were part of a robbery in which men were killed."

"But did they think of it as robbery?" Woolfolk insisted. "Was robbery in their minds, or was honor and vengeance and war against their white enemies?"

"We can try that, Joe," Ball conceded. "But nobody here believes the poor old Indian is just protecting what's his. There's too much blood between the folks here and the Indians. Back East we could point out the injustices to the Indians, but here nobody believes it. Even if they do, they don't give a damn. They'd say the government gave the Indian land and annuities and teachers to teach him, and he ought to be satisfied with his share and leave them in peace on their land. They'd say the Indians broke treaties same as white folks. Satanta barely signed the Medicine Lodge treaty before he was down our throats. We can try it, but it ain't going to hold up."

"Still, we need to point out the obvious. They were here first. . . ."

"And somebody was here before they were."

"Come on, Tom. I need some help here. Let's do this. You do the poor old Indian stuff, the white man's guilt . . . ," suggested Woolfolk.

"Joe, I know we've got to try the victims . . . that's the procedure. But the problem is every single man, woman, and child in that court identifies with the victims. The victims are *them*. We all came out here for the same chance to make a new and better life. If they agreed with everything we said, they'd have to vote against us in their own self-interest or pick up and move back East. Nobody's going to do that."

Woolfolk considered the words, then replied: "I'll pick the state's witnesses to pieces, if I can. We'll make every objection to jurisdiction, procedure, evidence, whatever. I'll make 'em hate me. Maybe that will get their minds off the Indians. You, on the other hand, will take the high road."

"I'll do what you say, Joe, but I think you'll pay a terrible price and still not get anywhere. Let's just take it by the book . . . like we would for any other client."

"Would you want *your* lawyer to just take it by the book? No, you'd want him to sweat blood for you. I would. I'd want to know he was doing everything he could, and, if I lost, maybe he lost too. It's the Indians' lives, Tom. How can we lose and just go home to dinner like any other day?"

"We can, because it's our job, Joe . . . our profession. We do the best we can. We keep doing it, win or lose, as long as we are in the profession. You're acting like a kid or a flaming martyr. We get paid for our knowledge and effort, not for destroying ourselves. We've got families, too. And if I have to choose between my life, my family, and Satanta and Adoltay, I know my choice right now." Tom Ball rose to his feet. "I really don't want to see you immolate yourself on a prairie fire."

"Fine," growled Woolfolk. "You stay safe. I'll take the spear."

"Whatever you say." Tom Ball picked up his hat. "I need some air."

Woolfolk stomped to the bed and threw himself on it. The corner of his mouth twisted as he thought about his words and Tom Ball's words. Tom was right. He couldn't throw away

161

his career for a couple of men who were guilty, whom he did not like, and who would never know whether he did or did not give his best shot. He crossed his arms and tried to think in the July heat.

When he awoke, it was late, dark outside. His shirt was soaked through with sweat. He rolled himself onto his feet. He did not bother to light the lamp, but moved desolately toward the open French doors and the night air. Woolfolk had not taken more than two steps into the cool night when he realized that someone else was already on the dark balcony. He closed his eyes.

"Missus Chastain," he whispered. "Sorry to have disturbed you, ma'am."

Adrianne Chastain leaned against the building wall in the deep shadows. Even after he spoke, she did not seem to hear or to move. He started back to his room. "You are Satanta's lawyer," she said from the shadows.

"That's right."

"Will you make a good defense?" she asked.

"I'll do my best," Woolfolk answered frankly.

"Who's paying you?"

"The State of Texas, ma'am."

"Is it enough?"

"Does this have something to do with thirty pieces of silver or some such, Missus Chastain? I mean, if you think I'm betraying the Christian white man, that's your business, but seeing these men get a fair representation is mine."

The woman moved out of the darkness. He could see her face now in the ambient light. "I meant is the money adequate for you to do a good job, nothing more?"

"You are, sure-fire, the only one that asked me that. Nobody seems to care what kind of job I do."

Woolfolk's eyes followed the line of the scar down her cheek

162

to her jaw. He lingered a moment on the throat as it slipped down into the neck of her dressing gown. "I can't believe you'd care." He started to add — "after what you've been through." — but thought perhaps it was indelicate.

"Do you think everyone, except yourself, is blind to the injustices done the Indians?" the beautiful Mrs. Chastain asked.

Woolfolk felt embarrassed. He had been thinking just that. He knew he'd gotten way out of hand if a strange woman could see what he was thinking. "I've thought that, yes. But perhaps I'm wrong. Still, it seems strange to me that you'd be one who was concerned about such things."

"Oh, I'm not concerned, Mister Woolfolk. Things will run their course with or without my concern. But my own misfortunes have not made me incognizant of crimes against the Indian. I grew up with that guilt. My father was a soldier. He fought with Andrew Jackson and the Cherokees at Horseshoe Bend. He felt Mister Jackson betrayed them when he refused to enforce the great court's order, protecting their claims. More than that he thought Jackson sold his character and his office to buy the approval of greedy men. I think he felt that his own word had also been broken by the President's studied inaction. It was a sad sight to see the people taken from their homes and farms with little or nothing for their old people and their babies."

"But you've come to see Satanta hanged for his crime against you," interrupted Woolfolk.

"It was a crime, Mister Woolfolk . . . killing my son and daughter, taking my grandchild, burning our home."

Woolfolk lowered his head. "Truly, ma'am, I am sorry to have questioned your right. I feel certain that Satanta will be found guilty and hanged. That should satisfy you."

The woman turned her head slightly. "Satisfy? His death will not satisfy me in the least. You see, sir, I need Satanta alive in order to get my granddaughter, Millie, back from the Kiowas. If money will help your defense, I shall gladly supply it."

Woolfolk almost gasped. "There's something more than money you can give. Don't go to court, ma'am. Your presence will assure his conviction. People will look at you and remember Elm Creek. They will remember Satanta was there. That he blew the bugle that caused you to open the door to the attack, the killings, the captivity. Lanham's going to use that bugle for sure."

"Satanta isn't the only Kiowa with a bugle," the woman stated. "They take special delight in counting coup on buglers. They've even forced captured buglers to blow calls for them. They commonly use bugles in their war dances."

"Do you know that for a fact, Missus Chastain?" asked Woolfolk.

"I know it for a fact."

"Missus Chastain, would you appear for the defense?" Woolfolk pushed. "For your granddaughter's sake, for Millie's sake?"

"You do not know the child, Mister Woolfolk. Do not bandy her name about to gain your own purposes. My testimony would do Satanta no good. Any man who knows the Kiowas well will know about the bugle."

"Your testimony would show you are willing to put the past aside. And if you are willing, the rest of us should be. You could say something good for his character perhaps." Woolfolk wanted this woman in his camp, not Lanham's.

"What shall I say, Mister Woolfolk? That I have been married three times and that that savage is the only man who ever held me after he had had his pleasure with me?"

Mrs. Chastain disappeared quickly into the darkness of her room.

Woolfolk remained on the balcony alone. He sat down with his hand on the railing and considered again the image of one of the only two people left on the earth killing the other. "Nice job, Joe," he said to himself.

Chapter Twenty-One

Monday, July 3, 1871
Jacksboro, Texas

At seven in the morning Sheriff Michael McMillan stood at the open front doors of the courthouse. The hallway was closed with a heavy bolt dropped across the back entrance. Armed soldiers stood on either side of the portly sheriff and his deputy. *The people will not like the soldiers,* McMillan thought, but he was glad to have them to keep things calm. He was equally glad that they lined the hallway and the courtroom upstairs. Any trouble-makers would think twice.

"If you have guns or knives or any other weapons, step aside and leave them with the deputy. You can't take them into the courthouse." He had said the phrase a half dozen times before he started the admissions.

As he allowed a few men and families to pass by him, he looked directly into the pale blue eyes of Isaac Lynn. He could not say the room was already full. It was too early. Lynn and everyone else would know that was a lie. He looked at the old man sternly and let him pass.

"Hey, Isaac, I hear Peyton's on the jury," a farmer said to the old man. "He'll hang 'em. He won't let Mary or Tom down. Your boy's a good man."

Lynn said nothing, but proceeded into the hallway and up the stairs.

John Wooten shouldered in behind Lynn. "Let me pass, Mike. I ain't armed, and I want to see how Joe Woolfolk does."

"Sure," the sheriff jerked his head. "Go on in. Keep an eye

on Mister Lynn, will you?"

The admissions and seatings continued until the courtroom was crammed with a hundred and fifty spectators and guards. Joe Woolfolk sat beside Tom Ball at the defense table. Neither man looked at the other or at the crowd. Prosecutor Lanham shook hands with some of the men entering the front rows. "Leave places through here," he said. "We're expecting some important guests from the fort. Save a spot there for Missus Chastain. I want her to have a good view of the jury."

"Shoot!" said Woolfolk, overhearing.

"What?" Ball inquired.

"Nothing," replied Woolfolk as he continued his examination of the bare table top.

A hand hit him from behind and squeezed the muscles of his tense shoulder into a painful knot. Woolfolk turned to see Isaac Lynn settle into the second seat. John Wooten still clasped his shoulder as he took the aisle seat. "Look real good there, counsel," the cowboy said. "How you doin', Tom."

Tom Ball shook his hand.

Woolfolk spoke almost in the cowboy's ear. "Have you seen Adrianne Chastain? Is she coming?"

Wooten shrugged. "I'm just the cow boss. She doesn't ask me for advice much even about cattle."

Fort Richardson

The guard escorted the freshly bathed and dressed Kiowa chiefs to the wagon out front. First Lieutenant Carter was in a near panic that someone across the river would get a clear shot at the men and eliminate the need for the trial. He had lain awake for days, figuring a strategy. This morning would see if it worked. The laundresses had been removed, lest one conceal a weapon to kill one of the Indians or pass one to him

167

as someone had to Satank. That must not happen again. Carter had a column of soldiers lined up — a human screen — protecting the emerging Indians from the gathering of onlookers across the river.

Dressed in soldiers' fatigues, still heavily manacled at hands and feet, Satanta and Adoltay struggled into the wagon. The hard soldier's brogans did not aid their movement. They had had little time to groom their hair and felt some consternation at their appearance. They sat on the floor. Three soldiers sat before them, three behind. Mounted troopers rode in tight formation at the wagon's sides. Getting a clear shot would not be easy. Carter checked his pocket watch. At precisely eighten, he nodded to his sergeant who directed the guard and their prisoners forward toward the wooden bridge over Lost Creek. It was the same bridge Tom Brazeal had crossed in the blinding May thunderstorm to report the events on Salt Creek Prairie. Every soldier was alert, and Carter did not relax.

Jacksboro Courthouse

By the time the escort and prisoners arrived, all the admissions to the courtroom had been made. The remaining populace, including many school children who had been dismissed to attend the historic trial so their teacher was also allowed to attend, were corralled away from the entrance by lines of soldiers.

"God'urn blue bellies thick as flies when you don't need 'em," one of the Texans spat out. "We wouldn't 'a' had the Injun trouble if you'd been half as hard on them as you been on us." The soldier ignored his words and pressed him back.

"I hear Mackenzie give out guns so the men could chase Injuns after them last horses was took. Looks like he's took 'em all back up again," commented a bystander.

"Ain't that shit," the first Texan said. "We're unarmed, but the Injuns ain't. Reconstruction ain't constructin' nothin' but coffins in Texas. By gad, that's a big damn' Injun."

"Other'n looks kind of skeered," the second man added.

"He ort to be," confirmed the first. "You childr'n look up thisaway." He lifted a small freckled boy onto his broad shoulders. "See that there is the ones done the killin'. Carried off and cut Miz Chastain, too."

"Oh, Papa," said the young girl, standing on tiptoes in front of him, "they are bad."

Holding the chains of the leg irons in their shackled hands, Satanta and Big Tree made the climb to the second floor between flanking soldiers. "Move along, men," the sergeant said evenly. "The judge is waiting."

When the back doors opened and the Kiowas entered the courtroom, the mass of Texans turned as a man to observe their enemies. Only the noise of the chains and their coarse shoes followed the Indians down the aisle toward the front. Satanta looked straight ahead, but Adoltay's eyes searched the room. He suddenly stopped and called out: "Wooten!" The guard quickly moved him on to the defense table where Woolfolk took in the scene of the Indian and his friend. As he was placed in his seat, the young Kiowa strained to keep his eyes on John Wooten.

The Indians had barely taken their seats when the officers, including Colonel Ranald Mackenzie, and their guests from Fort Richardson came down and took their seats behind Lanham. Woolfolk quickly noted that Mrs. Chastain was not with them or anywhere else in the courtroom. He sighed at the apparent favor.

"Oye, Oye! All rise!" called the bailiff. The courtroom rose with a great hollow sound. "The Thirteenth District Court of the great State of Texas is now in session. The Honorable

Judge Charles Soward presiding."

Soward entered and took his place at the raised bench. He studied the packed courtroom before he sat. "Be seated." Soward looked at the notes in front of him. "The court calls case number two hundred and twenty four, the State of Texas versus Satanta and Big Tree, an indictment for murder. How say you?"

Woolfolk stood and smoothed the front of his freshly brushed coat. "Your Honor, we plead the jurisdiction of this court in pursuing proceedings against the Kiowa Indian chiefs, Satanta and Adoltay. We contend that the proper jurisdiction is in a federal court, according to statutes that require all matters involving Indians and whites be tried before a federal magistrate."

"Exception," Lanham spoke, rising to his feet.

"Mister Lanham, what is your reasoning in the exception to this plea?" asked Soward.

"Your Honor, we contend that this is the correct jurisdiction since the federal law, to which Mister Woolfolk refers, deals with conflicts between Indians and whites arising in the designated Indian Territory. We contend that the intent of that statute was to provide a jurisdiction where none other exists. That is not the case here, where the State of Texas has jurisdiction. Further, your honor, Article Six of the United States Constitution states very clearly for all to see . . . 'accused shall enjoy the right to a speedy and public trial, by an impartial jury of the state and district wherein the crime shall have been committed. . . .' The crime was committed in the Thirteenth District of the State of Texas where we now are trying it. The jurisdiction of this court is indisputable." Lanham spoke clearly and thoughtfully.

Soward did not waste time, but stated: "It is considered by the court that the law is with the state. It is, therefore, ordered and adjudged by the court that the state's exception be sustained."

"Exception," said Woolfolk.

"Exception noted, Mister Woolfolk," Soward said. "Do you have further matters?"

"Sir, the defense takes exception to the indictment for murder as the incident purported to have happened could be considered an act of war as easily as of murder." Woolfolk waited for the coming exception to his exception.

Lanham leaned forward on the table. "The killings were committed during a robbery of wagons, carrying corn to Fort Griffin. Mules and personal belongings were also stolen. Sir, by any statute, that is murder."

Woolfolk pursued his exception. "The prosecution has chosen to selectively prosecute the prisoners in hand rather than the reported one hundred to one hundred and fifty men involved in the act."

"The prosecution will show that the accused were principal leaders in the robbery and killings. But aside from this, the mere presence and involvement of the defendants is sufficient for an indictment of murder."

"It is considered by the court that the law is with the state. It is, therefore, ordered and adjudged by the court that said defendants take nothing by their said exceptions."

"Exception," said Woolfolk.

"Noted," said Soward. "Anything else?" He looked at both lawyers for response. "Very well. Mister Lanham, is the state ready for trial?"

"We are, Your Honor."

"Mister Woolfolk, how say you? Are you ready for trial?" asked the judge.

"We are, Your Honor."

"The Defendants, Satanta and Adoltay, being duly arraigned, the court will consider their pleas." Soward seemed to be hunting for something on his bench as he spoke. Woolfolk and Ball lifted the two chiefs to their feet before the judge. "Satanta, how do you plead to the charge of murder? Guilty or not guilty?" Soward continued to prowl the papers on his desk, not looking at the defendants.

"Not guilty," said Woolfolk for his client.

"Big Tree, how do you plead to the charge of murder? Guilty or not guilty?"

"Not guilty," Woolfolk repeated.

"Sit down," said Soward. "The defendants plead not guilty to the charge of murder."

One of the court watchers, with arm resting on the window sill, leaned out to the gathering of citizens in the yard below. Joe Woolfolk heard his hoarse whisper across the room. "They plead not guilty. The bastards."

Soward ignored the commentator and proceeded. "A jury now comes from the venire heretofore issued for fifty good and lawful men in this call. The defendants by their counsels' waiving as to service of the list of names on said venire, and as to time in service of copy of indictment, we are ready to call the jury. Let the record show that the following named twelve men were duly elected, tried, impaneled, and sworn to try truly the issue joined and true deliverance made according to the law and the evidence, to wit, T. W. Williams, S. Cooper, Peyton Lynn, Lucas P. Bunch, John Camron, William Hensley, Peter Hart, James Cooley, Everet Johnson, W. B. Verner, John H. Brown, and Daniel Brown. Call the jury," he said to the bailiff.

In a few minutes the jury men began to shuffle into the room. Like the chiefs, they came down the center aisle of the room and up to the front. Some nodded to friends and relatives among the sea of faces. They filed into the elevated jury box.

Most were washed and shaved for the occasion. As most of the other Texans, their eyes seemed tired and weary as they looked out on the audience. Each man was serious as befitted their positions. A few had buttoned the top button of their shirts for the formal occasion. The ranchers and farmers bore the telltale mark of white foreheads and sun-baked faces and throats. Their protective hats were filed away downstairs. There was not a good haircut in the bunch.

Woolfolk came to his feet. "Your Honor."

Soward glared. "Mister Woolfolk."

"May the defense question the jury?" asked the lawyer.

Soward mulled the question. "This *is* the jury, Mister Woolfolk. But you may satisfy yourself, if you can do it quickly."

Woolfolk walked around the table and to the front of the jury box. He placed his hands on the rail that divided them. "Mister Hart, my notes show that you presented an affidavit to General Sherman as part of a citizens' committee. Is that so?"

"Yes," the man said softly.

"Was that affidavit part of a petition you and others signed called 'Statement of Murders and Outrages Committed upon the Citizens of Jack County by Hostile Indians?' "

"Yes," answered Peter Hart.

"You, according to the petition, have lost a lot of livestock," continued Woolfolk. "What kind of stock?"

"Horses mostly," said Hart.

"Indians stole your horses?" pursued Woolfolk.

"Sure they did. I seen 'em myself up at Fort Sill, but the soldiers wouldn't get them back fer me. You know that, Joe."

Woolfolk looked down at the floor. "Yes, I know that, Pete," he said. "You reckon you could be objective in your judgment of these two Indians, sitting here?"

Hart glanced at the judge.

"Can you be fair in deciding this case?" asked Soward.

Hart considered the question. "I believe they done it, sir," he said. "But I'll hear Joe out."

"We accept the juror," said Woolfolk.

"Damn' right, you do," muttered the judge to himself.

Woolfolk moved down the rail until he stood before William Hensley. "How's your wife doing, Bill?"

"Fine when I saw her last." The man smiled.

"She tell you anything to do in town, Bill?" asked Woolfolk.

The man reached in his vest pocket. "She don't tell me any more," he spoke, holding a note. "She writes it down, and I give it to Missus Teezer." The people in the room chuckled. "Saves lots of fretting around when I get back home," he added apologetically.

"She write on her list to hang the murdering Indians that killed her brother and scalped him?" Joe drove the words into the rancher.

"Hell, no," said Hensley. "My wife would never write that."

"But your brother-in-law was killed and scalped by Indians?"

"He was," agreed Bill Hensley. "This here is kind of pissy questioning, Joe."

Laughter ran through the room as the self-appointed court commentator repeated the remark out the window to the audience below.

Woolfolk looked at Soward. "It's sometimes hard for a man to go against his wife, isn't it?" he stated rhetorically. "I mean, it's one thing between men and another where your wife is involved, when her baby brother is killed and scalped."

"Get on with your questions?" Soward said.

Joe Woolfolk walked casually down the front of the jury, looking at the floor. In front of Peyton Lynn he raised his eyes. "Mister Lynn, you live out toward Lost Valley?"

"Yes, I do," Lynn said.

"In the spring of Eighteen Fifty-Eight, April, as I remember, there was an Indian attack in that area. Was anyone related to you hurt or killed?"

"My sister, Mary, and her husband, Tom Mason, were killed," the rancher said.

"Who buried their bodies?" asked Woolfolk.

"A bunch of men, following the Indians, found them two days after the massacre. They left Old Man Gage and his son, Dan, and Arch Hall to do the burying. The bodies was in bad shape, I heard later, so they had to bury them and the Cambrens right where they laid. Couldn't get their bodies to a cemetery or anything. The main chase party came over to our place to see if we was killed, too. I believe you was with 'em," Peyton Lynn volunteered without any protest from Woolfolk.

"What became of the children?"

"Well," the rancher continued, "my pa brought my nephews and the Cambren children, Mary and Witt, over to our place the day after the killing when he found Mary and Tom. W. C. Kootch came with his father and took the Cambren kids to relatives in Tarrant County. They still live there, I believe."

"Where are your nephews?"

"They live with me and my family," answered Peyton Lynn.

"Does that make a hardship for you?"

"Well, ranching ain't an easy business, but the boys try to help me and my pa," observed Lynn.

"Not much water this year," agreed Joe Woolfolk. "Not much water and lots of Indians. Did you recently have to sell out your cattle?"

"I sold 'em rather than lose 'em," said the rancher.

"Have you been paid for your cows?" asked Woolfolk.

Peyton Lynn studied his leathery hands. "No. I reckon I ain't goin' to get paid. I sold 'em to a buyer on his word that he'd pay me when he sold 'em. I heard he sold 'em, but he never paid."

Woolfolk drew himself up. "So, Peyton Lynn, the Indians have not only killed your sister and her husband and left you with two small boys to raise, they have bankrupted you. I'm through with my *voy dire*, Judge Soward."

"Let's proceed with the opening statements, gentlemen," the judge ordered. "It's getting hot."

Chapter Twenty-Two

Lanham opened with a quick summary of what he intended to prove — that Satanta and Adoltay were cold-blooded killers who participated in the Warren wagon train massacre. The jury listened attentively. Woolfolk looked pessimistically at the young prosecutor. S. W. T. Lanham was a wonder child — less than twenty-five years old, he was already favorably placed for political advancement through his office. At sixteen he had been a sergeant in his company of the Third South Carolina. Barely twenty after the war, he had married and headed for Texas in 1866. He had taught school two years in east Texas and had read for the law at night. Moving farther West, he had taught and studied until he had been admitted to the bar in Weatherford in 1869 and had become district attorney for the Thirteenth Judicial District that fall. Thinking about the boy's past achievements and glowing future wearied Woolfolk.

Woolfolk allowed Ball to make their opening comments. Ball was brief and sat down. Woolfolk studied the two Indians, watching the scene before them. "We need Donat in here to tell the damn' Indians what's going on."

Ball nodded.

The defense turned its attention then to Lanham's first witness, Thomas Brazeal. Brazeal limped to the witness chair, elevated beside Judge Soward's high bench and facing the jury. He was duly sworn.

"Mister Brazeal," began Lanham, "I noticed you limped as you came to the stand. What is the nature of your injury?"

Brazeal moved uncomfortably in his chair. A private man,

177

he did not like his handicap called to the jury's attention. In fact, all the attention focused on him since the attack had made him want to travel on. The Army had said he could not, until after the trial. "It's my foot," he said. "Can't put much weight on her yet. Doctor Patzki says the bullet entered my left foot. Just got shot in the side of my foot fur as I know."

"When were you shot, Mister Brazeal?" asked Lanham.

Thomas Brazeal did not look up. "During the attack on the train."

"Please speak up, sir," admonished the judge.

Brazeal cleared his throat. "During the attack on the train."

"What train?" led the prosecutor.

"The Warren wagon train."

"Mister Brazeal, will you tell us about the attack?"

"Well, Henry Warren had a government contract to deliver corn to Fort Griffin. It was a long, three-day trip, so we spent a good part of the Sixteenth getting the wagons in shape. You know, greasin' the axles, takin' the rims off the wheels, gettin' the wheels shrunk at the smithy, resetting 'em. It's bad to break down out that away. We finally picked up the corn at the railhead in Weatherford, late on the Sixteenth of May, and started out at five the next morning."

"Please describe the wagon train," interrupted the lawyer.

"Well, there was ten wagons . . . three with six mules and seven with four. . . ." The witness hesitated.

"Please continue," said Lanham.

"Well, Nate Long was the wagon master. There was ten drivers, including me, and one night watchman. On the Seventeenth we made it to Fort Richardson and camped down by the creek. We started out again early on Thursday. We didn't water the mules, but waited till we got to the tank at Rock Creek Station. It was already hot. Off to the west the sky was black. We knew a good storm was coming. We didn't take long for noon when we stopped again later. Seemed like there weren't no air, like it had been sucked out of the sky by the storm to the west. We drove on around that cut through the timber to the north of Cox's Mountain. By then the storm was just ready to pop. Nate said for us to try to make it on to the head of Flint Creek and camp at Murphy's Station. It didn't look like we could make it on into Belknap 'fore the storm hit. So's we tied down our covers good and checked the harness again before we rolled out onto Salt Creek Prairie. We could see the lightning in the clouds and count the thunder sound to see how far off it were. It weren't far off.

"We was about two miles out onto the flat, when we seen there was Indians comin' out from behind that pile of sandstone rock. I guess I heard the bugle first, amongst the thunder, but I don't know exactly. Anyway, Nate started yellin' to circle 'em. And I peeled off to do it, trying to figure room so that all the wagons could turn in with the mules in the center, once we got circled. I was thinkin' about that . . . goin' fast enough to close and slow enough not to turn over. My hands and them mules' mouths was plumb raw. Sometimes I glanced at the Injuns . . . looked like they were closin' mighty fast, almost on us."

Lanham interrupted his witness. "How many Indians, Mister Brazeal?"

"I swear it looked like there was a hundred and fifty. Lots of 'em, movin' like screamin' demons all around us. As I come around, closin' in on the last wagon, I seen the lead mule go down. An Injun, wearing a cougar-skin quiver with the head still on, hit that mule right behind his shoulder, just like they shoot buffalo with an arrow. It drove clean through the mule, and he went down. Well, that circle weren't goin' to close then. I tried to dodge around and catch up to the next wagon in front of that one, but the mules was crazy with the lightning and the wind and the yellin' of the men and the Injuns. I was fightin' 'em hard, and" — he lowered his head — "I couldn't do it. I seen Mullins squirt out of the last wagon as it flipped over and start running. The Injun who killed the mule rode down on him. I thought sure he was a dead man, but that Injun just bent over and tapped him with his bow as Mullins raised his gun. But the next one got him. An arrow in the chest. About that time, Nate Long was firing with a Henry and holding onto the frame beside me. He shouted . . . 'God A'mighty' . . . and fell off. He was dead, I reckon, 'fore he hit the ground. The wagons was a mess, turned this way and that, the teams tangled up in their harness. Four or five teams had mules down. The men were trying to get their guns and take some kind of cover. Some of 'em started throwing out grain sacks, trying to make a barricade they could get behind. Injuns was thick as fleas, everywhere. We was firing back, but we couldn't get no shots, because, as they circled us, they'd drop in behind their horses' necks and fire at us. It was sure enough the wheel of death I'd heard about, spinning around and around us a little closer at every pass. I seen Jim Elliott rise up, trying to pull an arrow out of his chest. He got hit square in the head with a bullet. He's dead, I thought. There weren't no way to defend that mess. Injuns was behind us, among us, outside us, everywhere. Pull back, I thought. Run for the timber. Maybe the damn' Injuns will let us be and get to lootin' the mules and wagons.

"So I started yellin' to the men, gatherin' them. 'We got to get out of here,' I shouted. 'We got to get to the timber. The Injuns want the wagons.' Well, pretty soon I gathered up the men that was alive . . . Dick Motor, Hobbs Carey, Charlie Brady, R. A. Day, Baxter, and Williams. 'Where's Sam Elliott?' I says. 'Gone,' says somebody. 'Over yonder by his brother.' I could see Jim sprawled over a pile of corn sacks, but I never seen Sam. I swear to God I did not know Sam Elliott was alive, or I'd never have left him. A man cannot leave a man alone for the Injuns. I couldn't do that. It sickens me to think I left him." Brazeal fell silent a moment. He looked up toward the courtroom. "I didn't know he was alive. I just looked and didn't see him. Someone says he was dead. 'Let's go then,' I says, and we started backin' out of there. We'd run a ways, and then show our guns and fire at the Injuns. It's funny what you can hear," he said softly. "There was some women somewhere, way over on the rocks, making that funny high-pitched sound, encouraging the fighters. Man, that sound'll make the hair on your neck stand up. *Women . . .* imagine that. The braves was taunting us, calling us cowards, I guess, 'cause we ran, mad 'cause we were shootin' back at 'em. I got hit and some of the other fellas did, too. As we ran, Baxter and later Williams fell behind and got cut off and killed. We seen 'em scalped. Once we were in the woods, the Injuns knew it would be a lot of trouble to get us out. They ain't fools. And they figured they were losin' out at the train, so they turned back and left us. That night I come on into the fort for help. And you know the rest of it."

Absolute silence had filled the courtroom as Brazeal, the wounded survivor, recounted the story of the attack. Now the audience sat stunned in its aftermath. Lanham allowed the words to sink deeply into the men and women around him. They had come to hear this with their own ears — Brazeal's words from his own mouth. Lanham hadn't deprived them.

"Thank you, Mister Brazeal," the district attorney said quietly. "Your Honor, the prosecution would like to introduce some items of evidence at this time." He walked toward the bench with a covered box.

Aw, hell, said Woolfolk to himself. *He's going to bring out the arrows.* Woolfolk rose and followed Lanham forward.

"The state offers the following items . . . five Kiowa arrows taken from the scene of the massacre and the bodies of the victims, marked state's exhibit one . . . a bugle taken by the Army from Satanta on his capture, state's exhibit two . . . and a cougar-skin quiver with the head still on it, arrows, and a bow taken by the Army from Big Tree at his arrest, state's exhibit three."

"Mark the exhibits," Soward said.

Woolfolk looked at the items. The broken, blood-soaked arrows removed from the victims' bodies were sure to cause an uproar. The bugle he could deal with later. The quiver . . . ?

Lanham grasped the bugle ornamented with a blond scalp. He moved quickly and set it in front of the witness. "This bugle was taken from the defendant, Satanta, when he was captured at Fort Sill."

"Objection," said Woolfolk. "The state is testifying in their own case."

"Overruled."

"Did you hear a bugle before the Indian attack?" pursued Lanham.

"I heard a bugle."

"Thank you, Mister Brazeal," said Lanham. He returned the bugle to the evidence table. Woolfolk returned to his seat.

Lanham lifted dramatically from the table the cougar-skin quiver and held it with both hands over his head, letting everyone in the courtroom have a good look.

"Looks like a bloody sacrificial offering," Joe Woolfolk whispered to Tom Ball.

Lanham placed the skin in front of Thomas Brazeal. "Tom, is this the cougar-skin quiver you saw?"

Brazeal considered it. "Looks like it. Has the head and all. I remember the head was on it."

"Thank you, Tom. I'm finished with the witness, Your Honor," Lanham said as he carefully carried the skin quiver to the evidence table.

"Mister Woolfolk, do you have questions for this witness?" asked Soward.

Joe Woolfolk stood, hitched his trousers, and walked around the table toward the witness.

"Mister Brazeal, you have told us in vivid detail about the attack on the Warren wagon train. You have said that there was a lot of confusion around you. Mules and men screaming. A thunderstorm thundering. You yourself were fighting the mules, trying to form a circle, rubbing your hands and their mouths raw in the struggle. With all that to think about could you really hear a distant bugle?"

"I believe I heard a bugle. It was faint, but I believe I heard it."

"Did you hear a bugle or not?" asked Woolfolk sharply.

Brazeal looked into the lawyer's face. "I believe I heard a bugle."

"There was noise all around you. Thunder. Screaming. How could you hear a bugle?"

"I don't know how I could, any more than I know how I heard those women's voices, but I believe I heard a bugle," Brazeal said again. "Way off, like the women's voices."

"The witness has answered Mister Woolfolk three times, Your Honor," protested Lanham.

"Move on, Mister Woolfolk," Soward instructed.

Woolfolk shook his head. "Mister Brazeal, the counsel for the state has shown you a panther skin to identify. You testified it looks like the one you saw, having its head and all. Are you certain that this was the exact quiver you saw?"

"I said it looked like it was."

"No, Mister Brazeal, was it *this* skin?" pushed Woolfolk.

"Well, I can't say that it is the exact skin." The witness sounded flustered.

"Thank you, Mister Brazeal." Woolfolk turned away from

the witness and caught Lanham's eyes. "You are an honest man. I can see that. Now, can you honestly identify any of the Indians you saw during the attack . . . even the ones who chased you and the other survivors across the prairie?"

Brazeal looked closely at the defendants. His voice was quiet and steady as he answered, "No, sir, I could not."

"Thank you, Mister Brazeal."

Woolfolk returned to the table and sat down.

Lanham rose. "Tom, you said in your direct testimony that the Indian who killed the lead mule on the closing wagon wore a cougar-skin quiver. I showed you a skin taken from Big Tree. Is it like the one you saw?"

"Yes."

"The man wearing a skin quiver opened the wagon train up for the others, did he not?" asked Lanham.

"Yes."

Lanham sat down.

Woolfolk stood. "Mister Brazeal, earlier you said that that Indian who killed the lead mule on the last wagon did not kill Mullins as he ran from the wagon, but merely touched him with his bow tip. How did he do that?"

"Well, he was riding down Mullins, I thought, and Mullins swung up his gun at him. The Injun just rode right past the gun and tapped Mullins" — he gestured — "like that on the head."

"Just tapped him when he could have killed him or been killed himself?" Woolfolk repeated the gesture made by the teamster. "Just tapped him? Didn't try to kill him? Just tapped him?" Woolfolk sat down meditatively and rested his hands on the arms of his chair.

"Are you gentlemen through with the witness?" asked Soward.

The counsels nodded.

"You're excused, Mister Brazeal. Call your next witness, Mister Lanham."

In quick succession Lanham called two other survivors of the wagon train attack. Like Brazeal, they conveyed the feeling of confusion and utter hopelessness against the large number of Indians and their own inability to form a protective corral. Like Brazeal, they, too, believed that Sam Elliott was dead when they made their desperate run for the sheltering timber of Cox's Mountain. Neither recalled hearing the bugle distinctly, but Hobbs Cary, like Brazeal, believed that he might have heard it. Neither saw the young Indian with the cougar-skin quiver take down the lead mule or strike coup on Michael Mullins. The defense was not defeated yet.

"The state calls Sergeant Miles Varily," Lanham said.

The old Indian fighter passed through the gate separating the mere spectators from the trial participants. His blue uniform was immaculate, tight over his flat belly. He carried himself like the top sergeant he was. Varily observed the courtroom and the soldiers around the wall with a critical eye, a quick private inspection of his troops and their effect on the proceedings. He was hardly sworn before Lanham brought forth the fistful of arrows and thrust them at him.

"Sergeant, Colonel Mackenzie recommended you to the state as an expert on Indian matters. Can you identify any of the arrows you see here?"

"They are Kiowa arrows," the sergeant said, after looking at the arrows carefully.

"How do you know that?" Lanham asked.

The sergeant took one of the arrows and held it up. "See here, how the feathers is set? That's Kiowa. It's fletched with owl feathers . . . blood doesn't ruin owl feathers. Then, there's these lines cut down the shaft, away from the point. That's Kiowa by design and color."

"You mean every tribe has its own kind of markings? Kind of a flag?" asked Lanham.

The sergeant nodded. "That's right, sir. These lines, running away from the point, would be curved if it was a Comanche arrow."

"Obviously, there is a great deal written on an arrow if a man knows how to read it," encouraged Lanham. "Is there anything else there, Sergeant?"

The sergeant sorted through the five arrows. "Well, they are man-killing arrows. You see the way the point is set sideways across the notch, so to speak? That's because men's ribs are set sideways. That way, if the arrow hits a man, it will go in between the ribs. If it was a buffalo arrow, the point would be turned up and down, at an angle to the notch and parallel to the string, because buffalo ribs is up and down to a man on horseback." The sergeant studied the arrow, then touched one of the corners of the head near the shaft. "The way the one point here is broken off? That's a killer. When that arrow goes in, it will sink and twist." The sergeant demonstrated the sinking and twisting of the arrow. "It would have to be cut out. Probably the man who took it would die of that, if not the arrow itself."

Lanham grimaced. "What did you say the lines running away from the point were for?"

"I didn't say, sir. But they are to let the blood run out so the victim will bleed, maybe bleed to death." Sergeant Varily laid the arrow down in front of him. "Then, of course, they probably weaken the shaft some, and it might break off easier in the victim and be harder to remove.

"Savage!" said Lanham.

"Objection!" shouted Woolfolk. "There's not a man here who's fought Indians who hasn't cut his lead so it would spread. Is that less savage?"

"Mister Woolfolk, you are overruled and out of order. Sit down now!" hammered Soward.

Lanham innocently pointed to the broken arrow in front of the witness. "Do you recognize that bloody, broken arrow, Sergeant?"

"Objection?"

"Overruled."

The continuing battle of objections and overrulings of Woolfolk by Soward little interested Lanham as he pursued his case. He was sure that there would be few or no sustainings. "Sergeant?"

"Yes, sir. I retrieved that arrow myself from one of the victims of the raid. Well, I picked up the part with the feathers from the ground, where he'd broken it off. Doctor Patzki took the tip out of the dead man's chest. It had penetrated his heart. You can see the two halves match." He held it up for the jury and courtroom to see.

"Good," muttered Woolfolk.

"Why did Doctor Patzki remove the tip from the dead man?" asked Lanham, pacing away from the witness.

"He was making a report for Colonel Mackenzie. Doctor Patzki is a curious fellow. He likes to see what's behind things. The victim had a head wound, and he'd been scalped, but the surgeon wanted to know what killed him . . . the arrow or the head wound? Some of the dead just seemed to have arrows stuck in them by hand, not shot from a bow." Sergeant Varily was speaking without emotion. After years in the bloody battles of the military, he was not squeamish. He was a professional.

"How could you tell that?" asked Lanham.

"Well, they were not deep set. They were fairly loose. The citizens had all been stripped naked, and the rain had washed away all the blood." A murmur spread through the room at this ghoulish information. The sergeant hesitated, but continued at Lanham's nod. "Well, it was very easy to see the wounds. Around those particular arrows there were many other wounds, like someone kneeled there and jammed the arrow in several times. . . ." The sergeant grasped one of the exhibit arrows and stabbed it into the rail a few times, then jabbed it deep and left it standing. "Like that."

Woolfolk closed his eyes and rested them on the butt of his palms as he leaned on the table. Tom Ball sat stoically.

"Donat, explain what he is saying to the Indians," the chief counsel for the defense instructed. Satanta and Adoltay listened to Donat intently.

"Did Doctor Patzki examine all the dead men?" Lanham was asking.

"No, sir. It was raining very hard. The bodies had been there for some time. We needed to bury them and get our report to Colonel Mackenzie and General Sherman."

"Your Honor," Lanham said from his table, "I would like to introduce another piece of evidence . . . a report made by Doctor Patzki to Colonel Mackenzie on May Nineteenth, Eighteen Seventy-One. We will mark this state's exhibit number four. Mister Woolfolk and Mister Ball have seen the document and have a copy of it."

Woolfolk nodded.

"Sergeant Varily, will you read for the court the report made by Doctor Patzki?"

The sergeant stretched out his arms to read the dated message of the surgeon to his commanding officer. " 'Colonel R. S. Mackenzie, Fourth Cavalry. Sir, I have the honor to report that in compliance with your instructions I examined on May Nineteenth, Eighteen Seventy-One, the bodies of five citizens killed near Salt Creek by Indians on the previous day. All the bodies were riddled with bullets, covered with gashes, and the skulls crushed, evidently with an axe found bloody on the place; some of the bodies exhibited also signs of having been stabbed with arrows. One of the bodies was even more mutilated than the others, it having been found fastened with a chain to the pole of a wagon lying over a fire with the face to the ground, the tongue being cut out. Owing to the charred condition of the soft parts it was impossible to determine whether the man was burned before or after his death. The scalps of all but one were taken. I have the honor to be, Colonel, your obedient servant, J. H. Patzki, Assistant Surgeon, U. S. A.' "

The spectators had become more and more agitated during the sergeant's reading. Now their words were clearly audible to the lawyers and the defendants. Some of the men near the back were on their feet. "Filthy savages! Burned Sam Elliott alive! Sonsabitches! Let's try 'em outside! Better'n the bastards deserve!"

Soward pounded his desk with the gavel. "Get quiet. I will not tolerate any outbursts. Bryant and the rest of you back there, sit down. Soldier, see that man sits down."

Black soldiers at the rear of the room moved quickly toward the vocal men, but the men had returned to their seats before the soldiers reached them.

"Now," said Judge Soward, "this is a court of law, *of law*." He was indignant. He rose and struck the bench in front of him with his outstretched hand, emphasizing his words. "In this place, we hear things through whether we want to or not. You will not hear things that are easy to hear in this court today. But you will hear them with the respect due in this setting and due the laws of this country. If you are unable to accept that, leave now." He paused. No one moved in the silent room. "If there is another outburst of any kind, it is fully within my power and my will to remove you from this room. Bear in mind, all of you, ladies *and gentlemen,* that this is *my* court, and that I may, at any time I deem it appropriate, clear this entire room." The judge's face had become red with anger during his outburst. He sat back down with a flourish. "Continue your questions, counselor."

"I have another piece of evidence, Your Honor," said Lanham.

"Objection," said Woolfolk. "May we approach the bench, Your Honor?"

The lawyers quickly huddled around the judge.

"Are you going to present the axe found at the scene in evidence, Lanham?" asked Woolfolk, glancing at Lanham to confirm his suspicion. "If you are, I strenuously object. You are inflaming this courtroom and prejudicing any chance of a fair trial."

"The axe is evidence, Your Honor," Lanham said quietly.

"Damn it to hell, Lanham, you don't have to use it. You're not in any great risk of losing this trial. The jury is yours, and they heard just now how their neighbors feel. What you are going to do is get these men hung here and now. I move for a mistrial, Your Honor."

"Be quiet, Woolfolk," said Soward. "He's right, Lanham. You bring in that blood- and hair-covered axe, and the trial is over. Do the best with what you already have."

"Thank you, Judge," Woolfolk said gratefully and returned to his seat. Before he sat down, he looked into Adoltay's eyes. The boy appeared strange. Woolfolk searched Satanta for a similar expression. He found none. Leaning over to Donat, Woolfolk whispered harshly, "What did you tell them? That we are going to take them out and hang them, turn them over to that pack of mongrels?"

"No, chief," the 'breed answered, "I just said the white folks was mad as hell about the way they tore up the freighters, like the Kiowas feel about the Tonks eating their people."

"Geezus," spluttered Woolfolk.

"Take it easy, Joe." Ball rested a hand on Woolfolk's arm. "The vein in the side of your head is standing out."

"What's wrong with the boy? Is he sick?" Woolfolk persisted at Donat.

"I don't know, chief," Donat admitted. He spoke to the boy. Woolfolk thought the language was Comanche, not Kiowa.

"*Ge,*" said the young Indian.

"No," translated Donat. "He ain't sick."

Lanham was again in front of the sergeant when Woolfolk looked up. "Doctor Patzki's report says all the men were scalped, but one. Why was that man not scalped?"

"He was bald, sir," answered the sergeant flatly.

"Can you tell us why Indians take scalps, Sergeant?" asked Lanham. "Is it a further act of humiliation?"

"Objection!"

"Overruled. Proceed, Sergeant."

"They take the scalp to keep the departed from going to the spirit land. It's kind of the ultimate insult, sir. Most Kiowas and Comanches as well as others braid a scalp lock into their hair. Some says it's to show contempt for death, to defy their enemies. Some says it's so the Great Spirit can snatch them up to their heaven by it. If you ain't got hair, He can't get hold of you. Either way, to take hair keeps the victim from a pleasing eternal life. Without it, he must wander forever between the winds."

"Counselors," the judge interrupted, "it's running up on eleven forty-five. Do you plan to conclude with this witness before noon, Mister Lanham?"

The prosecutor shook his head.

"Well, then, we are going to break now for lunch. Jury, don't discuss this case among yourselves or with anyone else.

191

The rest of you, cool off or don't come back. We'll reconvene at one o'clock." The judge rapped his gavel and left.

"You hungry, Joe?" asked Wooten, leaning over the rail.

"Oh, hell," said the lawyer. Suddenly he remembered he wanted Wooten. "Sit down, John. I want to talk to you."

Chapter Twenty-Three

After the jury exited, the courtroom slowly emptied. The black soldiers kept to the perimeter of the room, but again formed a protective barrier between the citizens and the accused. Many citizens strained to catch a quick glimpse of the Kiowa chiefs and their counsel and the two other frontiersmen, Wooten and Lynn, before they went downstairs and out into the open air and their lunches.

Woolfolk waited until the room was empty, then he turned to the young Kiowa. "You called out Wooten's name when you came in. Do you know him?"

Donat quickly asked the question.

"Yes," said Adoltay softly in English. "I know Wooten. Wooten save me. I save Wooten."

Woolfolk slumped back in his chair. "Well, damn. Why didn't you say you knew the boy, John?"

"Because I didn't know I knew the boy," was the cowboy's answer.

"How'd you save him?"

Wooten shook his head. "I don't remember."

"How'd he save you, John?" asked Woolfolk.

The cowboy had been studying the young man intently. "It was Elm Creek, the Elm Creek raid," he said thoughtfully, remembering. "He saved my life, sure enough. My horse went down in the open. My gun was full of mud. He and another boy had chased me long enough for their friends to leave me to 'em."

"Do I have to get a writ, or will you tell that to the jury?"

"Well, of course, I'll tell it," said John Wooten. "You're beginning to get on everybody's nerves, Joe, including mine."

"Good," barked the lawyer.

First Lieutenant Carter snapped to attention above the small group. Woolfolk looked up. "Sir, I have the responsibility for these men's food and exercise. Is it convenient, sir?"

Woolfolk gestured absently. "Take them wherever."

"Thank you, sir," said the lieutenant smartly. Donat spoke with the Indians. They rose and followed the young officer between two rows of black guards.

"Let's get something to eat, Joe," said Wooten. "Isaac and I worked up a lot of hunger, listening to you and Lanham. How about it, Tom?"

"Go on without me," Woolfolk dismissed them, sprawling over his chair. "I need to think." The three men started away. "Hey, John," called Woolfolk. "Thanks for the offer."

A smile touched the corner of the tall cowboy's mouth. "Sure," he said.

Satanta and Adoltay walked slowly down the stairs and out the back entrance of the courthouse. A narrow stockade ran out to a privy built for the trial. Water and sandwiches waited on a bench for the Indians. The shade of the building partially blocked the noon sun. Satanta quickly picked up his sandwich and began to eat. Adoltay sat beside him. He unwrapped the sandwich, but did not lift it to his mouth.

"You must eat," said the older man.

"Yes," agreed Adoltay, but he did not eat. "What do you think these white men are doing?"

"They are telling about our raid." Satanta spoke with his mouth full.

"Yes, but they are very angry."

"That is natural," said Satanta. "We beat them."

"No," said the boy. "It is more than that. We have done something more."

"We beat them. I showed Kicking Bird and the others that I could beat white men, too. That is all. It was a fight. We beat them."

"It is *more*," Adoltay repeated.

"They want to hang us because we beat them. Woosinton will not allow them to hang us. Do not be afraid. I will remind them of that when I talk . . . they can do nothing to us without Woosinton's approval."

"I will ask Donat to tell me more closely what they say," Adoltay murmured softly to himself.

"Such matters are between the Kiowas and Woosinton, not with the *Tejanos*. You will see. Woosinton will give us presents, and we will agree not to raid for a while. That is the way it has always been."

The young Kiowa considered his sandwich. He stuck one corner in his mouth and chewed slowly.

Wooten, Ball, and old Isaac Lynn strolled over to the Wichita Hotel where lunch had been laid out for the crowd — one price, one meal for everybody. They paid their money and took a plate of food and a piece of pie from the checked tablecloth near the door. Fritz brought them coffee at the table.

"You know Woolfolk better than I do," said Tom Ball. "Is he always like this?"

"He is," the cowboy stated.

Isaac Lynn smiled.

"He worries me," Ball said.

"He worries everybody," agreed the cowboy. "Some do things one way . . . some do them another. Joe is just doin' things the way he sees 'em. Mostly he gripes and scares hell out of you, but he comes through."

"He is not going to come through this, and he's making enemies," observed Ball.

"Does that worry you, counselor, makin' enemies?" queried the cowboy gently.

"Sure." Ball nodded. "I haven't been here that long. I've got to live here."

"Well," said John Wooten, "there are folks here who will never forgive Joe, that's for sure. But there ain't many people can hate forever, and, in time, some of them will come to think he's done right. The way I see it, you keep livin' and tryin', and things come around in the end, or it don't matter by then. Ain't that so, Isaac?"

Isaac Lynn chewed his food steadily. "Human beings can't kill each other out of existence. It ain't in our self-interest. Cultivated hate takes too much tendin' for most folks, anyway. They got to get on with things."

"You're saying that all this anger we saw today will pass?" queried Ball. "I don't think so."

"Nobody spit on you, did they?" asked Wooten. "I mean, you just walked in here, paid your money, and got your dinner same as any other day. That's Texas. That's America."

"You sick sonsabitch," the words addressed to Tom Ball came from behind Wooten. "You Injun-lovin' sonsabitch. I want to puke up my dinner, just lookin' at you."

"Ah, the sweet voice of Lucius Bryant," observed Wooten.

"Shut up, Wooten. What in the hell are you doin', havin' dinner with this Injun-lovin' sonsabitch?" Bryant answered his own question. "Hell, if you can stomach Joe Woolfolk, this one ain't nothing, I guess." He snorted.

The cowboy looked at the table, his plate, his coffee cup between his outstretched hands, and sighed. "Well, Bryant, I was just tryin' to digest my food here with a little peace and tranquillity with the Injun-lovin' son-of-a-bitch. But you've ruined that."

"Ain't that big Injun the one who raped your boss and passed her over the prairie?" shot back the other man. "Don't you know he had a good time with that white woman? Hell, who wouldn't? I'd have took all I could get 'fore *he* had her. You gettin' any, Wooten? Hell, you're even behind that nigger, Britt Johnson. What's it like, sharin' an Injun's leavin's? What's it like kissin' that scar, knowing what else he done to her?"

Wooten's outstretched hands closed slowly. "You stink, Bryant. Your whole crowd stinks. Everything you touch stinks. Every thought you think stinks, because it comes out of that cesspool you call a brain."

"I don't have to take that from you," blustered Lucius Bryant.

Wooten rose and stood, looking at the belligerent boaster. He removed the napkin from his shirt and stepped up to the other man's face. "Yes, you do," he said evenly. "You see, you're a coward, Bryant. You've called me, and now you must face me down or crawl out of here on your belly. I know you won't face me. So. . . ." The cowboy dropped his napkin onto the table.

"Stop this," came Adrianne Chastain's voice.

"The squaw saved her little toady," said Bryant, backing away from John Wooten. "You call me a coward, but what's a man called who hides behind her Injun-dirty skirts?"

Wooten's jaw set hard. "Push this, Bryant, and they'll carry you out of here in spite of the lady."

Bryant consistently moved away from the big cowboy, putting tables and diners between them. At the door he pushed roughly past Mrs. Chastain. He touched his hat. "Pardon me, *squaaaaw*."

Adrianne Chastain never acknowledged the coarse man or his words. Her eyes held John Wooten's, half a room away.

Chapter Twenty-Four

The afternoon session resumed with the usual formalities. Sergeant Miles Varily returned to the stand. Lanham strolled contentedly up to the witness, hands on his hips, pushing his coat back away from his vest. *Somehow,* Joe Woolfolk thought, *he doesn't look hot, but fresh and perky as in the morning.* "Shoot!" he muttered aloud.

"What is it, Joe?" asked Ball.

"That's why Jinny put in that other shirt. She meant for me to change at noon like Lanham."

Ball's eyebrows drew together in a frown. He shook his head.

"Sergeant," Lanham was saying, "you gave us some interesting testimony this morning about the arrows. You read us Doctor Patzki's report. Now, I'd like your own testimony concerning what you saw, what had taken place on Salt Creek Prairie, and what you did. Tell us why you went to the scene? What was your purpose?"

"A civilian, Thomas Brazeal, had come into the fort after midnight on the Nineteenth. He reported a large number of Indians had attacked the Warren train. We left Fort Richardson shortly after noon with Companies A, B, E, and F of the Fourth, about one hundred and fifty men, with Colonel Mackenzie himself in command. We had supplies enough to stay in the field for a month. The orders were to ascertain that the attack had taken place and pursue the hostiles, even into the reservation at Fort Sill, if necessary. I led an advance party. We reached Salt Creek Prairie late in the afternoon. It was raining. It had been raining all day, since the afternoon before."

"If you will, describe the scene as you found it May Nineteenth." Lanham was continuing his stroll.

"Well, sir, I fought in the War Between The States, and I have seen some hard and bloody action, but I never saw anything like that. The wagons were broken up and set on fire. Some had burned and were smoldering in the rain. The wheels on most had been taken off and rolled out on the prairie. Out of the ten wagons, a man might have made one or two from what was left. I counted five mules down. They were swollen, and the birds and coyotes had torn open their bellies. Most of the harness was missing." Sergeant Varily paused and looked at his hands.

"Go on please," said Lanham.

"There were five citizens in the immediate area of the wagons. They had been stripped, scalped, and mutilated."

"How exactly were they mutilated?" pushed Lanham.

"Objection," said Woolfolk.

Soward looked at Lanham closely. "Approach the bench, counselors."

"Goes to the point of prejudice and incitement made earlier at the bench, Your Honor," Woolfolk contended.

"It is important to establish the nature of this attack. It was more than a mere robbery. It was particularly vicious. I think that must be established," argued Lanham.

"Watch your step on this, Lanham," cautioned the judge quietly. "We do not want a riot or a lynching." For the court, he said: "Objection overruled. Proceed with your witness. I warn this court again that outbursts will not be tolerated. Do you hear me, Lucius Bryant?"

Lanham returned to Sergeant Varily on the witness stand as Woolfolk ambled back to his seat. "By God, Lanham, you may have made a mistake," Woolfolk muttered to himself.

"Sergeant Varily, please continue describing the scene your

party encountered on May Nineteenth. Exactly how were the men mutilated?"

The sergeant straightened in his chair. He fixed his eyes and spoke directly to a spot in the back of the room. "Sir, three of them had been beheaded and their skulls split open. Their brains had been scooped out. All the men's skulls were smashed. Some of the men had been stabbed, as I said earlier, with arrows. A couple of them looked like porcupines, there were so many arrows in them. All the men's toes, fingers, and private parts had been cut off and stuffed into their mouths. Their bowels had been gashed with knives. Masses of burning coals had been carefully heaped inside their exposed abdomens. The rain had, of course, extinguished the fires. In general, their bodies had bloated from lying in the rain, what with several inches of rain since the day before. The mutilations and bloating made all chance of recognition impossible."

The courtroom sat in stunned silence.

"One man, I believe, was identified," Lanham almost whispered. "Tell us about Samuel Elliott."

The sergeant took a deep breath. "Mister Elliott's body was found, chained face down, between the front wagon wheels. A fire had been made from the wagon pole under his head. He was burnt to a crisp."

"Doctor Patzki said in his report that he could not tell whether Elliott was burned alive. At the time that report was written, you had not even found one of the men's bodies. That report was written shortly after you arrived, after the briefest of perfunctory examinations, was it not, Sergeant?"

"Yes, sir."

"Do you agree with that report today, Sergeant?"

"It is not for me to say, sir. I'm a common soldier, not a surgeon."

"Were Elliott's limbs drawn up and contracted?"

"Yes."

"Would a dead man do that?"

"No."

"Had Elliott's teeth been broken and his tongue cut out?"

"Yes, sir," the sergeant answered hoarsely.

"Why?"

"Well, maybe he was screaming so loud they couldn't stand it." The sergeant's voice was barely audible.

Lanham pivoted sharply. "Your witness, Mister Woolfolk."

Joe Woolfolk rose and walked toward the witness. The sounds of his steps echoed in the still silent room. He observed the white faces of the men in the jury box. Their anger and outrage had been driven deep by the ordered silence.

"Sergeant Varily, you have described a truly horrible scene. Was it, do you think, a scene of a simple robbery?"

"The mules were gone and harness and other things," said Varily.

"Yes, that's so, but would the attackers have done so much destruction just for a few mules with a thunderstorm crashing around them?"

"Probably not, sir," Varily answered, looking into Woolfolk's eyes.

"Probably not." Woolfolk paced toward the jury, observing their faces. "I agree, probably not. Could something else have caused such acts?"

"I don't know, sir."

"Come now, Sergeant, you were willing to speculate that Elliott's teeth were knocked out and his tongue was cut out because of his screaming. What could provoke such viciousness?"

"Anger, I guess," said Varily.

"Anger. That's possible, Sergeant. Please continue," said

Woolfolk, looking at the jury.

"I can't think of anything else, sir."

"Revenge?" asked Woolfolk. "Hatred?"

"Yes," answered the soldier.

"What kind of men do we hate, Sergeant Varily?"

"Sometimes we hate our enemies, sir, if we think they are out to destroy us and what we believe in."

"Has it been your experience as a soldier that armies sometimes hate each other?"

"Not in the War Between The States, sir," the sergeant replied. "In that war we had too much in common, I think. But in Europe, when Napoleon's troops went into Spain, there were incidents like that on Salt Creek Prairie . . . men beheaded, disemboweled, even impaled on trees, widespread rape, robbery, and massacre of citizens."

"Was that war or robbery, Sergeant Varily?" asked Woolfolk, turning to the witness.

"That was the worst of war, sir."

"When atrocities occur in war," pursued Woolfolk, "does every man participate equally or are some not involved?"

"I guess, knowing men, that some men don't participate. I think it would make some men sick."

"Do you think those men could stop such an action by their fellows?"

"I doubt it, sir, not without getting killed or killing their own men." Sergeant Varily's voice had become more hoarse.

"Would you say that the leaders had no control? Had lost control? They could only get it back by killing their own men?"

"That's possible, sir."

"Sergeant Varily, you've had great experience with the American Indians. The prosecution has presented you as an expert on their weapons. You can tell one tribe from another

202

by looking at their arrows?"

"Yes."

"Do Indians ever trade between tribes . . . arrows, horses, things like that?"

"Sure they do."

"It is possible, then, for a Kiowa to use Comanche arrows, or a Comanche to use Kiowa arrows."

Varily nodded.

"I didn't hear you," Woolfolk stated.

"Yes, sir."

"Is it possible from what you know of Indian warfare for a chief or a warrior to kill another Indian because he thought he was out of control?" pressed Woolfolk.

"No, sir," Varily admitted. "They don't fight as a unit. Each man does as he sees fit. Each man fights for his own prestige and honor. Some of the men may be able to direct things like the time and place of attack, maybe even the strategy, but not the individual soldiers. In their system, one man does not interfere with another. It's their way. I don't think they would even think of it."

"What would those . . . that, say, had shown their courage and wanted no more of the action . . . do?" asked Woolfolk out of his own curiosity.

"Most likely they would leave," speculated Varily.

"They wouldn't participate, and they wouldn't try to stop the others?"

"No," the sergeant said flatly.

"Thank you, Sergeant. You have informed us well on the ways of war."

Woolfolk started toward his table as Lanham rose for his redirect of the witness. Woolfolk paused and turned back to Varily. "Sergeant, the state has presented in evidence a bugle. Have you ever known Indians to use a bugle?"

"Satanta carries a bugle," said Varily.

"Is he the only Indian in all the world that has a bugle?" persisted Woolfolk.

"Probably not, sir . . . ," stated Varily, and stopped.

"I'm waiting to hear more, Sergeant," shot Woolfolk. "Is it not a feat common among the Kiowas to capture buglers and have them blow charges and recalls to confuse troopers? Is it not a fact that the Kiowas often use bugles in their war dances?"

"I've heard that, sir."

"Is it true, Sergeant?"

"I know that they do use bugles in their dances."

"Commonly?"

"Commonly."

"Then it is likely that Satanta is not the only Kiowa Indian who owns and toots a bugle, is he?"

"No, sir."

Woolfolk sat down.

Lanham walked to the witness. "Sergeant, did Satanta have a bugle in his possession when he was arrested and taken prisoner at Fort Sill?"

"Yes, sir."

"Were mules stolen from the Warren wagon train?"

"Yes, sir, forty-one head."

"When anything is taken which does not belong to the taker, what is it? War or robbery?"

"Robbery, sir."

"That will be all, Sergeant."

The courtroom remained silent as Sergeant Varily made his way down the center aisle and out the back. A few men, including Lucius Bryant, shook his hand quickly and offered to buy him a drink later. The sergeant thought about that drink as he left the courthouse. He walked steadily toward Mollie's place. He didn't want to drink with anyone. He wanted to go upstairs with a bottle and one of the girls and forget about the crushed skulls and severed heads and body parts. He didn't want to have enough sense left to see the carnage on the back of his closed eyelids, as he had every night since he and the other troopers of the Fourth dug a seeping, water-filling grave on Salt Creek Prairie and lowered the collected remains of the seven dead teamsters in a casket made from a wagon box into the soggy pit. He really didn't care if the Army busted him to private.

After Varily, the prosecution called Matthew Leeper, interpreter for the Kiowa-Comanche Agency run by Lawrie Tatum. Leeper was young, conscientious, a wiry man without much physical substance. He sat quietly on the witness stand, waiting for Lanham's questions.

"Mister Leeper, were you in the office of Agent Lawrie Tatum when Satanta and Adoltay and the other chiefs came for rations?"

"Yes."

"Is it customary for the agent to summon the chiefs to his office before he issues their rations?"

"No."

"It was unusual, then?" pursued the prosecutor. "You would remember it well, because it was unusual?"

"Yes."

"Do you know why the agent called the chiefs into his office?"

"General Sherman had visited with him the day before and told him about the wagon train attack. Agent Tatum had agreed to ask the Indians about the raid. That's why he asked them to his office."

"Had all the chiefs been at the agency during the previous month?" Lanham strolled casually.

"Satanta, Big Bow, Satank, Adoltay . . . or Big Tree, Eagle

Heart, and Fast Bear had been away for about a month."

"What happened when Agent Tatum asked the Indians about the wagon train?"

"Satanta said he led the raid. He was proud of it and claimed he was the leader."

"Objection. The witness does not know the state of mind of the witness," Woolfolk protested without enthusiasm.

"Overruled. Continue with your case, Mister Lanham," decided Soward.

"Satanta claimed he led the raid. Did he name any others involved?" asked Lanham.

"He named Satank, Big Bow, Eagle Heart, Fast Bear, Woman's Heart, Adoltay, and Mamanti," said Leeper.

"Were these men all present to hear Satanta and deny their involvement if necessary?" continued Lanham.

"Mamanti and Big Bow were not present."

"But all the others were?"

"Yes."

"Did any of them deny their involvement?"

"No, sir, none of them denied taking part in the raid."

"Satanta said he led the raid?" repeated Lanham.

"Yes," agreed Leeper.

"Satanta said Adoltay, or Big Tree, was part of the raid?"

"Yes."

"Did Adoltay deny his involvement?"

"Adoltay did not deny his involvement."

"At the end of the meeting, what did Agent Tatum do?"

"He wrote a note and had me deliver it to Colonel Grierson at the post."

"The prosecution wishes to introduce into evidence the note written by Lawrie Tatum to General Grierson on May Twenty-Seventh, Eighteen Seventy-One. We mark this as prosecution exhibit five. The defense has seen the note."

Woolfolk had grown tired of sitting. He and Ball walked up to the evidence table and re-read the Tatum directive to Grierson. The Defense accepted the paper submitted into evidence and returned to their chairs.

"Please read the note, Mister Leeper," directed the prosecutor.

" 'Fort Sill, Indian Territory, Office of Kiowa Agency, Fifth Month, Twenty-Seventh Day, Eighteen Seventy-One. Colonel Grierson, Post Commander. Satanta in the presence of Satank, Eagle Heart, Big Tree, and Woman's Heart has, in a defiant manner, informed me that he led a party of about one hundred Indians into Texas and killed seven men and captured a train of mules. He further states that the chiefs, Satank, Eagle Heart, Big Bow, and Big Tree, were associated with him in the raid. Please arrest all of them. Lawrie Tatum. Indian Agent.' "

The interpreter had read carefully without any inflection or emotion.

"You delivered the message, and, then, what happened?" asked Lanham.

"Colonel Grierson sent me to bring as many chiefs as I could find to his headquarters," said Leeper.

"Were you present when the chiefs arrived at the general's porch?"

"No, sir, I was still carrying the message to the various chiefs."

"Thank you, Mister Leeper. The prosecution is finished with the witness, Your Honor."

Woolfolk stood up, but did not bother to walk toward the witness. "Mister Leeper, how would you know whether an Indian was absent from the reservation?"

"He would not come for rations."

"If he disdained to come for rations, even though he was on the reservation, you would conclude he was absent?"

"Yes, sir. We would probably ask the others about him and go and look for him, if he missed several issues."

"Several issues? How many is that, Mister Leeper?"

"I'm not sure, sir. Two or three, maybe."

"You think Satanta missed two or three rations then, Mister Leeper?"

"I don't really know, sir."

"Did you ask about him among the other Indians?"

"Yes."

"And . . . ?" Woolfolk waited.

"They said he had left the reservation."

"Did you go out and look for him, or was it just hearsay that led you to think Satanta was off the reservation?"

"We did not go and look for him," admitted Leeper.

"It was hearsay, then, that made you think he was away?"

"Yes."

"You didn't know it for sure. You just accepted it, is that right, Mister Leeper."

"That's right."

Satisfied with the answer, Woolfolk formed his second question. "White men brag sometimes, Mister Leeper. We sometime overestimate our deeds, our importance, our money, our exploits with women." Some in the court chuckled at that. "Do Indians ever exaggerate?"

"I suppose so, being human," agreed Matthew Leeper.

"Could Satanta have exaggerated his importance in boasting to Agent Tatum?"

"I suppose he could have."

"Did you ever quietly agree to something you knew was not true rather than make an issue of it, especially when the others involved were your superiors and you felt that you were the low man on the totem pole?"

"I have done that," said Leeper sheepishly.

208

"You suppose a young chief, like Adoltay, might do the same thing as a young white interpreter, Mister Leeper?"

"Yes."

"Thank you, Mister Leeper." Woolfolk sat down. "Call your next witness."

Soward glared at the usurpation of his power. "Mister Lanham, call your next witness."

Horace Jones passed young Leeper on his way out of the courtroom. He was neatly attired as usual, wearing a tie. His hat had been left outside, and his hair was oiled and combed neatly into place. He swore appropriately on the Bible as to his name and promised that he would tell the truth, the whole truth.

"Mister Jones, are you post interpreter at Fort Sill, Indian Territory?" asked Lanham.

Jones nodded. "I am."

"Did Satanta come to your house on Saturday afternoon, May Twenty-Seventh of this year?"

"Yes, he did," said Horace Jones.

"What did he want?"

"He wanted me to go up to Colonel Grierson's with him and translate for him. He said he wanted to talk to the big general. He meant General Sherman."

"Did you go with him and translate for him?"

"Yes, I did."

"What happened?"

"Well, we rode across the parade ground, up to the colonel's house. There wasn't anybody around, and that made Satanta nervous." Woolfolk withheld his objection, regarding testimony about the defendant's state of mind. He merely glanced at Soward who shook his head and mouthed, overruled.

"When we reached the porch, Satanta and I tied our horses and started up the stairs. General Sherman was waiting for us.

He stopped Satanta at the top of the stairs and asked him straight out if he was the man who had led the raid."

"And what did Satanta say?"

"He said . . . 'Yes, I am the man.' "

"What next transpired, Mister Jones?"

"General Sherman asked him facts about the raid. Satanta answered him."

"Why would the general do that?"

"Your Honor . . . ?" protested Woolfolk.

"Overruled," said Soward. "Answer the question, Mister Jones."

"Well, I guess to check how much he really knew about the raid. It was a way to verify his statement that he led the raid."

"Was the general satisfied with Satanta's answers, Mister Jones?"

"Yes."

"General Sherman ascertained Satanta's involvement to his satisfaction?"

"Yes."

"At any point, did Satanta deny his involvement?"

"Well, sir, when the general began to ask about burning Elliott alive, Satanta began to back water some."

"Then when he felt that he might be in danger because of his actions, Satanta began to recant his confession?"

"That's right. I think he realized that maybe he had said the wrong things earlier."

"During the following dangerous situation, when the assembling Indian chiefs were faced with armed soldiers, did Satanta say anything?"

"He asked me . . . 'What is this?' "

"What did you tell him?"

"I didn't get time to tell him anything. General Sherman

told me to tell him he was not to try to leave. If he did, he would be shot."

"What did Satanta say to that, Mister Jones?"

"He said he was a fool, that he'd been deceived by Sherman as he had been by Custer. He'd come under a white flag, so to speak, and he'd been arrested again."

"Did he say at any time that he had not been involved in the raid, either as its leader or as a participant?"

"When the other chiefs arrived, General Sherman had me explain that he wanted to know who had led the Warren wagon train raid. He wanted to know from the others if Satanta really did. He wanted the chiefs to tell him who helped Satanta, who killed the men, and who burned the man over the wagon tongue. Kicking Bird told the chiefs not to say anything more about the raid. But Satanta took the stage and said again that he was the man who led the raid. He said it was for the young men. He said he did not kill or burn anybody. He even asked Sherman how he could know that anybody was burned, maybe the white men were lying."

"He admitted leading the raid twice before Sherman?" summarized Lanham.

"Yes."

Chapter Twenty-Five

"Mister Jones," said Joe Woolfolk, leaning on the witness box, "did you say that Satanta had no knowledge of the burning of Sam Elliott?"

"He said he didn't know about it. He said that he thought the white men were making it up."

"Thank you, Mister Jones. Do you find Indians to be truthful?"

"They can be, mostly are, in my experience."

"So, if we are willing to believe Satanta about leading the raid, we probably ought to believe him, as well, about not instigating or even knowing about the death of Sam Elliott?"

"I guess, if you believe one, you have to believe the other, don't you? If you're fair."

"Well, we are fair men here," said Woolfolk, looking at Judge Soward. "Now, Mister Jones, you are knowledgeable about the Kiowas. Is there any politics among Indians? I mean, do they try to get ahead of each other like white men?"

"I'd say that they do. Place is very important among the Kiowas."

"About three or four years ago" — Woolfolk paced away from the witness toward the jury — "did their old chief . . . Little Mountain . . . Dohausen . . . die?"

"He died in the summer of Eighteen Sixty-Seven," the interpreter stated.

"What happened then? Was there a power struggle between the band chiefs to see who would take his place?"

"Yes, a lot of the small chiefs began to go their own way.

Satanta and Guipago were vying for the position of principal chief. Kicking Bird was trying to get the Kiowas to stay on the reservation and make peace. So he was another contender. The old warriors like Satank and Satanta called him a coward, said he was afraid of white men."

"What did the peace chief, Kicking Bird, do?"

"Kicking Bird led a war party into Texas. He fought with soldiers from Fort Richardson. I think the Army refers to the engagement as the Battle of the Little Wichita. To the Indians' thinking, he won a major victory. After that Satanta and Satank had to be quiet. Kicking Bird was holding his own."

"What did the war chiefs do then?" queried the defense attorney.

"The war chiefs wouldn't give in to him, or let him become principal chief. It was little things mostly, irritating him, stealing his horses, grazing their ponies so close to his herd that the grass was eaten up, so he'd have to move his band often. The Comanches and the Cheyennes were in on it, too. The young men were sneaking off and raiding. Sometimes he'd catch them. Sometimes not. The situation was like a boat with a lot of little leaks. Kicking Bird was bailing water. But nobody else had enough power to really be chief of all the bands."

"How would a contender try to tip the scale in his favor, Mister Jones, sink Kicking Bird's boat?"

"He'd have to lead a bigger, more successful raid in which the young men could gain honor. The older warriors would then recognize his leadership."

"Something like the wagon train attack?" asked Woolfolk.

"Yes."

"Could a war chief do it alone?"

"He'd need the help of his supporters. He wouldn't want his enemies to come along or get any credit."

"Would he boast about his dominance in leadership, even

if there were several other men involved?"

"Well, that's the point. He'd have to claim the credit to get to be principal chief."

"He would magnanimously name the others he wanted to influence to his side, but he would take the credit for all his supporters?"

"Yes."

"Is Adoltay thought of as a leader of the young men?" asked Woolfolk. "Would a principal chief need his support among the young men?"

"Adoltay is well thought of. Even Agent Tatum thinks he will be a leader of the Kiowas."

"Not after we hang him," someone in the courtroom said loudly.

Judge Soward turned his attention from the witness to the room. "Guards," he said, "remove Lucius Bryant and the men with him from the courthouse."

"I didn't do it," protested Bryant, as the guards began to hustle him and his friends toward the door.

"I do not really care, Mister Bryant," Soward returned. "At this moment, I am not concerned with justice, but with retribution." The clamor in the back of the room soon subsided. "Proceed with your examination of the witness, Mister Woolfolk."

"Is it fair to say, Mister Jones, that in the absence of a principal chief, that a man who wanted to be chief would try to make himself big by boasting, by exaggerating his leadership, and by flattering the leader of a faction whose support he needed to become chief?"

"I think that's a fair statement," agreed Jones.

"That's all I have for the witness, Your Honor."

"Redirect, Mister Lanham?" questioned Soward.

Lanham stood in place. "Mister Jones, would Satanta have

boasted of his leadership if he had not been involved in the raid?"

"No," said the interpreter. "The others would not have put up with it. He'd have been out completely. Guipago or Kicking Bird would become principal chief."

"The state rests its case," said the prosecutor.

Soward surveyed the audience from his high bench. A steady sweep of fans had failed completely in cooling the close-packed spectators. Faces were red and wet with perspiration. The jury was little better. The buttoned collars were soaked through. Neatly-oiled and combed hair now clung in wet strings to clammy scalps.

"We'll take a thirty-minute recess," the judge decided. "Jury, do not discuss this case among yourselves or with anyone else. Folks, go out under the trees, get something to drink. I want to get some air back into this room."

Soward left the room with his clerk at his side, his robe open and billowing behind him as he descended the staircase toward his office. "Hell's bells," the judge confided to the clerk, "Margaret Wisdom is as red as a fox's ass. A three-hundred-pound woman like her could die of the heat in that room. How'd that look? You get that back door of the hallway open whether the Army wants it or not. We need some circulation in this building."

Isaac Lynn stretched out on one of the benches, catching a breeze from the floor-to-ceiling windows that surrounded the empty courtroom. The guards came and took the two Kiowas away for a bit of exercise and personal necessities. The counselors for the defense adjourned to the shade of a pecan tree and figured the final details of their case. In the courthouse, John Wooten rested his boot heels on a window sill and tipped back in Lanham's chair. Below him, the crowd on the grounds was catching up on the testimony. The cowboy was willing to bet that the hideous fury of the raid and the killing of Sam Elliott were getting a good play. He doubted whether anyone was considering that Satanta and Adoltay might not have played much of a part in either.

He saw Lucius Bryant exit the Wichita Hotel with a pack of mongrels that passed for men. They sauntered over to get the details of what they had missed of the afternoon session. Pretty soon they were stirred up and stirring up those fool enough to listen. Wooten let his chair drop to the floor, as he pulled his long legs out of the window. He sat with his hands on his knees for a few minutes, then stood, and stretched.

"Lucius out and about?" asked Isaac Lynn.

"He's running his mouth, it looks like," commented the cowboy.

"I reckon the world would go to hell without men like Lucius settin' it straight," Lynn said.

"How come you ain't killin' Injuns no more, Isaac?" asked Wooten, looking again out the window.

"Too much competition," answered the old man. Then he said very quietly: "I had to forgive to be forgiven, son. It's required."

"You think Woolfolk has a chance?"

"No."

"Neither do I," said John Wooten, as he moved now along the row of windows. "Neither do I. Then, why in hell are we going through all this effort?"

"Why do you lance a boil? To get out all the putrefaction, so the healing can start."

"You think this hate between white men and red will ever heal?" asked the cowboy, as he stopped to stare again out another window.

"I don't know that. But it will not heal with men like Lucius

Bryant, putting everything in perspective. Men like Woolfolk and Lanham, well, we need 'em. Sometimes one slips something by, and sometimes the other. But it's out in the open where the free wind can blow away the chaff. It damn' sure ain't done by night with a torch and a lynch rope."

"You know, Isaac, I've fought a lot of Indians and killed some and been near-killed by some. And I never really thought much about it. I just did it. I didn't hate them or even dislike them as men. But that Satanta irritates me as much as Lucius Bryant. I'd really enjoy tying into him."

"Well, I reckon that's good."

Wooten turned to see the old man's face, but he still lay on the bench with one leg thrown over the back. "How's it good to want to beat the hell out of a man?"

"One on one in a good fight is good exercise for a man's body and his soul," Isaac Lynn said. "There's just some things a man should not tolerate from a white man or a red man, or any other kind of a man. But I doubt you'll get a swing at Satanta."

Chapter Twenty-Six

Judge Soward hammered in the last session of the afternoon. He smiled. "It's your turn, Mister Woolfolk. Call your witness."

"John Wooten."

Wooten opened the swinging gate and raised his hand for the oath, as the bailiff shoved a Bible under his other. "Do you swear to tell the truth, the whole truth, and nothing but the truth, so help you God?"

"So help me God," repeated Wooten.

"State your name and occupation and sit down," said the bailiff.

"John Wooten," said the cowboy. "Ranch foreman." He sat down.

Woolfolk ran a hand through his already tumbled, blond hair and stood in front of the witness for several moments, looking at the floor. He took a breath and asked: "John Wooten, do you know personally either of the defendants?"

"Yes, I do. I know Adoltay."

"How do you know Adoltay?"

"He saved my life," said the foreman. A murmur of voices came from the spectators as they displayed surprise at this testimony.

"When did he save your life? When you delivered cattle to the Brazos Reserve?"

"No," Wooten said, "it was during the Elm Creek raid." Again the murmur ran across the rows of citizens.

"Let's see, when was the Elm Creek raid?"

"October Thirteenth, Eighteen Sixty-Four," said Wooten without hesitation.

"Was it a bad raid?"

"Yes, very bad . . . eleven killed, including five Rangers, eleven wounded, two women and five children carried off. Some said a thousand Indians rode up and down Elm Creek that day."

"How did Adoltay save you?"

"Well, I was riding with the Rangers. We got word of the attack and rode out to do whatever we could. We rode into an ambush. Five of the fifteen were killed and five more wounded before we could get turned around and headed back to Fort Murrah. My horse was shot out from under me. When he went down, I was thrown over his head, and my rifle barrel end was jammed full of mud. It was three miles to any kind of cover. I knew I could not make it with the Indians closing in, but I ran anyway. There were two young boys right on me. But they let me run. I ran, and they ran behind me. When I couldn't run any more, I stopped and pointed my gun at them. Adoltay pointed his bow at me. He could have killed me right then. But he said . . . 'Don't shoot me, Wooten. You know me. You run, Wooten.' Every time I had to stop, I'd raise my gun. And he'd say, 'Run, Wooten, run!' He called me by my name and told me to run a half dozen times, I guess. I noticed that the main party had dropped off, leaving me to the two boys who.were chasing me. Adoltay and his friend chased me right into the trees and safety. Then they turned around and trotted back to the others. I went on in to Fort Murrah when it got dark."

"Adoltay could have killed you several times?" asked Woolfolk.

"Sure, he could have," agreed Wooten.

"But in his continued pursuit of you, he deceived the other raiders and got you to safety?"

"Yes, he saved my life that day."

Woolfolk turned, anticipating Lanham's question. "Why did he do that?"

"I think he knew me from the time I drove cattle to the Brazos Reserve. We didn't get time to talk much about that."

There was light laughter among the courtroom spectators.

"He could have killed you, but he did not because he knew you," summarized Woolfolk. "Did you know or remember him?"

"No, I did not. I did not recognize him until today when he said 'Wooten.'"

"So on that October day in Eighteen Sixty-Four, you didn't beg him for your life on your friendship, or try to get him to help you out in any other way?"

"No, I thought he was going to kill me."

"He took all the initiative, not only in not killing you himself, but in taking you away from the main party to safety?"

"Yes."

"Thank you, John Wooten." Woolfolk shoved his hands into his pockets and walked past Lanham to his own chair.

"Mister Lanham," Judge Soward directed.

Lanham stood, resting his finger tips on the table. "Let's see, Mister Wooten, Eighteen Sixty-Four, that's seven years ago. Adoltay couldn't have been over, say, fourteen, could he?"

"Probably not much over that."

"Couldn't what you thought was saving your life have been mere inexperience?"

"I don't think he'd have needed much experience to kill me. My gun was plugged, and he had the drop on me with a strung bow and arrow. Besides, as a young man, he had a lot to gain by killing me. He could have used my scalp to get honor."

"You're a big man, Mister Wooten, and even seven years later, Adoltay is slight. Have your client stand up, Mister Woolfolk?"

Judge Soward nodded to Woolfolk. The young Kiowa stood up. Every eye focused on his five-foot-seven-inch frame.

"Please stand up yourself, Mister Wooten," the prosecutor directed.

The cowman stood. The difference in their sizes was obvious to every observer.

"Perhaps what you thought of as compassion was simply the fact that he did not feel he had the experience to take you, if you fought him?"

"The boy had the difference, sir. And he had enough experience to take me out of harm's way."

Wooten sat down as Woolfolk directed his client back into the chair.

"So no qualifications, he saved your life, Mister Wooten?"

"That's right. No qualifications, he saved my life."

"And now you are trying to save his, is that not so?" thundered the prosecutor, slamming the table with his hand.

Wooten flinched at the attack upon his integrity. He gripped the chair arms tightly with his hands. "I'm telling the court what I know about this man," Wooten replied. "I believe it is right to tell the good, as well as the bad."

"His goodness is a pea on the scales of justice against the crimes he has done," said Lanham.

"Objection," said Woolfolk.

"Overruled," said Soward. "Are you finished with the witness, Mister Lanham?"

Lanham nodded as he sat back down.

"Have you other witnesses to call in the defendants' behalf, Mister Woolfolk?"

"Not at this time, Your Honor."

Soward looked at him quizzically, then rapped the block in front of him with his gavel. "The court will hear closing arguments tomorrow morning. Guards remove the prisoners."

The bustle and shuffle of the heavy guard almost masked the young Adoltay's words. "Wooten, come and see me," he said as the guard led him away.

When Soward was satisfied that the prisoners were safely removed and in the Army's secure custody, he struck the gavel again. "Court is adjourned until tomorrow morning at eight-thirty."

Chapter Twenty-Seven

"We can't put Adoltay on the stand, if that's what you're thinking, Joe," said Thomas Ball as he almost ran along beside Woolfolk. "We can't put on that Indian and have him say the Indians tore hell out of those bodies and burned a man to death, because the men they were robbing made them mad. We cannot say that. That's no excuse . . . my victim fought back, so I tore him to pieces."

"That *is* no excuse," conceded Woolfolk, as they entered the door of the Wichita Hotel. "It's over, Tom. No matter what we say or do, the Kiowas killed those men on Salt Creek Prairie. We can point to all the wrongs and crimes against them, and it won't help. We can't even make it a case of war, really. In their savage fury, they mutilated the dead men in every way. Maybe they were furious because they were all dead except Sam Elliott. Maybe they couldn't kill them enough, so they just obliterated them as men. Even in war that won't work, not if we want wars to stop."

"So who is this 'not at this time' witness?" asked Ball. "Have you got a witness?"

"Yes, I've got a witness. Get Wooten for me, will you?" Woolfolk wasn't demanding or arrogant. He simply needed Thomas Ball to find the cowboy. "I need him to learn some things."

"Come and see me," the boy's words echoed in John Wooten's mind, as he walked away from the throng of people still gathered around the Jacksboro square and its saloons and eating establishments. He picked up his horse at the livery and trotted out of town across the now famous bridge on Lost Creek and into the grounds of the fort. After making his arrangements with Mackenzie's staff, he went to the stone laundry prison. The guard searched him and allowed him into the cell where Satanta and Adoltay's empty supper plates remained to be picked up.

Satanta rose in front of the visitor and faced him squarely. "What do you want with me?"

Wooten stood eye to eye with the big Kiowa. Like dogs about to fight, each took the measure of his opponent. "I came to see Adoltay." The words came hoarsely from the cow boss's constricted throat.

"Wooten!" greeted the young chief.

"Adoltay," the cowman spoke softly and offered his large hand.

The boy took it and shook it vigorously. "Wooten, thank you for speaking for me. You are still a good man." He motioned Wooten toward a stool. "Sit, Wooten."

The cow boss sat awkwardly. "Look, what I said probably won't help you much." It was an earnest confession from the man. He wanted the boy not to get his hopes up.

"Yes, help me much," the young man said.

"No," Wooten said. "You don't understand. What I said won't help." He began to speak in a mixture of Spanish and English and Comanche, hoping to convince the boy not to hope in his testimony.

The young man listened intently. He gestured at his chest and responded in the same language soup. "In here, Wooten. Help in here. You are the only white man I know, and you spoke for me."

"I only told what I know for fact," replied the cowman. "Say, when did I save your life? That sounds kind of grand to

224

me. I cannot remember that for all my trying."

The boy smiled. "Is it that you do so much good, Wooten, that you cannot remember one small boy trapped in a burning barn?" The image struck Wooten's mind. "You stood for me then against men of your own kind, and now you have done it a second time. This puzzles me. I have thought about it, and I would like to hear why you have denied your own people twice for a Kiowa."

"There are things that are right," said the cowboy. "It doesn't have anything to do with you being a Kiowa or me being a white man. It's just the way of things."

The young chief thought a moment about the Texan's words. "What are these things?"

"Well, one is not letting a gang jump a kid. Another is telling the truth about things. I ain't got a corner on them, kid. You did a right thing yourself when you helped me escape, because I'd helped you in a bad place. You had more to gain from your friends by killing me, but you paid your private debt, instead."

"Wooten, I want to ask you something else. I do not understand much of this trial. I know Joe talks for us. But I do not understand, when the soldier spoke, why the people in the room were so angry? Donat said it was the same way we act toward Tonkawas. But we did not eat the wagon drivers."

Wooten rubbed his eyes. "Do you know what the sergeant said?"

Adoltay shook his head.

"Well, he told about the way the bodies were found . . . stripped, stabbed, shot over and over, heads pounded in, brains dug out, fingers, toes, genitals stuffed in the mouths, fire put on the men's bellies . . . and Sam Elliott, one of the men, burned alive. That was all too much . . . excessive. Killing a man to white people is one thing, but tearing him to bits sort of denies him being human. It's trying to steal all he is, or was."

225

"The men were angry because of the boy, Gunshot," said Adoltay. "They did not want those men to take anything away. They wanted to wipe them out completely."

"That's what I mean. It's too much hate. I guess we think there's a limit on a man. Americans don't try to kill a man's soul. We think it belongs to God. It ain't ours. Sometimes we kill . . . think we have to, to stay alive . . . but then we are finished. We think that there is something wrong, evil . . ." — Wooten groped for a word that could contain the horror he meant and he settled for — "bad medicine, about a man that enjoys another man's pain or his eternal damnation."

Adoltay watched Wooten's face closely as he spoke. He listened with eyes and ears. "I did not do this. Satanta did not do this. We are warriors, men of honor."

"But you let the others do it. You were part of it, because you were there and did not stop it," explained the cowboy. "White men believe that a man is responsible for what other men do around him."

Adoltay turned his head away, thinking. "This is strange to me. I am responsible for myself. I am responsible for my people's food and well being. On a raid, I am responsible for a plan that will satisfy and keep my men alive. In council, I am responsible for thinking wisely for others. But I have never been responsible for what other men do."

"You cannot be responsible for what other men do," growled Satanta. "Each man is himself. You cannot violate that."

"White men believe a man has a right to his own way, too," countered Wooten. "But some men are too weak or powerless to do much for themselves. And some men are too dangerous to be allowed to do what they want. We say a man's rights end at his neighbor's nose. It's always a balance."

"They would kill us, if we tried to stop them," said Satanta. "You speak foolishly."

The corner of Wooten's mouth twisted. "Maybe you need some new thinking yourself, chief. Maybe you need to have more on your side than a strong arm and a 'let 'er rip' attitude. Maybe you need some check that ain't just another man with a weapon. Maybe you could use a common understanding that some things ain't acceptable."

"We have such understanding," said Satanta.

"Yeah," said Wooten, rising. "You understand that the strong man runs things. And he don't interfere with other strong men, if he's smart."

Thomas Ball caught Wooten on his return to the Wichita Hotel. They went up to Woolfolk's room together. Woolfolk yelled through the door for them to come inside as he washed his bearded face.

"Here's the deal, Wooten," he said without preface, as he dried his ears and burning eyes. "I want to know what that Quaker agent told the citizens' committee from Jacksboro. He might want the chiefs punished like a white man, but he damn' sure would not want them or anybody else killed. The whole Quaker establishment has got to be beating down President Grant's door on this. Get me something from the Quaker, Wooten."

"Now how am I going to do that?" the exasperated cowboy asked, sitting on the bed.

"With your usual charm," smiled Woolfolk. "And a few drinks with W. M. McConnell ought to help. I saw him in the bar as I came up from dinner."

Wooten remembered aloud that he had not eaten.

"Look, don't sit here," berated Woolfolk. "He might leave. There's plenty of food in the bar. Go on."

Wooten looked at Thomas Ball. The words — "Why can't . . . ?" — had barely formed themselves in his mind when Woolfolk shouted. "Because we are defending the Indians. Nobody in town would drink with us."

Wooten shrugged himself off the bed. "And what are you going to do?"

"I am going to see a lady," said Woolfolk.

Wooten and Ball exchanged glances. "You worry me when you get cheerful, Joe," Wooten said flatly.

"Not to worry, old friend," said Woolfolk, ushering Wooten out the door. "When you can't win one way, maybe you can win another. There's always a higher court."

"Watch him," Wooten called to Thomas Ball as he descended the stairs. He heard Joe Woolfolk humming behind him in the hotel room.

Chapter Twenty-Eight

Tuesday, July 4, 1871

After the usual preliminaries, the Thirteenth District Court of the great State of Texas settled into expectant waiting for the final moments of the trial of the Kiowa chiefs. The Kiowa verdict was at hand.

Soward looked fresh and rested as he spoke. "Mister Woolfolk, have you found another witness?"

"Not at this time, Your Honor," Woolfolk said politely.

Thomas Ball tossed his pencil at the table in exasperation. It rolled onto the floor.

"Well, your time is up. We are now ready for the closing arguments, gentlemen. Mister Lanham proceed."

"I thought you were doing something last night," whispered Ball.

Woolfolk looked at him with peculiar attention, amazement even. "Take it easy, Ball. I did do something." He smiled sweetly and turned his attention to the prosecutor.

Young Lanham stuck his thumbs into his vest pockets and strolled to the jury. He stopped a few feet in front of the jurors. He observed them as they observed him. The room became slowly silent as the spectators anticipated the orator's words. Lanham knew he had them.

"This is a novel and important trial and has, perhaps, no precedent in the history of American criminal jurisprudence," he began. "The remarkable character of the prisoners, who are leading representatives of their race . . . their crude and barbarous appearance . . . the gravity of the charge . . . the number of the victims . . . the horrid brutality and inhuman butchery inflicted upon the bodies of the dead . . . the dreadful and terrific spectacle of seven men, who were husbands, fathers, brothers, sons, and lovers on the morning of the dark and bloody day of this atrocious deed, and rose from their rude tents bright with hope, in the prime and pride of manhood, and found at a later hour, beyond recognition in every condition of horrid disfiguration, unutterable mutilation and death, 'lying stark and stiff, under the hoofs of vaunting enemies,' all conspire to surround this case with extraordinary interest! Though we were to pause in silence, the cause I represent would exclaim with trumpet-tongue!

"Satanta, the veteran council chief of the Kiowas . . . the orator . . . the diplomat . . . the counselor of his tribe . . . the pulse of his race, and Big Tree, the young war chief who leads in the thickest of the fight and follows no one in the chase, the mighty warrior athlete with the speed of the deer and the eye of the eagle . . . are before this bar, in the charge of the law. So they would be described by Indian admirers, who live in more secured and favored lands, remote from the frontier . . . where 'distance lends enchantment' to the imagination . . . where the story of Pocahontas and the speech of Logan, the Mingo, are read, and the dread sound of the war whoop is not heard.

"We who see them today, disrobed of all their fancied graces, exposed in the light of reality, behold them through far different lenses. We recognize in Satanta the arch fiend of treachery and blood . . . the cunning Cataline . . . the promoter of strife . . . the breaker of treaties signed by his own hand . . . the inciter of his fellows to rapine and murder . . . the artful dealer in bravado while in the pow-wow, and the most abject coward in the field, as well as the most canting and double-tongued hypocrite when detected and overcome. In Big Tree we perceive the tiger-demon who has tasted blood and loves it as his food . . . who stops at no crime how black 'soever . . . who is swift at every species of ferocity, and pities not at any sight of agony or death. . . . he can scalp, burn, torture, and has no feeling of sympathy or remorse. They are both hideous and loathsome in appearance, and we look in vain to see, in them, anything to be admired or endured.

"Still, these rough 'sons of the wood' have been commiserated, the measures of the poet and the pen of romance have been invoked to grace the 'melancholy history' of the red man. Powerful legislative influences have been brought to bear to procure them annuities, reservations, and supplies. Federal munificence has fostered and nourished them, fed and clothed them. And from their strongholds of protection, they have come down upon us 'like wolves on the fold.' Treaties have been solemnly made with them, wherein they have been considered with all the formalities of quasi-nationalities. Immense financial 'rings' have had their origin in, and drawn their vitality from, the 'Indian question.' Unblushing corruption has stalked abroad, created and alive through 'the poor Indian, whose untutored mind sees God in clouds, or hears him in the wind.'

"Mistaken sympathy for these vile creatures has kindled the flames around the cabin of the pioneer and despoiled him of his hard earnings, murdered and scalped our people, and carried off our women into captivity worse than death. For many years, predatory and numerous bands of these 'pets of the government' have waged the most relentless and heart-rending warfare upon our frontier, stealing our property and killing our citizens. We have cried aloud for help. As segments of the grand aggregate of the country, we have begged for relief. Deaf ears have been turned to our cries, and the story of our wrongs has been discredited. Had it not been for General W. T. Sherman and his most opportune journey through this section, it may well be doubted whether these brutes in human shape would ever have been brought to trial. For it is a fact, well known in Texas, that stolen property has been traced to the very doors of the reservation and there identified by our people, to no purpose."

Lanham spoke directly to Peter Hart as he stirred the embers of horse stealing. Hart, completely enthralled with the prosecutor's words, nodded his agreement. Lanham turned from the jury to the courtroom itself. He moved toward Colonel Mackenzie and his party, observers for the United States.

"We are greatly indebted to the military arm of the government for kindly officers and co-operation in procuring the arrest and transference of the defendants. If the entire management of the Indian question were submitted to that gallant and distinguished Army officer, Colonel Ranald Mackenzie, who graces this occasion with his dignified presence, our frontier would soon enjoy immunity from these marauders."

"Here! Here!," came from random spectators.

Encouraged, Lanham pursued the vein of gold. "It speaks well for the humanity of our laws and the tolerance of this people that the prisoners are permitted to be tried in this Christian land, and by this Christian tribunal. The learned court has, in all things, required the observance of the same rules of procedure . . . the same principles of evidence . . . the same judicial methods, from the presentment of the indictment down to the charge soon to be given by his honor, that are enforced in the trial of a white man."

Lanham walked back to the jury.

"You, gentlemen of the jury, have sworn that you can and will render a fair and impartial verdict. Were we to practice *lex talionis,* no right of trial by jury would be allowed these monsters. On the contrary, as they have treated their victims, so it would be measured unto them."

Heads bobbed in agreement.

232

"The definition of murder is so familiar to the court, and has been so frequently discussed before the country, that any technical or elaborate investigation of the subject, under the facts of this case, would seem unnecessary. Under our statute, *all murder committed in the perpetration, or in the attempt at the perpetration of robbery is murder in the first degree!*" Lanham's voice punctuated, emphasized, and italicized the words. "Under the facts of the case, we might well rest upon this clause of the statute in the determination of the grade of the offense."

"He's not going to quit there," wagered Ball.

"Not on your life, he's not," agreed Woolfolk.

Lanham seemed to hear. He turned briefly to the co-counsels. "But the testimony in this trial discloses these salient features."

"Here it comes," muttered Woolfolk.

Lanham was back at the jury. "About the time indicated by the charge, the defendants, with other chiefs and a band of more than fifty warriors, were absent from their reservation at Fort Sill. They were away about thirty days . . . a sufficient length of time to make this incursion and return. Upon their return, they brought back booty . . . forty-one mules, guns and pistols, and camp supplies of the deceased. Satanta made a speech in the presence of the interpreter, Lawrie Tatum, the Indian agent at Fort Sill, and General Sherman, in which he boasted of having been down to Texas and had a big fight . . . killing seven *Tejanos,* and capturing forty-one mules, guns, pistols, ammunition, sugar and coffee, and other supplies of the train. He said, if any other chief claimed the credit of the victory, that he would be a liar. He said that he, Satanta . . . with Big Tree and Satank, who was present and acquiesced in the statement . . . were entitled to all the glory. Here we have his own admission, voluntarily and arrogantly made, describing minutely this whole tragic affair.

"Besides his own words, we have the evidence of one of the surviving teamsters, Tom Brazeal, who told of the attack upon him and his comrades by a band of as many as one hundred and fifty Indians . . . of the killing of seven of his comrades and the escape of four others, with himself. Then, we have the testimony of the orderly sergeant, Miles Varily, himself an old Indian fighter and familiar with the modes of attack and general conduct of the savages. Varily, with a detachment of soldiers, went out from Fort Richardson to the scene of blood, to bury the dead. He describes how the seven teamsters were scalped . . . mutilated with axe . . . shot with arrows . . . how Samuel Elliott was chained and burned, evidently while living. He told you of the revolting and horrible manner in which the dead bodies were mangled and disfigured. Everything betokened the work and presence of Indians. He further described the arrows as those of the Kiowas. We learned from him that Indian tribes are known by the peculiar manner in which their arrows are made, like civilized nations are recognized by their flags."

Lanham seemed thoughtful as he strolled the length of the jury box. "The same amount and character of testimony were sufficient to convict any white man. 'By their own words let them be condemned.' The conviction and punishment of Satanta and Adoltay cannot repair the loss nor avenge the blood of the good men they have slain. Still" — he leaned on the rail for emphasis — "it is *due to law and justice and humanity* that they should receive the *highest punishment*. This is even too mild and humane for them. Pillage and blood-thirstiness were the motives of this diabolical deed . . . fondness for torture and intoxication of delight at human agony impelled its perpetration."

Lanham straightened. "All the elements of murder in the first degree are found in the case. The jurisdiction of the court is complete. The State of Texas expects from you a verdict and judgment in accordance with the law and the evidence." Lanham spoke his last line straight to the jury calmly, softly: "It is expected."

There was hushed silence within the room. As the citizens realized the moving oratory was over, a thunderous applause broke out. Soward let it run for a while, then rapped for quiet. "That's enough," he said. "Mister Woolfolk."

"Grand, wasn't it?" quipped Woolfolk. "You ready to follow that, Thomas?"

The color left Thomas Ball's face. "I . . . I didn't prepare. . . ."

"That's fine with me," said Woolfolk cheerfully. "I did." Woolfolk rose and walked around his table behind the two chiefs. Every eye in the courtroom followed him.

"It is expected," he began softly. "It is expected that you will think as a servile, monolithic unit and find these men guilty. Under Mister Lanham's supposition, you might not even have to leave the jury box to make your judgment. Guilty! Guilty! It is expected.

"Most of you have lived on this frontier as long as I have. You have seen families robbed, burned out, and killed. You have thrown yourselves into the saddle as I have to catch the thieves, arsonists, and killers. When we came here, we expected to fight for what we got, whether it was with the land or other men, red or white. We wanted land and all that that means to a man. Texas told us we could have that land. But Texas did not own it. There was a previous title holder. We put that out of our minds . . . we did not see his improvements upon the land, no houses, no gardens, no barns, or corrals. Yet, though his title was as tenuous and pervasive as the wind and the sun that burned us white men red, it was there. In our hearts, as honest men, we knew it was there. But we wanted the land, and all that that means to a man . . . independence, family, purpose. Some of us put aside all pretense and took what we wanted, saying the Kiowas and Comanches took the land before us from those who occupied it. Most of us, as honorable men, felt we should make some agreement with the title holder. Our government met with the Indians. Treaties were signed and broken . . . by both sides. It was not fair, we said, for the Indians, who our taxes paid with annuities, to raid us and take our goods and our lives. And we were right. And the Indians arrogantly used the reservations for their protection, as safe havens, to strike from and to flee to. That was not fair, we said. And we were right."

Woolfolk moved closer to the jury. "We killed the buffalo on our way to the treaty signings and turned the hide hunters loose on the great herds that were the Indian's life. The Indians said that was not fair. And they were right. We took the open prairies of a people who had lived by moving over the land for as long as their old people remembered and put them on reservations that were large to us and very small for their needs. The Indian said that was not fair. And he was right.

"So, gentlemen, what are we to do? Mister Lanham says you are expected to find these men guilty of murder under the statutes of the great State of Texas. He says his evidence proves that they are guilty.

"I do not agree. He showed you Kiowa arrows, but his own witness, Sergeant Varily, admitted that there is trading among the Indians. A Cheyenne might trade for Kiowa arrows or the other way around. The prosecutor showed you only selected arrows, Kiowa arrows, when his witness says that there were arrows belonging to other tribes at the scene. Two witnesses for the state said they *believed* they heard a bugle. Is it really possible that they heard a faintly blowing distant bugle above the sounds of guns and wind and thunder, above the screams of men and mules? Mister Lanham set down a bugle taken

236

from Satanta and concluded that he blew that bugle during the attack. Sergeant Varily again said that many Kiowas know the use of bugles. Bugles flourish in their society. Reliable witnesses have said that Satanta confessed his leadership before Agent Tatum and General Sherman and implicated Adoltay. I do not believe the witnesses would lie. But neither do I believe that this man knew what he was confessing. The Constitution of this country has from the beginning protected a man from self-incrimination. We say a man must know what he is saying, and what the consequences of his saying it are. This man did not."

Woolfolk saw a glimpse of something in Peyton Lynn's eyes, then it was gone.

"Mister Lanham would paint the Kiowa chiefs as all bad, and ourselves as all good. This, I suppose, is another of those things that Mister Lanham feels is expected of Texans. But you and I, as Texans, know that is not true. There is good in the worst villain and bad in the best of men. He calls Satanta and Adoltay the worst of their race, meaning the best examples of the savage Indians. He tells us of the terrible butchery of the dead men in the Warren wagon train. He tells us of the terrible death of another who lived to die over a heap of coals. I do not understand the mind behind such atrocities myself any more than you do. But I am certain that the men who sit before you to be judged did not participate in these atrocities and could not have stopped them any more than you or I have been able to stop those committed by our people. Satanta, we learned from the state's witness, did not know about the killing of Sam Elliott. He thought his accusers were making it up. Young Adoltay, Tom Brazeal said, killed a mule in what to the Indians was a feat of extraordinary bravery and leadership as he rode through the white men's guns. When he could have killed Mike Mullins, he tapped him, counting coup instead.

When he could have killed John Wooten, he saved him, let him run to safety, instead."

Woolfolk leaned over the jury rail. His words were quiet and straight.

"What is expected of us, gentlemen? It is what has been expected of all honest men in all times. We are expected to put aside our anger and our hatred and our own past experiences. We are to hear the evidence presented and weigh it . . . not being moved by our emotions or outrage. We are to look at these men before us as men and decide what they did as fairly as we can." He straightened. "That is what is expected."

Woolfolk received no thunderous applause. He had not expected it. But he thought he had done his job. He settled back in his chair to wait for the judge's charge, the exit, and return of the jury. The faces of the jury showed him that these men would think about what he had said before they returned from the tiny room downstairs toward which they were now filing.

"Nice job, Joe," said Wooten.

"Think I won?" teased the lawyer.

"Well," said Isaac Lynn, "you damn' sure created some doubt in my mind. I'm kind of getting to like Wooten's Indian. Maybe even that damned puffed up Satanta didn't know what they did to Sam Elliott."

"We'll see," said Woolfolk. "But I'm not counting on a not guilty." He turned and hit Adoltay on the knee. "How you holding up, son?"

The young Kiowa nodded as he looked at the rumpled white man. "You talk good, Bearded One. I could see that the men who decide were listening to you."

"How about you Satanta?" asked Woolfolk.

Donat talked with Satanta who could not communicate his ideas in English. "He says he wants to talk for himself. You

238

know, chief, he's quite an orator himself."

Wooten pulled out his fat watch and laid it on the table in front of him. He could hear and feel its ticking through his skin.

Many people had stood to stretch in the room. But no one had left — they did not expect a long wait. They visited as neighbors with a common interest do. All in all, the trial had been successful. They had had a trip to town to see history made. They had seen their friends. They had heard first hand the shocking details of the Salt Creek Prairie massacre. And they had heard one of the best young orators on the plains. That S. W. T. Lanham would go to Congress one day, maybe be governor of Texas. No Texan could expect more.

Joe sighed and studied his hands. He had to admit they didn't really suit a lawyer. They were brown and callused, scarred from brush and thorns. In fact, as he considered himself, he did not look like a lawyer at all, even with Jinny's fixing him up. His collar was never buttoned, and his tie was never in place. His hair couldn't stay straight for more than the time it took to lay down the comb and turn away from the mirror. And there were the slippers. Joe Woolfolk couldn't wear slippers. They weren't secure. And they made his feet cold. A man needed a foundation, he told Jinny. Boots were what a man needed to stand on. No, Joe Woolfolk did not see himself in Washington. There was nothing about him that said attorney-at-law but his sign and the burning hunger in him to see that no man went down without a fight.

Woolfolk could not hold his eyes off the watch a moment longer. Fifteen minutes had passed. He bent to pick up Ball's pencil from the floor. He stood and stretched his back. He strolled down the aisle, not expecting hearty handshakes, but not intimidated by the fear of his fellows' disapproval. He mingled until he caught a glimpse of Bill and Helen Inlow near the aisle.

"Before you leave town," he said, as he shook Bill's hand, "come over to the hotel and get your papers. The title on your land is clear now." The young couple smiled.

Woolfolk moved deeper into the people.

"Say, Joe," a hunter said, "you still want a pup?"

"Out of Bear Dog?" asked Joe incredulously. "You bet I want a pup."

"Good," said the hunter. "We'll call it even on my bill, then."

Woolfolk smiled. A good hunting dog was a lot better than the bag of green pecans he got last time. As a matter of fact, Joe Woolfolk felt rich. He was feeling almost good as he saw Tom Ball and John Wooten moving easily among the crowd.

"Wooten, ain't you skeered to be out alone?" Woolfolk knew the voice, and he knew his bubble had burst. Lucius Bryant had squared off with a pack of bullies against John Wooten. "I mean your Injuns chained up, and Missus Chastain ain't here to protect you, neither."

Woolfolk saw the color rising above John Wooten's collar. He pushed toward the men. "Bryant," he joked, "I thought you got thrown out of here."

"I sneaked back, Injun lover," the chief bully taunted. "But the smell of you and Wooten is drivin' me out."

Woolfolk had just started to say good, when a fist hit him in the jaw. He didn't know where it came from, or who threw it. The whole corner swarmed around him and Wooten, pushing, shoving, twisting them toward the ground. The black soldiers descended on the courtroom brawl with the speed of experience. They pushed the belligerents apart, pinning Bryant's men against the wall and shoving them toward the door. Woolfolk rubbed his stinging cheek and wondered where Bryant was.

"Get back," a soldier pushed against John Wooten.

"*Awww,*" growled Lucius Bryant from under Wooten's feet.

As Bryant was jerked up and driven with his friends from the room, Wooten and Woolfolk returned down the aisle. The crowd parted before them.

"What did you do, you brute?" asked Woolfolk.

"Nothing," said Wooten. "He slipped. I reckon, when I took my boot off his head, all the blood rushed back in and hurt him."

"Nothing personal, then?"

"Not a thing," said Wooten.

Woolfolk noticed Wooten shook the fingers of his right hand to get the sting out.

The two friends resumed their seats. Woolfolk checked his watch. Forty minutes had passed.

Ball bent over the table. "Forty minutes!" he said enthusiastically.

"They probably took 'em to the privy first." Woolfolk downplayed the length of time. "Takes twelve men a long time to go to the privy."

Sheriff McMillan's voice came from the back of the room. "All right, folks. Take your seats now. The jury is coming."

Woolfolk did not turn or look up to see the men enter. He could not.

Soward hammered the court into session as the jury reseated themselves. "Mister Foreman," he calmly asked, "do you have a verdict."

"We do, Your Honor," said T. W. William. He handed two pieces of paper to the bailiff who passed it on to Soward.

The judge opened the papers and looked up. "Read your verdict."

Thomas W. William read from the papers he had signed as foreman. "We, the jury, find the defendant, Satanta, guilty of murder in the first degree, and assess his punishment at death."

He shuffled the pages. "We, the jury, find the defendant, Big Tree, guilty of murder in the first degree, and assess his punishment at death."

A whoop of jubilation went up from the Texans. The verdicts were shouted out the window to the crowd below, and an echoing shout returned to the room. Soward hammered with ferocity. "Sit down. Be quiet. That's enough."

Woolfolk watched it all at a great distance. The words of guilt and death barely created a ripple on his calm mind. Tom Ball dropped his head.

Without thought Woolfolk put a hand on his back. "It ain't over, Tom," he heard himself say. "Your Honor," said Woolfolk then, rising quickly to his feet. "The defense moves for a new trial."

Soward pounded his gavel. "Guards," he yelled. "Prepare to clear this room at once."

The spirit within the room subsided under the continued pounding and the efforts of the black soldiers.

Satisfied at last, Soward turned his attention back to the lawyer. "On what grounds, Mister Woolfolk?"

"On the grounds that this court has no jurisdiction in this matter, that it belongs in a federal court. On the grounds that the defendant incriminated himself without knowledge of what he was doing or what the consequences were. On the grounds that because of the volatile situation existing in this county, a fair and impartial jury could not be found."

"We have heard these arguments before, Mister Woolfolk. It is considered by the court that the law is with the state. It is, therefore, ordered, adjudged, and decreed by the court that the said motion be overruled."

"Exception."

"Exception noted," barked Soward. "Does the defendant, Big Tree, have anything to say regarding why the sentence of the jury should not be passed upon him?"

Woolfolk turned to the boy. "Donat."

"He understands, chief," the 'breed said.

Woolfolk looked at the young Kiowa.

He shook his head.

"No, Your Honor," reported Woolfolk to the judge.

"Does your client, Satanta, have anything to say?" continued Soward.

Woolfolk said to the Kiowa chief. "Now is your time to talk, Satanta."

Chapter Twenty-Nine

Satanta rose from his seat, no longer awkward in his chains.

"Mister Jones," Soward directed, "will you translate for the court?"

Woolfolk settled back to listen as the post interpreter, Horace Jones, delivered the chief's words behind him in English. Woolfolk looked at the dark copper skin, the broad shoulders, and chest of the chief. The wide plane of his face and high cheekbones, the carriage of his body had been transformed in some way. Satanta was no longer the prisoner, but the orator — a powerful man, comfortable in the discourse of decision.

"I cannot speak with these things upon my wrists." Satanta lifted his shackled wrists, revealing the iron bracelets. "In chains, I am as powerless as a woman. Has anything been heard from the Great Father?" He turned. "I have never been so near the *Tejanos* before. I look around me and see your families, your men, your women, and your children. I have said in my heart, if I ever get back to my people, my family . . . I myself have three sons and five daughters . . . I will never make war upon you again because I have seen you. You have fed me. You have not treated me harshly as your prisoner. You have protected my life.

"I did not kill the *Tejanos*. I came down Pease River as a powerful medicine man to doctor the wounds of the braves. I am suffering now for the crimes of bad Indians . . . for Satank and Lone Wolf and Kicking Bird, for Big Bow and Fast Bear and Eagle Heart. If you will let me go, I will kill Big Bow, Fast Bear, and Eagle Heart with my own hand.

"It is to your advantage to let me go. I am an important leader among my people. I have great influence among the warriors of my tribe . . . they know my voice and will hear my word. If you will let me go back to my people, I will speak for you. I will withdraw my warriors from *Tejas*. I will take them all across Red River with me, and that river shall be the line between us and the white men. I will wash out the spots of blood on the land and make it a white land. There shall be peace. The *Tejanos* may plow and drive their oxen to the river.

"But if you kill me, my death will be a spark on the prairie. There will be a great fire, and it will burn everything before it."

The assembled citizens muttered. They would not be threatened by this windbag of an Indian. Who, after all, did he think he was, offering terms to them when he was about to die for his crimes? Soward stifled the outburst with a sour look and several raps on his bench.

"It is ordered, adjudged, and decreed by this court that the defendants, Satanta and Big Tree, be taken by the sheriff of Jack County, and hanged until they are dead, dead, dead, and the Lord have mercy upon their souls.

"It is further ordered by this court that the sheriff do take the defendants into close custody to await the sentence of this court. And to take the defendants, Satanta and Adoltay, on Friday, September One, in the year of our Lord, Eighteen Seventy-One, to some convenient place near the courthouse, at the town of Jacksboro, and between the hours of six A.M. and noon of said day, and said defendants to hang by the neck until they are dead, dead, dead, and may God have mercy upon their souls."

Donat gave the judge's words to the two Kiowas as the judge spoke them. There was no expression on either man's face. Death was something they had accepted long before. The soldier guard came down the aisle to get them and turned them to leave. Satanta looked out over the faces in the room. They had waited to see his face, too. Woolfolk had gathered his materials and was preparing to follow Satanta when the Indian stopped short and straightened. The Indian spoke softly. *"Taukkoyma!"*

Woolfolk struggled around him to see what had drawn him up. In the door of the courtroom stood Adrianne Chastain.

Chapter Thirty

"Blazes, it's hot," complained Judge Soward as he quickly signed the papers laid on his desk.

"It's cooling off now," said James Robinson, picking up the sentencing documents, the last details of the July session of court. He carefully sorted them and placed them in the file for Case 224. "The crowd is almost out of the building. And it's getting on toward sundown. Reckon most folks will stay in town for the rest of the Fourth of July. I hear they're going to ask Lanham to speak tonight."

"Hmm," said Soward. He removed the stifling robe from his shoulders and tossed it over the back of his chair. He stepped down from the high bench and walked over to the first large window. A strong breeze ran across him. The air on his wet shirt made him feel almost cool. "Well, Jim, it's over. The people are happy. They're down there, celebrating the soon coming deaths of their enemies. They'll all come back in September for the hanging. Meanwhile, all the Army has to do is see that the celebrating doesn't end with a lynching. That's the Army's problem, isn't it? We've done our part rather well, I think. It's all gone pretty well. And now our part is over."

"Not quite, Your Honor," Joe Woolfolk said quietly from the door.

Soward turned to face the pesky attorney. "Take those papers and go on downstairs, Jim," he directed. "I'll be there in a few minutes."

The clerk bundled them quickly and scuttled past the lawyer.

"Woolfolk . . . ," Soward began.

"There's one more piece of evidence and one more witness."

Soward closed his eyes. "You know it's over, Joe."

The attorney still stood at the door.

"Damn. All right, counselor, present your evidence, call your witness." The judge walked away from the noise of the celebrating Texans, away from the cooling air of the long Texas twilight. He retrieved his robe and sat back in his chair.

"The defense calls Adrianne Chastain." Woolfolk opened the door wider and escorted Mrs. Chastain into the room and down to the front. The woman stepped into the witness box.

"Get on with it, Woolfolk," growled Soward.

"The defense offers in evidence this letter from Lawrie Tatum to S. W. T. Lanham. The letter is dated June Twenty-Ninth, Eighteen Seventy-One. It is marked defense exhibit one." Woolfolk handed the letter to the judge who jerked it impatiently from his hands. The judge started to read it to himself. "Please read it out loud, Your Honor."

Soward's look cut into Woolfolk, but he read: " 'To S. W. T. Lanham, Esquire, District Attorney, Sixth Month, Twenty-Ninth day, Eighteen Seventy-One. In view of the trial of Satanta and Big Tree, Kiowa Chiefs, of this agency, permit me to remind thee that two characteristic traits of the Indians are to seek revenge, and a great dread of imprisonment. From my knowledge of the Indians, I believe if the prisoners should be convicted of murder, it would be more severe punishment to them to confine them for life, than to execute them, and it would probably save the lives of some white people; for, if they were executed, it is more than probable that some of the other Kiowas would seek revenge in the murder of some white citizens. This is judging the case from a policy standpoint. But if we judge it from a Christian standpoint, I believe, we should in all cases, even murder in the first degree, confine a person for life, and leave to God His prerogative to determine when a person has lived long enough. Lawrie Tatum, Indian Agent.' "

Soward laid the note down in front of him. "Where did you get this, Mister Woolfolk?"

"I took it from Lanham's room," the lawyer said honestly. "I know, of course, that you had no idea it existed."

"Of course," agreed Soward. "Do you have a point here, counselor?"

"My point is, sir, that Satanta's words, taken defiantly by this courtroom full of people as arrogant brag, a challenge to their will, were, indeed, truth. His death and Adoltay's death will be a spark on the prairie. Aside from the facts that this court has no jurisdiction, that the Satanta confession violates Article Six of the United States Constitution regarding self-incrimination, not counting its words about a fair and impartial jury, and that for all intents and purposes the raid was an act of war by a sovereign people upon their enemies, us. Aside from all that, I have a witness who will speak to the point."

Woolfolk moved to the witness box. He did not lean on it, but stood respectfully at a distance, allowing Judge Soward to observe the beautiful Mrs. Chastain.

"Missus Chastain, have you appeared before Judge Soward before?"

"Yes," Adrienne Chastain said softly. "In January of Eighteen Fifty-Nine and again seven years later, February, Eighteen Sixty-Three."

"What was the nature of those appearances?"

"On the first I sought custody of my son, Joe Carter, and upon my daughter Susan's petition, I was found to be incompetent, and it was denied," the woman answered.

"And the second?"

"On that occasion I received custody of my son and posted a bond for it."

"Your daughter did not contest it?"

"No," Mrs. Chastain said. "Susan did not contest it."

"What had happened in those years, Missus Chastain?"

The woman sighed. "I guess we both grew up. I had worked very hard to put the ranch on a strong financial footing by paying off all the creditors. And my daughter and I had gotten to know each other, to trust each other."

"You valued that trust because it was hard won?" asked Woolfolk.

"Yes, I did."

"What happened to your daughter?"

"She was killed on October Thirteenth, Eighteen Sixty-Four," the woman whispered hoarsely.

"Who killed her, Missus Chastain?"

"A band of Kiowa Indians." Adrienne Chastain's voice was normal again.

"Who led those Kiowa Indians?" Woolfolk glanced up as the door opened and Wooten and Isaac Lynn slipped into seats near the door.

"Satanta."

"Will you describe the raid and its aftermath for the court," directed Joe Woolfolk.

"I only know what happened at our place," Mrs. Chastain began. "It was early. We heard a bugle as we were eating breakfast . . . my children and Susan's daughters, Britt Johnson's wife, Mary, and her children. The men were away. I opened the door. I thought it was troops from Fort Belknap. But the yard was full of Indians." Mrs. Chastain paused. "Susan grabbed a gun and pushed past me. Britt's oldest boy and his little bulldog followed her. The dog was having a fit. And the Indians began to shoot him. Susan yelled and raised the gun. They shot her and the boy. Then they stormed the house and set it on fire. Mary and I were trying to get the little children out and fighting the Indians who were pushing us about. Joe Carter was not well. But I got to him and Lottie and . . . ," the woman shook her head slightly as if she were trying to clear it of the scene.

"Lottie is your granddaughter?"

"Yes. I had Joe Carter and Lottie, but not my daughter's youngest child, Millie. She had crawled under the bed. Satanta caught hold of me and pulled me toward the door. I brought the other children with me, but I couldn't see Millie. I could see the house was really beginning to burn, and I struggled with him to get back to her. He tossed Joe Carter and Lottie onto horses ridden by other Indians. I broke away for the house, but he caught me again and put me on his horse. The horse was spinning, and I was trying to see where Joe and Lottie were. I saw Susan in the yard. They had stripped her and cut her open. When the horse turned again, I saw a man come out of the house with Millie in his arms. He was gentle with her.

"We rode without stopping for the next two days. On the Pease River, the party split up. Mary Johnson and her children, Jube and Cherry, were taken by one group and Millie was taken away by the Kiowa who brought her out of the house. Joe Carter, Lottie, and I were taken by Satanta. Joe Carter was coughing and having a lot of trouble, staying on the horse. I pleaded with Satanta to let me take care of him, to let me ride with him and hold him. He took Lottie and let me ride with the boy. We rode all day without stopping again. I could feel Joe Carter, slipping away. When we stopped, Satanta gave me the little girl. I just looked down at her, and, when I looked up, he had cut Joe Carter's throat. My son was sliding down the side of the horse where he had been leaning. He fell to his knees and rolled onto his side. I held Lottie away, but I had to go to him. He was already dead." The woman stopped and took several deep breaths.

Joe Woolfolk waited for her to regain herself. "After that, you became Satanta's woman?"

"Yes," Mrs. Chastain answered clearly.

"Did you try to run away?"

"No," she said.

"Did you attempt to kill yourself? Surely a decent white woman would prefer to kill herself than become one of the squaws of a Kiowa who had killed her daughter and cut her son's throat?"

"I did not try to kill myself."

"Why not?"

"I had my daughter's children. I had to find Millie and get them home," Mrs. Chastain explained.

"What made you think you could do that?"

"One has hope, Mister Woolfolk. One must try. I knew I must put aside my feelings and use my mind. I saw that Satanta was not brutal in his camp among his people. He was kind to Lottie. He gave us our own lodge when he knew I could not and would not run away. I had begun to talk to him about Millie, and he knew I would stay. As time passed, I realized that Satanta liked to trade. I was a wealthy woman, fully capable of providing him a hundred horses, if necessary. We talked about this."

"I'm curious, Missus Chastain, how did you speak to Satanta?"

"He speaks Spanish very well. I knew that language, and I learned some Kiowa."

"Did the chief bargain?"

"He was willing, for so many horses, but we needed an emissary, someone to arrange for and deliver the horses to him. That was a problem. Finally, Britt Johnson appeared, looking for his family. I made the arrangement for him to act for me. The bargain was a hundred head of horses for Lottie and Millie and I and for Mary Johnson and her children. Britt had to bring the horses to the camp."

"Was the bargain kept?"

"Satanta kept his part. He allowed Lottie and me to go. He was not able to get Millie and the Johnson family away from their captors."

"Missus Chastain, do you want to see Satanta killed for what he has done to you and your children and grandchildren?"

"No."

Soward leaned forward. "Surely you have every reason, Missus Chastain."

"Killing Satanta will not stop the killing, Judge Soward. It will only get worse. Holding him in prison opens the opportunities for negotiation. Satanta will deal with you. The other chiefs will deal with you because they cannot leave him to you, and because they are practical men. I have been to the Army, to General Sherman himself, and they cannot get my daughter's child back. Satanta and the Kiowas can. I want my granddaughter back much more than I want Satanta's death. I want to see other people live in peace on this frontier much more than I want Satanta's death. There are debts made in blood that cannot be paid in man's blood. These debts must be forgiven."

Soward drummed his fingers on the arm of his chair. "What have you done, Joe Woolfolk?" he asked quietly. "A thousand voices are yelling in my ears to kill Satanta and Adoltay. And you have brought two quiet witnesses to whisper to me louder than all the others. I will have to think. The jury and the people have spoken. I dare not cross them, but I will think about what your witnesses have said."

"Thank you, Your Honor," said Joe Woolfolk sincerely. "We are grateful for your patience and your consideration."

Woolfolk ushered Adrienne Chastain from the stand and

toward the men sitting at the back of the room. Wooten and Lynn rose and followed them. The three men stood together as the woman walked down the stairs ahead of them. She did not ask their assistance or their presence in returning to the hotel. In fact, she had asked nothing but the return of her daughter's child.

"Isaac," asked Woolfolk, "what does *Taukkoyma* or something like that mean?"

The aged Indian fighter scratched his bearded chin. "It's a term of endearment . . . a way of pointing at a difference that doesn't really exist between two people. It means 'white woman.' "

Six days later, in his office in Weatherford, Judge Charles Soward wrote the following letter:

Weatherford, Parker County, Texas
July 10, 1871
Governor E. J. Davis

Sir:
   I have the honor to say that the last term is regarded of more interest to our frontier than any court that has ever been held in the state. Upon arriving at Jacksboro, we dispatched a posse of five citizens to Fort Sill for the necessary witnesses, and through the assistance of Colonel Mackenzie, commanding United States Army at Fort Richardson, General Grierson, commanding at Fort Sill, and Lowrie Tatum, Indian agent, we obtained the necessary witnesses for the state, and after a fair and impartial trial, the defendants having the best counsel at the command of the court, the jury returned a verdict of murder in the first degree and fixed their punishment

at death. Mr. Tatum expressed a strong desire that they should be punished by imprisonment for life instead of death, but the jury thought differently. I passed the sentence upon them on the 4th of July, and fixed the time of execution at Friday, September 1st, next.

I must say, here, that I concur with Mr. Tatum as to the punishment simply, however, upon a politic view of the matter. Mr. Tatum has indicated that if they are tried, convicted, and punished by imprisonment, that he would render the civil authorities all the assistance in his power to bring others of those tribes on the reservation who have been guilty of outrages in Texas to trial and just punishment.

I would have petitioned Your Excellency to commute their punishment to imprisonment for life, were it not that I know a great majority of the people on the frontier demand their execution. Your Excellency, however, acting for the weal of the state at large, and free from the passion of the masses, may see fit to commute their punishment. If so, I say, Amen!

Now, while entertaining the opinion that the present policy of the United States toward these wild tribes is founded on supreme folly, nevertheless, I see in this new phase of the Quaker policy (which has culminated in the trial and conviction of the chiefs, Satanta and Big Tree, by civil authority) a solution of our difficulties. If we only use our vantage ground, I think we will speedily be redeemed from the ravages of all the reserve Indians on our borders.

During the trial of Satanta and Big Tree, it appeared from legitimate testimony that Big Bow, Fast Bear, and Eagle Heart were in the last raid that resulted in the murder of seven men and the capture of forty-one head of mules. Now, I most earnestly request Your Excellency to issue your requisition for the above named Indians, to be turned over to the sheriff of Jack County. You will please send your commission through General Reynolds, to Colonel Mackenzie at Fort Richardson. Colonel Mackenzie informs me that he is ready and willing to execute the commission and Tatum, the agent, is under promise to render all assistance in his power.

With many wishes for your good health. I remain with much respect.

> Your very obedient servant
> CHARLES SOWARD
> Judge – Thirteenth Judicial District,
> Texas.

The peculiar events of the evening of July 4, 1871 and Mrs. Chastain's name were never mentioned in any official correspondence. Governor Davis's reply to Soward was swift and to the point.

Dear Sir:

Your communication of the 10th ult., has been received recommending the commutation of sentence in the case of "Satanta" and "Big Tree." I have thought your recommendation a good one, and have accordingly directed that the sentence of these two Indians be commuted to imprisonment for life.

> Respectfully,
> Edw'd J. Davis, Governor

On August 2, 1871, the commutation was signed and published to the people of Texas. The legal phraseology incorporated many of Joe Woolfolk's ideas. No mention was made of the part played by Mrs. Chastain because no one outside the twilit courtroom ever knew of her testimony or the price she paid. The commutation said:

THE STATE OF TEXAS: TO ALL TO WHOM THESE PRESENTS SHALL COME —

Whereas, at the July Term, A. D. 1871, of the District Court of Jack County, in said state, one Satanta and Big Tree, known as Indians of the Kiowa tribe were tried and convicted of a charge of murder and sentenced therefore to suffer the penalty of death on the first day of September, A. D. 1871, and imprisonment for life will be more likely to operate as a restraint upon others of the tribe to which these Indians belong; and,

Whereas, the killings for which these Indians were sentenced can hardly be considered as a just consideration of the animus as coming within the technical crime of murder under the statues of the state but rather as an act of savage warfare;

Now, therefore, I, Edward J. Davis, Governor of Texas, by virtue of the authority vested in me by the constitution and laws of the state, do hereby commute the sentence of Satanta and Big Tree to imprisonment for life, at hard labor, in the state penitentiary, and hereby direct the Clerk of the District Court of Jack County to make this commutation of sentence a matter of record in his office.

EDWARD J. DAVIS, Governor
JAMES P. NEWCOMB, Sec'ty of State

Davis's instructions were followed:

THE STATE OF TEXAS
COUNTY OF JACK

I hereby certify that the foregoing is a correct record of the original commutation of punishment recorded this August 14, 1871, at 9:00 A.M.

In testimony of which I hereto set my hand officially at office in Jacksboro this day and date last above written.

JAS. R. ROBINSON
District Clerk, Jack County,
Texas

The final record of the trial was made by a clerk and entered into the history of the American West.

THE END

Cynthia Haseloff was born in Vernon, Texas. She was named after Cynthia Ann Parker, perhaps the best-known of 19th-century white female Indian captives. The history and legends of the West were part of her upbringing in Arkansas where her family settled shortly after she was born. She wrote her first novel, *Ride South!*, with the encouragement of her mother. Published in 1980, the back cover of the novel proclaimed Haseloff as "one of today's most striking new Western writers." It is an unusual book, with a mother as the protagonist searching for her children out of love and a sense of responsibility, rather than from a desire for revenge or fame. Haseloff went on to write four more novels in the early 1980s. Two of these focused on unusual female protagonists. *Marauder*, of the two, is Haseloff's most historical novel and it is also quite possibly her finest book. As one review put it, *"Marauder* has humor and hope and history." It was written to inspire pride in Arkansans, including the students she had known when she taught in a high school while trying to get her first book published. Haseloff's characters embody the fundamental values—honor, duty, courage, and family—that prevailed on the American frontier and were instilled in the young Haseloff by her own "heroes," her mother and her grandmother. Haseloff's stories, in a sense, dramatize how these values endure when challenged by the adversities and cruelties of frontier existence. Her talent, as that of Dorothy M. Johnson, rests in her ability to tell a story with an economy of words and in the seemingly effortless way she uses language. Haseloff once said: "I love the West, perhaps not all of its reality, for much of it was cruel and hard, but certainly its dream and hope, and the damned courage of people trying to live within its demands."